Contents

Your FREE Ebook is waiting! — v
Acknowledgments — vi
Dedication — vii
Primordial Earth - The Beginning — 1
Primordial World - Prologue — 3
Chapter 1 - Rogue — 16
Chapter 2 - Ridley — 21
Chapter 3 - Rogue — 27
Chapter 4 - Ridley — 37
Chapter 5 - Jessica — 44
Chapter 6 - Ridley — 52
Chapter 7 - Seth — 62
Chapter 8 - Rogue — 68
Chapter 9 - Ridley — 75
Chapter 10 - Jessica — 83
Chapter 11 - Ridley — 92
Chapter 12 - Seth — 98
Chapter 13 - Jessica — 103
Chapter 14 - Ridley — 112
Chapter 15 - Ridley — 119
Chapter 16 - Ridley — 123
Chapter 17 - Ridley — 129
Chapter 18 - Ridley — 136
Chapter 19 - Ridley — 141

Chapter 20 - Jessica	147
Chapter 21 - Rogue	153
Chapter 22 - Ridley	162
Chapter 23 - Ridley	171
Chapter 24 - Jessica	176
Chapter 25 - Ridley	184
Chapter 26 - Ridley	191
Chapter 27 - Ridley	199
Chapter 28 - Ridley	207
Chapter 29 - Ridley	215
Chapter 30 - Ridley	226
Chapter 31 - Jessica	233
Chapter 32 - Rogue	237
Chapter 33 - Ridley	248
Chapter 34 - Ridley	256
Chapter 35 - Rogue	264
Chapter 36 - Ridley	271
Chapter 37 - Ridley	279
Chapter 38 - Ridley	286
Epilogue I - Ridley	289
Epilogue II - Rogue	292
Epilogue III - Seth	296
Do you want more?	300
Primordial Earth - Sneak Peek	311
Your FREE EBook is waiting!	322
About the Author	323
Glossary	324

Your FREE Ebook is waiting!

If you'd like to learn more about my books, upcoming projects, new releases, cover reveals, and promotions, simply join my mailing list. Plus, you'll get an exclusive ebook absolutely FREE just for subscribing!

Yes, please. Sign me up!
   https://www.subscribepage.com/i0d7r8

Acknowledgments

A huge thank you to Alex for the stunning book cover design. You can check out his portfolio on Facebook at 187Designz. He's an amazing artist!

Dedication

This book is dedicated to Ronnie Galloway, a wonderful reader and supporter of books and authors all over the world. Thanks a million, Ronnie. People like you make this job worth doing, and I hope you enjoy this book of prehistoric adventure. May you experience many more great stories in your lifetime. Happy Reading!

Primordial Earth - The Beginning

42 years ago, an experiment gone wrong caused a catastrophic event that tore apart the very fabric of time. Entire cities and chunks of land were sent millions of years into the past, along with the living creatures that inhabited them. Left to fend for themselves, they were cast into a savage world filled with prehistoric predators.

Orphaned and alone, Rogue is forced to survive on the streets of Prime City, one of the few strongholds against the wilderness and its native creatures. Governed by a tyrant, food is scarce, and hunger is an ever-present threat.

When she is caught thieving, Rogue is sentenced to exile and thrust into the adventure of a lifetime. Along the way, she meets many people, some friends and some foes. She helps to defeat a tyrant, suffers tragic losses, establishes a new era, and finds love.

Finally, she settles down in her new home, The Zoo, with her husband, Seth, and daughter, Ridley. Becoming a pillar of the community, she strives to forge a new world for them all. A place where people can live and grow in prosperity and peace. But safety is an illusion, and trouble looms on the horizon. Only this time, it involves her daughter, Ridley.

***

If you want to know more about Rogue and the many adventures she survived, check out the Primordial Earth Series, and learn where it all began: 75 million years in the past.
***

Or, turn the page if you wish to embark upon an epic journey through the primordial world with Ridley and her wolf companion, Loki. Meet diverse characters, and discover the creatures that populate her world, both beautiful and dangerous.

Primordial World - Prologue

Ridley eased through the brush with smooth grace. She slipped between the trees, the rough bark scraping against the soft leather of her pants and sleeveless tunic. Although it was late in the season, the weather was warm, and sweat trickled down her back. Midges buzzed around her face, but she ignored them. They were a minor inconvenience and wouldn't deter her from her mission. Pausing to look around, she spotted a narrow game trail. Fresh tracks marred the ground, and she studied them with minute care. The hoof prints were small and belonged to herbivores—precisely the kind she wanted.

With a predatory grin, Ridley followed the trail, the thrill of the hunt singing through her veins. She loved being out in the wild and relished the sense of freedom and the lack of responsibility. Out here, it didn't matter who or what you were. All that mattered was your will to survive and your ability to navigate the dangers of the prehistoric world.

Armed to the teeth, she was well-equipped for the perils of the wild. Her clothes were made from camel leather and encased her body like a second skin. Tough and durable, it allowed her to move with ease and kept insects at bay. A hunting knife rode on her hip, its sheath worn and polished.

A gift from her father, the edge was razor-sharp, and the handle perfectly balanced. A hatchet sat on the other hip, a deadly missile in her practiced hands.

In addition, she carried a crossbow and a quiver of bolts on her back. Handcrafted from cedar wood, it packed a hefty punch at close range but was light enough not to weigh her down. A second knife rode inside her boot, an ace up her sleeve. Along with her natural agility, strength, and skill, she was at home in the worst of environments.

But her state of readiness was no accident. Her father, a respected man and part of the community council, was also a lone wolf. He often disappeared into the forest for days, returning bloodied, dirty, and unkempt but never empty-handed. He always brought something with him—either news of new hunting grounds, territories, supplies, or resources.

Ridley envied his freedom. It was something she'd never had. As the only child of two council members, one of whom was the community leader, she was expected to set an example. Her mother's words rang in the back of her mind, a constant reminder of the rules that made up her existence.

"Stand up straight, Ridley. Don't slouch."

"Put away that bow. You must practice your manners, not just your archery skills."

"Lift your chin and speak clearly. Don't mumble."

"No hunting! No fighting! And above all, no leaving the compound!"

It never ended. Day and night, it carried on. *Don't do this. Don't do that.*

It was exhausting, and Ridley chafed against the many restrictions placed upon her. Whenever possible, she snuck away from her mother and the community, her heart bursting with the need to fly. Though she knew she'd get into trouble if caught, she didn't care. *I'll take my freedom, and no one will stop me.*

Giving in to the urge to forget, she forged ahead, each step taking her further from home. It wasn't long before she closed in on her quarry, a small herd of Thescelosaurus. The gentle herbivores grazed in a grassy clearing, making the most of the late afternoon sun. Soon, the sun would set, giving way to the night and its perils. The herd would retire, huddled together for protection under the watchful gaze of the matriarch. Grizzled by the passing of many seasons, she watched over her daughters and their adolescent young with the keen sense of a true survivor.

Ridley singled out her prey, a small but plump female feeding at the far edge of the herd. The animal had wandered off from the rest, unaware of its encroaching danger. It presented the perfect target, and Ridley's mouth watered at the thought of its rich, fatty flesh sizzling over an open flame.

She edged closer to the clearing. The soft soles of her moccasins allowed her to feel the terrain, and she avoided stepping on any twigs or branches. A vine tugged at her hair, and she paused, letting the tendril unfurl. It sprang free, and she continued until she came within firing range.

Reaching for a bolt, Ridley honed in on the target. She breathed out, her hands steady on the seasoned wood of the crossbow. With a pull of the trigger, the deadly missile shot through the air, the barbed metal head flashing in the sun. It thudded into the female Thescelosaurus' side, penetrating the tough hide and piercing the heart and lungs.

The mortally wounded herbivore threw back its head with a squeal, crimson blood gushing from its lips. It managed to take two faltering steps before it collapsed, sending the herd into a panic. The matriarch bugled a warning cry and signaled the retreat. As one, the frightened dinosaurs stampeded across the clearing.

Ridley jumped to her feet, ready to dash toward her fallen prey, but a thunderous roar froze her on the spot. The trees across the clearing shook and shivered under the onslaught of a fearsome predator. A branch as thick as her middle snapped in half and crashed to the ground. Ponderous footsteps sent vibrations rumbling through the earth. Each thump caused fresh fear to spurt through her veins, leaving a sour taste on her tongue.

A monstrous head topped with two stubby horns thrust into the open, the thick, scaly hide a rusty brown. Ridley's heart quailed at the sight. Easily seven meters long, the carnivore loomed above her, and she instantly recognized the species. *A Carnotaurus!*

That knowledge both shocked and surprised her. They were scarce and hadn't been seen in the area in years. No large predators frequented the site close to her home. It was too busy, trafficked by traders' caravans and hunters alike. Carnivores were quickly discouraged and chased away by parties of armed guards and soon learned to steer clear. However, that didn't mean rogue predators wouldn't take a chance at a quick meal.

The Carnotaurus peered around the clearing, its gaping nostrils sucking in the scent of fresh blood. Panicked, the Thescelosaurus' stampeded in the opposite direction. They honked with panic, but the predator ignored them. Instead, its colossal form turned toward Ridley's fresh kill, stomping across the clearing. An opportunist, the beast would much rather scavenge than expend the energy necessary to catch its prey.

Ridley had little time to react. She was caught out in the open, mere feet from the carcass, a sitting duck. The dino didn't take long to spot her, and it roared with fury. She was too close to the kill, and the carnivore brooked no competition.

Aware of her peril, Ridley scrambled backward, scrabbling through the rough grass as the monster approached. Thorns and stones cut into her palms, but she hardly noticed. The distance between her and the meat eater closed until it filled her entire field of vision. She tried to run, but her legs wouldn't work. Besides, she'd never outrun the Carnotaurus. *This is it. I'm dead.*

Boom!

Boom!

Boom!

Ridley opened her mouth to scream, but a hand clapped over her lips. Strong arms dragged her behind the scant cover of a bush. She whirled around, a fist raised to punch but stopped when she saw a familiar face. Her father, Seth, looked angry enough to catch hornets.

"Dad!" Ridley gasped. "I'm so sorry, I—"

"Shh," her father said, raising one finger to his lips. He pulled her deeper into cover, burying her into the moss and earth like a worm. One hand rested on his rifle, the safety flicked off. She'd only seen him fire it once, but he looked ready to take on anything that moved. *For me,* she realized. *He's willing to risk his life for me.*

A low rumble vibrated through the air, and the stench of rotten meat filled the air. Ridley swallowed hard and twisted her head, her eyes widening at the sight. The monstrous dinosaur was close, so close it loomed above them. Legs the size of tree trunks stood mere feet from their hiding spot, vicious claws tipping each toe. A head the size of a boulder hovered above the ground, sucking air into its gaping maw while teeth that looked like daggers glinted in the sun.

Ridley smothered a horrified gasp. She'd never been that close to a predator before, especially one that big. It was the stuff of nightmares, and she was sure she'd have trouble sleeping for many weeks. *If we make it out of this alive.*

The proximity of death was enough to send her into a panic. All her training immediately deserted her, and her brain turned to mush. Tears burned her eyelids, and her lips began to quiver. She was on the verge of a panic attack and had no idea how to stop the slippery descent into chaos.

As if he knew what was happening, Seth looked at her with dark eyes. Eyes she'd inherited. Her mother always said she looked and acted just like her father. Ridley had always taken pride in that fact, trying to live up to his reputation for courage and bravery. But at that moment, she felt like a scared little girl. Not brave at all.

Seth placed one hand on hers, his touch steadying her nerves. With silent words, he reassured her, mouthing the phrase, "It will be all right."

It was enough to pull Ridley from her funk, and she snapped back into focus. If her dad said everything would be okay, she believed him. He'd never lied to her in his entire life, and she knew she could trust him. They'd always had a special bond forged in blood and bone. With a slight nod, she showed him she was back in control, and he relaxed slightly. Together, they waited in hiding, praying the predator would move on.

The Carnotaurus lingered for several moments, its fearsome presence like a cloud of acid in the atmosphere. It swept the ground, looking for anything out of place, any smell or trace of the tiny creatures it had seen scuttling away like crabs. But the scent of fresh blood proved irresistible, and it finally returned to the Thescelosaurus' carcass.

The sound of cracking bone and tearing flesh caused Ridley to wince, but she stayed in place, not moving an inch. Neither did her father, his patience endless. It took the better part of an hour for the Carnotaurus to devour its meal. Afterward, it took the time to mark its newly claimed territory before it lumbered into the distance, searching for fresh victims to terrorize.

As it disappeared through the trees, Ridley heaved a sigh of relief. Her tense muscles melted into a puddle of goo, and she stood up on wobbly legs. Shooting her father a look, she uttered a mumbled apology. "I'm sorry, Dad." Seth stared at her for several long moments, and she squirmed on the spot. "I'm really, really sorry. Please don't tell Mom about this. You know what she'll do."

"She'll ground you for life. That's what she'll do, and it serves you right," Seth said, his expression stern.

"No!" Ridley burst out, unable to contain her horror. "I can't. I'll die within those walls."

Seth sighed. "I know. You're just like me."

"Yes! I'm nothing like Mom!" Ridley cried. "She's old and stuffy. Boring. She never does anything fun."

"Don't speak about your mother like that," Seth interjected, his voice thunderous. "You know nothing about her."

"That's because she doesn't tell me anything. She lectures me all the time," Ridley protested.

"Your mother is trying her best to turn you into a responsible young adult, and you're not making it easy for her," Seth said.

"I don't care about any of that. I want to be free to do what I want," Ridley said.

"It doesn't work like that, sweetheart. Life doesn't care what you want. Ask your mother. Do you think she was always like she is now? She had dreams too."

"So, what happened?"

"Life did. The community needed a leader after the drought, and she was the only one willing to step up to the plate. It weighs heavily on her, but she never complains. You would do well to remember that and give her the respect and credit she's due."

Ridley's shoulders sagged. "I know. It's just… I can't be what she wants me to be. I want to be free."

"One day, you'll be able to make your own decisions. You'll be a grown woman and in charge of your own life. But right now, you're just a teenager. Barely fourteen, and you will obey your mother. Got it?"

Seth's tone brooked no resistance, and Ridley had no choice but to agree. "Yes, Father." However, she could not hide the rebellious note in her voice, and Seth noticed.

Softening, he added, "That doesn't mean you can't have a little fun in the meantime. Just don't give your mother a heart attack. Okay?"

"Okay," Ridley agreed.

"And no more solo hunting missions. Next time, you ask me," Seth added. "It's a lot more dangerous out here than you realize."

Ridley sighed. "Fine. No more solo trips."

"Good. Now let's go home. We need to get back before dark," Seth said.

Ridley followed him through the woods, sticking close to his side. She was still slightly rattled by their encounter with the Carnotaurus, and she hoped the rest of the journey would be uneventful. Thankfully, it didn't take long to reach their home, the Zoo. They broke through the trees and emerged into the open, pausing to take in the sight.

Situated in a vast clearing, the Zoo formed a bastion against the wilderness, standing in defiance of the primordial forest that loomed on its borders. The walled compound was built like a fort, each corner guarded by watchtowers and armed guards. Cobbled roads led the way between the various animal enclosures, buildings, and housing units. Outside, crops flourished in the rich soil, delivering a burgeoning bounty each year. It was nothing short of a miracle, built with its inhabitants' blood, sweat, and tears.

Still, life was harsh at times. The winters were brutal, and the rains often poured into the valley, causing flash floods and mudslides. The river, their primary source of trade, turned treacherous, with white-water rapids forming on the bends to claim unsuspecting victims. Sometimes the crops failed, or hunting was scarce. Disease was an ever-present threat, and hunger a looming specter. But it was their life. The only life Ridley had ever known, and she wouldn't trade it for anything.

"Come on. We'd better hurry," Seth said, jogging toward the gate.

With a heavy heart, Ridley followed. She didn't want to go home. Didn't want to face her mother. Didn't want the long lecture that was sure to follow her return. If everything had gone to plan, she'd have been home hours ago, but the Carnotaurus had ruined everything, and now she was late. Late enough for her mother to know she'd slipped out of the compound. *I am in so much trouble.*

They were greeted by a trio of armed guards and an angry-looking woman who paced the perimeter like a caged lion. Ridley's mother, Rogue, was small in stature but more dangerous than a spitting cobra. She led the community with an iron will and militaristic efficiency—a force to be reckoned with and an impossible ideal to live up to. Ridley had ceased trying years before.

"Ridley! Where have you been?" Rogue cried, rounding on her daughter. "You know the rules. You are not allowed outside these walls on your own. You're only fourteen!"

"Mom, I'm sorry. I—"

"No, I don't want to hear it. You are grounded, young lady," Rogue said. "Plus, cage cleaning duty for a month."

"A month!" Rogue cried, her jaw dropping. "But—"

"I said, not another word," Rogue said, raising one hand.

"Rogue, honey," Seth said, interjecting. "Calm down, please."

"Calm down? How can you say that?" Rogue asked. "Our daughter was out there alone, in the wild, without supervision or backup. What if she got attacked? Or killed. You know how dangerous it is."

"She wasn't alone. I went on a day trip and decided to take her with me," Seth said.

"You went on a day trip together? Without telling me?" Rogue asked, her voice heavy with suspicion.

"It must've slipped my mind. I was in a hurry," Seth said with an apologetic shrug.

"I see. So, you just decided to go out on the spur of the

moment. Without my knowledge," Rogue added, folding her arms.

"Exactly, and I know it was wrong. I should've told you and spared you the worry," Seth said, offering her his most charming smile. "I'll make it up to you. I promise."

Rogue stared at him for several seconds before she relented. "Fine, but don't think I can't see right through you. She's still grounded and reporting for two weeks of cage duty starting tomorrow."

"Mom!" Ridley protested.

"Okay. One week," Rogue relented.

"Fine, but no lecture," Ridley replied.

"Deal," Rogue said.

"I'll take it," Ridley said, knowing it was the best offer she would get.

"Now come along. Dinner is getting cold. Plus, I have a surprise for you," Rogue said, walking toward their home.

Ridley ran to catch up. "A surprise? What for?"

"Call it an early birthday present," Rogue said with a grin.

"What is it? A new crossbow?" Ridley asked, excitement bubbling in the pit of her stomach.

"No, it's not a bow," Rogue replied with a frown.

"Oh," Ridley said, momentarily disappointed.

"Don't worry. You'll love it. I promise."

"The last time you said that, it was a dress," Ridley said with a shudder.

"It's not a dress. See for yourself," Rogue said. They'd reached their home, and she pointed at a wooden crate on the patio.

Ridley ran toward the crate, not wanting to wait for another second. There was no lid, and the inside was filled with a soft hide. A ball of dark grey fur lay in the middle, and Ridley's heart stopped. "A cub? You got me a wolf cub?"

"Yes, I did. Jamie dropped it off. It's the runt of the litter, and it won't survive on its own. It needs a mother. A nurturer," Rogue said. "Are you up to the task?"

"Of course I am!" Ripley cried. She reached into the crate and picked up the tiny ball of fluff. The wolf cub mewled, its eyes still closed. When it sensed her warmth, it immediately tried to suckle. "It's hungry."

"There is milk inside the kitchen and a bottle. You'll have to feed him every three hours. Got that?" Rogue said with a stern look.

"Got it," Ridley said with a grin. She lifted the cub in the air, noting the three white paws. "Look, Dad. Isn't he the cutest?"

"That he is," Seth said with an approving nod. "What are you going to call him?"

Ridley thought about it for a moment. "Loki. I'm calling him Loki."

"That's a good name," Seth agreed.

"As long as he's not as mischievous as the Loki from myth," Rogue said.

"We'll see," Ridley said, gazing at her new charge. Already, the tiny wolf had crawled into her heart, and she knew she'd love him forever.

"Come on. Let's go inside," Rogue said. "We're all hungry. Loki too."

Rogue led the way inside with Seth on her heels. As they entered the house, Seth said, "You did good, honey. Now she won't want to leave the compound. At least not until the wolf is grown."

"Exactly," Rogue said with a smug smile.

Ridley rolled her eyes. Her mother was right. It was a clever ploy to keep her in line, but not for long. Snuggling Loki's warm fur, she whispered, "One day, you and I will have grand adventures. That's a promise." Loki growled in reply, and she smiled. "That's the spirit. We'll show them. We'll show them all."

Chapter 1 - Rogue

4 Years Later...

Rogue's eyes snapped open, and she stared into the darkness that shrouded the bedroom. It pulsed around her, the atmosphere tense and ominous. She knew the feeling wasn't real or even rational, but it was hard not to be scared when the remnants of her latest nightmare still hovered in the back of her mind.

Seeking comfort, she reached out to Seth's side of the bed but encountered nothing but empty space. Bitter disappointment filled her heart, and tears stung her eyelids. She'd forgotten he was gone. *It's been so long.*

Four months, two weeks, and three days had passed since Seth left the Zoo, accompanied by a small group of people. A mixture of hunters, trackers, and traders. They'd embarked on an exploratory expedition looking for a city to the east, a place rumored to be advanced and self-sufficient. Seth had hoped to open up a trade route with the new town, but he never returned from the trip, and neither did any of the others.

Numerous search parties went out looking for them, following their route to the east. They all returned empty-handed, reporting that the trail, clear at first, quickly petered out. It was as if Seth and his party had been plucked off the face of the earth. There were no signs of their bodies, possessions, or the rumored city, and Rogue was deathly afraid that the worst had happened to them. *Please, not him. Not Seth. He's my life. My world. My everything.*

The idea that she might never see him again was enough to bring her to her knees, but she couldn't afford to languish in self-pity and despair. She had responsibilities. Too many to count. One of them being her daughter, Ridley.

Rogue shook her head and sighed. Ridley had always been a handful. Stubborn, adventurous, and impetuous, trouble seemed to follow her like a shadow. Since her father's disappearance, she'd gotten even more difficult, neglecting her duties and sneaking off at all hours of the day. "What am I going to do with you, Daughter? Anything I say just seems to make it worse."

Swallowing her fear and loneliness, she dragged herself out of bed, shivering in the cool air. Dawn was still an hour or more away, judging by the gray light seeping through the curtains, but she got up anyway. Sleep held nothing but terror for her now.

Dressed in a woolen nightgown, robe, and slippers, Rogue headed toward the kitchen. The room was cold and dark, but she quickly approached the wood-burning stove in the corner. Inside, a pile of neatly stacked wood waited, packed the night before.

Reaching for the flint and steel on top, she struck them together to create a spark. One flew through the air and landed on the kindling, catching alight. Smoke curled from a wooden shaving, and she blew on it until a proper flame burst free. "Yes!"

Feeding the fire, she waited until it was blazing hot inside the steel belly of the oven. Next, she filled a kettle with water, using the hand pump in the washbasin, and added a scoop of dried, ground chicory root.

After a terrible frost killed their coffee bean fields years before, chicory became the new brew of the day. Sadly, it lacked the oomph of the real thing, not containing a drop of caffeine. She missed the kick of energy, especially now that she was getting older, feeling every single one of her forty-eight years.

With the kettle heating on the stove, Rogue opened the curtains and windows. Fresh air flooded the room, and she sucked in a deep breath, but a hacking cough ruined the sensation.

Doubled over, she clung to the kitchen counter until the coughing fit passed, leaving her faint and lightheaded. Her lungs burned, and it took several moments before she was strong enough to continue her daily chores. Finally, she straightened up and grabbed a lantern. After lighting it with a flame from the stove, she went to the bathroom.

Inside, Rogue used the compost toilet, sprinkling a layer of sawdust and dirt over the evidence. Afterward, she washed her hands, brushed her teeth, and combed her hair. A second coughing fit left her hanging onto the sink for support. *I'm getting worse. The antibiotics aren't working.*

Terror flared inside her chest, but she suppressed it with an iron will. There was no time for weakness or lazing about. Her chores waited, and without Seth around to help, the brunt of the work fell on her shoulders.

CHAPTER 1 - ROGUE

Back in her bedroom, Rogue pulled on clean underwear, a shirt, and a pair of slacks. The garments were made of finely woven wool, light and comfortable against her skin. Leather sandals finished off the ensemble, and she styled her hair in a thick braid that hung to her waist.

If Seth were there, he'd tug the braid with a smile playing on his lips. Despite her advancing years, he maintained that she was the most beautiful woman in the world, appearing blind to the fine lines around her eyes and the gray streaks in her hair. He never failed to make her feel special.

Thoughts of her missing husband caused her knees to wobble, and Rogue sank down on the edge of the bed. *I miss you, Seth. Where are you?*

She wanted to cry and rail at the heavens but couldn't. Not with Ridley sleeping in the room next door. She had to keep going for her daughter. No matter what the cost.

"Come on. You can do it," Rogue said, standing up with a groan of effort.

Wearily, she made the bed, opened the curtains, washed the dishes, wiped down the counters, and made breakfast. After setting the table for two, she knocked on her daughter's bedroom door. "Ridley? Are you awake?"

Silence.

Rogue knocked a little louder. "Time to get up, sweetheart. Breakfast's ready."

Nothing.

Frowning, Rogue opened the door and stepped into the room. "Ridley?"

An empty space greeted her, the bed still made and one window yawning wide open. A quick check revealed that Ridley's treasured crossbow and backpack were missing, along with her outdoor jacket and moccasins.

Rogue's lips compressed as anger and frustration flooded her veins. "Damn it, Ridley! Where did you run off to this time?"

But the anger quickly faded, replaced by exhaustion. She simply didn't have the energy to deal with her wayward daughter anymore. A free spirit, Seth used to call her, his eyes shining. *Free spirit, be damned. More like a monumental pain in my ass.*

Taking a deep breath, Rogue attempted to calm herself, but yet another coughing fit seized hold of her body. An iron fist closed around her lungs, squeezing the breath from her body. She doubled over as one hacking cough after another wracked her fragile frame until she sank to her knees, one hand pressed to her chest. Spots danced before her eyes, and she wondered if it was the end.

Finally, the fit passed, and Rogue was able to suck in a precious lungful of oxygen. As her vision cleared, she focused on the polished floorboards mere inches from her face. Crimson spots dotted the surface, and she frowned. *Is that....?*

She dragged one trembling hand across her lips, and it came away wet, tarnished with crimson blood. The liquid bubbled up her throat and frothed on her lips, and her heart sank as she realized the truth. *I'm dying.*

Chapter 2 - Ridley

Ridley jerked upright with a start and blinked at her surroundings with confusion. Gray light filtered through the leaves, casting a greenish tint over the wooden platform nestled within the limbs of an ancient tree. High off the ground and lodged inside a clump of knotted branches, it was safe from predators. A haven in the prehistoric world. But it was not meant to serve as an overnight shelter. Especially when she was supposed to wake up in her own bed long before her mother could discover her absence.

"Crap! I overslept," Ridley cried, kicking aside the blanket that shrouded her form. She accidentally kicked Loki in the ribs, and the wolf yelped with startled surprise. Patting him on the head, she said, "I'm sorry, boy. I didn't mean to do that."

He affected a haughty look and stood up, his fluffy tail hitting her in the face. She sputtered and waved it away with one hand, laughing. "Watch it, fur ball!

Loki ignored her and walked toward the end of the platform. He peered over the edge, his nose twitching as he took in the scents and smells brought to him by the fresh morning breeze.

A flock of pterosaurs swept past overhead, the force of their wings causing the forest canopy to shake and shudder. Harsh caws filled the air as the prehistoric birds sought their nests. Nocturnal by nature, they wanted no part of the sun and hunted during the dark hours of the night.

Alerted by their presence, Ridley reached for her pack. She pulled out two strips of dried meat and called to Loki. "Here, boy. Eat up."

Loki walked over and sat down, waiting for her to present the food. Ridley held it out, and he took it from her fingers with careful deliberation. The sight made her smile, and she rewarded him with a pat on the head. "Good, boy."

Aware that Loki was both wild at heart and dangerous by nature, she'd taken care over the years to train him well. She also made certain they shared a strong emotional bond forged from mutual companionship and respect. He was her best friend, and she was his, but she was in charge. There were no doubts about that.

Once they'd eaten, Ridley poured Loki a bowl of water from a bottle and took a few sips herself. It was all they had time for. Already the forest echoed with the familiar whoops and calls of birds readying to greet the dawn, and they had to get back before her absence was noticed.

Ridley got to her feet and slung her crossbow and backpack across her shoulders. She walked to the edge of the platform and reached for the rope that controlled the pulley system her father had built.

The tree house was his handiwork, a hideaway up in the trees where a couple of hunters could rest in relative safety or even overnight. It was small but solid, reachable by a series of wooden steps nailed to the tree. The pulley was added afterward at her insistence, as Loki couldn't climb trees. It also came in handy when they had a lot of supplies to ferry

CHAPTER 2 - RIDLEY

up and down.

Thoughts about her father caused a knot to form in her throat. She missed him so much it hurt, and she hated the thought of him lost out in the wilderness, hurt and in pain. He wasn't dead. Of that, she was certain. Her dad was one of the toughest people she knew. Strong, tenacious, determined, and brave, he'd never give up. Never stop trying to return to his family. It killed her that she couldn't go out looking for him, but her mother had forbidden it. Yet another reason they didn't get along lately. *She treats me like a child when I know I can find him. All I need is a chance.*

But now was not the time to get lost in morbid thoughts. She had to get home before her mom noticed she was gone. If Rogue found out about Ridley's nocturnal trips into the wild, there would be hell to pay. So far, she'd gotten away with it by sneaking in and out of the Zoo undetected. She usually made it back to her bed before her mom discovered her gone, though she'd had to lie on occasion. Pretending she'd gotten up early to feed the horses or head out to the fields with the farmers. Either way, she had to get moving, or no amount of excuses would help her out this time. "Come on, Loki. Let's go."

As usual, he balked. He wasn't fond of the experience and had to be coaxed onto the platform. Being stuck on a small wooden square high up in the air wasn't his idea of fun, and he whined with anxiety.

"It's okay, boy. I'm right here," Ridley said, her voice low and soothing.

Gingerly, Loki stepped onto the board and huddled against her legs. He shivered with fear, and she rubbed his head with her free hand. "Don't worry, boy. I've got you. I promise."

While lowering them to the ground, she kept up a stream of comforting words. At the same time, she looked around for danger, making certain the area was clear. The thought of a T-rex lumbering up and snapping them out of the air as an early-morning snack was not a comfortable one. Fortunately, the woods were quiet, and nothing stirred beneath the trees.

Once they hit the bottom, Ridley hid the platform and tied up the rope. After a quick look around, she struck out for home. The sun was up, and she needed to be back in her room before Rogue noticed she was gone. If it wasn't too late already. Her mom was an early riser, never one to lay in bed when there was work to be done.

Thoughts of her mother made her frown. She didn't like thinking about their relationship. The tense atmosphere, the strained silences, and the constant fighting. It had always been bad, but ever since her father disappeared, it had gotten even worse.

Her mom insisted on keeping her close, not allowing her an inch of freedom. It was both aggravating and infuriating, and she chafed at her invisible bonds. *Why won't she let me be? Why does she try so hard to turn me into something I'm not?*

Ridley did not possess the answers, and she wasn't about to ask either. That only led to more arguing, and she was tired of always being at odds with her mother. *I just want my freedom. Is that too much to ask?*

Shaking her head, Ridley focused on her surroundings. Not paying attention was a quick way to end up inside a predator's stomach. With her senses on high alert, she said, "Come on, Loki. Time to run!"

Loki yipped and forged ahead, cutting a path through the ferns. She followed, ducking underneath the hanging vines

CHAPTER 2 - RIDLEY

and branches. Leaves brushed against the leather of her pants and tunic, and her soft-soled moccasins flew across the trail. Each step took her closer to home, and her muscles sang with vigor. Blood pumped through her veins, and she felt young and alive. Vital.

For a brief moment in time, she forgot about her troubles. She forgot about everything except the need to run with Loki at her side. He was the only one who understood her desire to be free and wild. To exist in the moment and not care about the morrow.

Staying a few steps behind Loki, Ridley jumped across a fallen log and sidestepped a moss-covered rock. A twig tugged at her hair, but she ignored it, twisting around a corner in the trial. It led to a steep embankment, and she slid down the muddy slope to the stream below.

Leaping from stone to stone, she crossed the creek and climbed up a steep hill until she reached the top. There, she paused, taking a moment to survey the area. The trail she followed wound between the trees, their slim brown trunks reaching to the heavens. A thick carpet of dead leaves rotted on the forest floor while moss covered the rocks and fallen logs in different hues of green and brown. The first rays of dawn filtered through the canopy overhead, and the distant cawing of pterosaurs echoed through the air.

It was a captivating world, and it promised to be a beautiful day, the kind Ridley would've liked to spend outdoors, hunting, fishing, and exploring. It was not meant to be, however, and she resigned herself to going home. From where she stood, it was a straight shot to the Zoo, and she should be able to sneak back inside without anyone noticing. With any luck, she'd arrive at the same time the guards changed shifts, the perfect moment to slip into the compound.

Ridley glanced at Loki. "Come on, boy. We'll be home in no time."

Or so she thought until she noticed movement across the trail and in the trees surrounding it. Her heart sank when she realized what caused the movement, and frustration bubbled up her throat. A herd of Styracosaurus blocked the way, and there was no way she'd make it back in time. *Ah, crap. Mom's going to kill me.*

Chapter 3 - Rogue

Rogue dragged herself into the kitchen, feeling drained and nauseous. The Zoo's homegrown variety of penicillin wasn't strong enough to treat her illness, an advanced form of tuberculosis. Despite her and the local doctor's best efforts to treat it, she'd steadily worsened over the past few months.

Seth's disappearance was an added blow. He'd always been her rock. The steadying influence in her life. Whenever she embarked on some crazy adventure, he was the one who backed her. He also provided her with a safe place to lick her wounds when it all went wrong, as it often did. She wasn't sure she had what it took to carry on without him.

A knock on the door pulled her from her thoughts, and she sat upright, plastering a smile on her face. "Come in!"

The door opened, and a familiar face popped into the gap. "Good morning. It's me, Jessica."

"Jessica!" Rogue exclaimed, jumping up. "You're back!" She rushed forward, and they shared a warm hug. "I've missed you."

"I missed you too," Jessica said, peeling off her muddy boots. She dropped them on the porch and stepped inside on bare feet. "It's why I came straight here the moment we arrived."

"You just got back?" Rogue asked, warming up the pot of

coffee.

"We arrived last night, but it was after dark, so we decided to camp out in the fields and hit the gates first thing this morning," Jessica explained.

She placed her backpack against the wall, her hunting rifle, and the rest of her gear. Although covered in the dust and muck of the trail, she still cut an impressive figure with her dark good looks and athletic build. The room seemed to shrink around her, made smaller by her larger-than-life presence and sheer vitality.

Suddenly, Rogue felt the loss of her youth and freedom. While younger than Jessica by a few years, she felt and looked older. It was the price she paid when she gave up her freedom and settled down with family and community responsibilities. A burden that weighed heavy on her shoulders.

Still, she wasn't sorry she'd made that choice. Her loved ones and her people flourished partly because of her leadership and efforts. Without her, the Zoo wouldn't be what it was: A beacon of safety, hope, trust, and partnership in a brutal world.

"Coffee?" she offered.

"Yes, please," Jessica said, sinking into the nearest chair.

Rogue poured them each a cup before taking her seat. "Where's Bear?"

"Taking a bath. The man stinks to high heaven," Jessica said. Wrinkling her nose, she sniffed her armpits. "So do I, but I had to come here first. I knew you'd want to see me right away."

"Of course. I'm glad you came," Rogue said, her hands clenched around the hot cup of coffee. Despite her assertion, she wasn't sure she wanted to hear what Jessica had to say. So far, she'd avoided asking the question that burned inside her heart, afraid of the answer. "Did you find him?"

Jessica shook her head. "No. I'm sorry, but there's no sign of Seth anywhere."

Rogue slumped in her seat, despair settling over her like a suffocating cloud. "Nothing? Nothing at all?"

"Bear and I followed the route on the map you provided and saw signs of his group's passage. We stuck to the trail for days until...."

"Until what?"

"Until it disappeared."

"How's that possible?"

"The rain, the elements. It's been months, and the trail has gone cold."

"But, there has to be some clue as to what happened to him and the others. Did you ask the other traders? Go to the towns?" Rogue asked. "Someone must know something."

"No one has seen him or anyone of his team, and they haven't been to any of their usual haunts either," Jessica replied. "It's like they vanished into thin air."

"What about the place he was searching for? This mystery city everyone is talking about?" Rogue said.

"We looked but couldn't find anything. No trails, no signs of passage or people. If there is such a place, they do not want to be found." Jessica shook her head. "I'm not even sure it exists. The rumors are very vague, and no one I've spoken to, has actually been to it."

Rogue stared at her friend with dismay. Jessica had been her last hope. Her last shot at finding Seth. The woman was an ex-big game hunter and an excellent tracker. Where everyone else had failed, she was sure to succeed. Now, it was over, and she struggled to cope with the knowledge that Seth might genuinely be gone.

Unable to sit still, Rogue jumped up from her chair. She paced the length of the room, a storm of restlessness and fury brewing inside her chest. *No. He can't be dead. I refuse to believe it.* "I'm not giving up on him. I won't."

"What are you thinking of doing?" Jessica asked, looking concerned.

"I'll go out looking for him myself. Like I should've done from the beginning instead of leaving it up to others."

"You can't!" Jessica said, stunned.

"Why not?"

"You haven't been out there in years," Jessica protested. "Not for more than a day or two at the most, anyway."

"So?" Rogue said, dismissing her words. "Seth would never have given up on me. How can I abandon him now?"

"You wouldn't last a day," Jessica said. "Besides, you're needed here. What about Ridley?"

Rogue paused. Ridley was the only reason she hadn't gone out looking for Seth herself yet. The reason she'd been forced to sit around and wait for news that never came. *No more.* "He's out there somewhere, and I'm going to find him."

"Be reasonable, please," Jessica pleaded.

"Four months. It's been four months of utter hell," Rogue cried. "I need to know what happened to my husband, Jessica. I need to know!"

Suddenly, her chest convulsed, and she broke into a series of hacking coughs. Desperate to keep it under control, she turned away from Jessica and clung to the nearest chair. Bloody saliva frothed on her lips, and the taste of iron filled her mouth as she fought for air.

CHAPTER 3 - ROGUE

Firm hands gripped her shoulders, and Jessica's voice sounded in her ears. "What's wrong? Are you alright?"

"I... I'm fine," Rogue gasped in between coughs.

"No, you're not," Jessica said, fussing around the kitchen. She returned with a wet cloth and pressed it to Rogue's forehead.

"Thanks," Rogue muttered, the cool material reviving her somewhat. After patting her entire face, she wiped the blood from her lips.

"You're coughing blood."

"It's nothing. Just a chest infection," Rogue insisted.

"Don't try to bullshit me," Jessica said, her voice stark. "It's tuberculosis, isn't it?"

Rogue nodded.

"How long have you had it?"

"Six months," Rogue admitted.

"Six months! Why didn't you tell me?" Jessica cried.

"I didn't want to worry you," Rogue said, waving her off. "I'm not an invalid."

"Did Seth know?"

"Yes. It's one of the reasons he went looking for that other place. The supposedly advanced one. He was hoping to trade for stronger antibiotics," Rogue said, guilt churning inside her chest. *It's my fault he's missing.*

"What about Ridley? Does she know?"

"No, she doesn't, and you can't tell her," Rogue said, grabbing Jessica's hand. "Promise me."

"Rogue, you have to. She deserves to know."

"Not with her father missing," Rogue said. "She's got enough on her plate for now."

"She'll have even more on her plate if she loses you too."

"Don't say that. Seth isn't dead. He's still alive," Rogue said.

"It's been so long, Rogue. Maybe it's time you accepted the truth."

"Truth? What truth? That he's dead? That some horrible accident befell him, and he died alone? Hurt and in pain?" Rogue asked, bitter tears stinging her eyelids.

"I'm sorry. I don't mean to hurt you," Jessica said. "I just can't stand seeing you like this. Pining for him day after day."

"What else can I do?" Rogue said. "He's the love of my life, Jessica. He's part of my soul."

"I know, sweetie. I can only imagine how much it must hurt to lose him, but you still have Ridley," Jessica said. "You still have your daughter."

"Do I?" Rogue asked with a bitter laugh. "My daughter has become a stranger to me."

"What do you mean?" Jessica frowned. "I know you've struggled in the past, but surely, it can't be that bad."

"She hardly speaks to me," Rogue shook her head. "Ever since Seth disappeared, I don't even know where she is half the time."

"Would you like me to talk to her? She listens to me," Jessica said.

"She idolizes you, but no. This is my cross to bear," Rogue said.

"Are you sure?"

"Yes," Rogue said, chewing on her bottom lip. "Maybe you're right. Maybe it's time I told her the truth."

"About your illness?"

"That, and Seth. Maybe it's time we both faced the facts. He's not coming back, is he?" Rogue said, hot tears spilling down her face.

CHAPTER 3 - ROGUE

"Oh, sweetie. I'm so sorry," Jessica said, drawing her into a hug.

Rogue clung to her, heartbroken.

"You'll be okay; you'll see," Jessica said. "The pain will get less with time."

"I hope you're right," Rogue said, pulling away. "I really hope so because if it doesn't, I don't know how I will make it through another day."

"You'll make it. You're one of the strongest people I know," Jessica said. "Besides, you have Ridley to take care of."

Rogue choked out a broken laugh. "Do I?"

"She'll come around. Just give her time."

"That's the thing. I don't have a lot of time. A few months at most," Rogue said. She wiped the tears from her face and poured them a fresh cup of coffee.

"Don't say that," Jessica said, looking distraught. "There has to be something we can do."

"I've tried everything," Rogue said. "The doctor too. Herbal remedies. Antibiotics. Nothing works. My condition is too advanced."

"Then we'll get stronger antibiotics. The good stuff," Jessica said.

Rogue snorted. "Where would I get that? Vancouver's the only place I know of that might have what I need, but I can't be sure, and traveling by river takes weeks. On foot even longer. I'd never make the trip."

"I could do it for you," Jessica suggested.

"I could never ask that of you," Rogue said. "Besides, I can't afford it."

"Oh, please. Imogen owes us both," Jessica said. "It's because of us that her mom had to step down as the Mayor, remember?

Paving the way for her to take over."

"I remember, but you'd never return in time."

"I can damn well try," Jessica said. "You're my best friend, and I'm not giving up on you yet."

Rogue smiled. "At least Ridley will still have you once I'm not around anymore."

"That's quite enough of that. You are not dying, and that's final," Jessica said, two bright spots marring her cheeks.

"Jessica, please. It's not like I want this."

"Isn't it? Because it seems to me like you've given up already," Jessica said. "This isn't like you, Rogue. You're a fighter, so fight."

"Fine. I'll try," Rogue said, secretly wondering if she even wanted to. It would be so much easier to give up and die. Especially with Seth… Even in her head, she couldn't complete the thought.

"What happened to the Rogue who took down General Sikes and liberated an entire city? What happened to the Rogue who traveled to an unknown city, through unknown territory, took down a crooked mayor, and stopped another time-traveling disaster from ripping us apart?" Jessica asked.

Rogue sighed, too tired to argue. "She got old and boring, remember?"

"You are neither old nor boring. You are an inspiration. The fearless leader who took this community into a future it could never have imagined," Jessica said, her tone fierce. "Don't you ever sell yourself short."

"Thanks," Rogue said. "Now, if only Ridley could see that. Maybe she'd stop fighting me on everything."

"Maybe you need to give her some space. You're a lot alike. Stubborn, crazy, adventurous, and impulsive."

"I know. That's the problem," Rogue said, thinking back over the years. In hindsight, it was a miracle that she hadn't died a million times over and didn't want Ridley to take the same chances.

"The harder you hold on, the more she'll pull away," Jessica added.

"I know, but letting go is hard. She's my child," Rogue said.

"Maybe, but she's not a kid anymore. At some point, you've got to trust that you raised her right and that she'll make good decisions."

"As usual, you are right," Rogue said with a frustrated groan. "I'll try not to be so hard on her in the future."

"Promise?" Jessica asked, one eyebrow cocked.

"I promise," Rogue said, rolling her eyes.

"You have to promise to look after yourself too. At least until I get the chance to figure something out," Jessica said.

"I'll try."

"I mean it, Rogue. I couldn't find Seth, but I swear I won't let you down."

"I know you won't," Rogue replied, her heart full of gratitude. "You're a good friend."

"The best," Jessica said with a grin. "Anyway, thanks for the coffee, but it's time for me to go. I stink of dust, sweat, and horse. Not a pleasant combination."

"I'm just happy you're back in one piece. You and Bear," Rogue said, escorting Jessica to the porch.

"Me too. We had a few hairy encounters out there," Jessica said, pulling on her dirty boots and slinging her backpack across her shoulders.

"Tell Bear I said hello," Rogue said, sad to see her friend leave.

"We'll probably make a turn again later this afternoon," Jessica said. "Just to ensure you and Ridley haven't killed each other yet."

"We'll find out soon enough," Rogue said, looking at the sun. It hovered just above the horizon, well past dawn but still early. "She should be home soon enough, and I'd love to find out what she's been up to."

"Just remember what I said," Jessica cautioned.

"I will," Rogue promised, though she wasn't looking forward to the encounter.

The last thing she wanted was another argument with her daughter, but she had no choice. Seth was gone, and he wasn't coming back. Hiding behind false hope wasn't an option anymore. Not when she was dying. Ridley needed to know the truth. She needed time to prepare for the future—a future as an orphan.

Chapter 4 - Ridley

Ridley watched the Styracosaurus from the shelter of a moss-covered tree. The large herd of herbivores filled the area, numbering in the dozens. They were identifiable by their large neck frills and the curved horn that sprouted from their snouts, flanked by two smaller ones on their cheeks.

Licking one finger, she tested the wind, relieved to find it was blowing toward her. The last thing she needed was for the stocky, horned dinosaurs to catch a whiff of her scent and panic. Though not as large as their cousins, the triceratops, each styracosaurus weighed between two and three tons. Enough to grind her and Loki into a bloody pulp should they be caught in a stampede.

Even worse, it was a breeding herd led by an old and scarred matriarch filled with the wisdom granted by many seasons. The younger females grazed around the edges of the group while the juveniles stayed in the middle, where it was safer. Mid-spring, the young were still small, easy prey for the many predators that populated their world.

Ridley studied the herd, hoping they'd move on, but they seemed content to stay they were. They grazed on the rich undergrowth, slicing through the tough ferns with their beaks. She craned her neck, looking for a way around or through the herd, quickly realizing she was doomed.

Going around was the safest option, but it would take several hours. By then, her mother would have the entire Zoo in an uproar looking for her missing daughter. Going through the herd was too dangerous. If she was spotted, it meant certain death.

Suddenly, an idea hit her, and she ran back to the river, scooped up handfuls of mud, and rubbed it across her exposed skin. Much to his disgust, Loki got the same treatment, and he tried to back away with a low growl.

"Oh, come on. This will work," Ridley coaxed, rubbing the stuff into his fur. "You don't want them to smell you, do you?"

Loki wrinkled his nose and tried to shake off the muck clinging to his body, his tail rigid.

"I don't get it. You love rolling around in dinosaur poop and other horrible stuff, but you can't stand a bit of mud," Ridley said with a low laugh. "You are a mystery."

Loki responded with a vigorous shake, splattering her with leftover muck, and she stifled a squeal. Wiping her eyes, she beckoned to the wolf. "Alright, you've had your fun. Let's go."

Together, they returned to their previous position and scouted a route that led around the outer edges of the herd, away from the juveniles. It was safer than cutting straight through but shorter than bypassing the herd altogether.

Clutching her crossbow with shaky hands, Ridley waved to Loki. "Come on, boy. Hide!"

She accompanied the last word with a hand signal, a downward thrust with her flat hand. Loki immediately went into stealth mode. It was one of the first commands she'd taught him as a puppy, knowing there were many dangers in the world, and he needed to know how to stay hidden.

CHAPTER 4 - RIDLEY

Taking the lead, Ridley navigated a path through the trees and undergrowth. She stayed low to the ground and did not step on a twig or brush against a tree trunk. Even the tiniest noise could alert the styracosaurus and set them off.

In a low run, she crossed a few feet of open space before she dropped down behind a bank of thorny bushes. She slithered through a gap in the brush on her hands and knees, pushing through to the other side. Halfway there, a thorn dug into the palm of her hand, and she hissed with pain. Using her teeth, she dug out the barb and spat it aside. *Ow, ow, ow!*

Blood oozed from the hole, and she paused to rub mud on it to disguise the smell. However, there was no time to waste, and she carried on until she reached the far end of the brush. There, a gigantic log blocked her path. Ancient and covered in moss, it had fallen in one of the many big storms that plagued the region in summer.

Just as she prepared to climb over, a lumbering foot thudded down mere inches from her hiding spot. A tail as thick as her waist flew past overhead and smashed into the log. The rotten wood splintered into a gazillion pieces, releasing a flood of insects onto the forest floor. Worms and grubs writhed about in the open, quickly burrowing into the soft soil while beetles scuttled for shelter.

A fat spider crawled up her arm, and it took all of her willpower not to scream and run around in a panic. She hated the creatures and couldn't stand them anywhere near her with their thick, armored body and beady eyes. Horned fangs topped the list of their nasty characteristics, and she flung her arm out with all her might. *Get it off; get it off!*

The violence of her movement dislodged the spider and catapulted it into the air. It hit the nearest tree with a muted splat, and green goo oozed down the rough bark.

Ridley shuddered and looked away, afraid that her actions had alerted the herd. But the styracosaurus appeared oblivious, and they continued to graze unperturbed. She heaved a sigh of relief, but the sensation was short-lived when Loki sniffed at the spider's remains with grizzly interest. *Eeuw! No! Yuck!*

She pulled the wolf away from the spot and wagged a stern finger at his face. Loki answered with a silent laugh, his tongue lolling from his open jaws.

Rolling her eyes, Ridley returned to the task at hand: Getting through the herd of styracosaurus without being spotted and causing a stampede.

Inching forward, she crawled across the remnants of the rotten log with Loki close at her side. She kept a wary eye on the dinosaur looming above her head the entire time. It lumbered across the forest floor, chewing on ferns and leaves mere feet from her side. Each step caused deep vibrations to run through her body, and its scaly hide was so close she could almost reach out and touch it.

It was a tense couple of moments, with visions of her being stepped on and squashed like a bug flashing through her mind. The cloying smell of musk and dung filled her nostrils and clung to the back of her throat. Finally, the dinosaur moved away, and she could scramble past it without being seen.

In a low crouch, she crossed a small clearing, skirted a knot of trees, and circled a handful of juveniles. They gamboled through the trees, chasing each other with squeals of joy underneath the watchful gazes of their mothers. Their antics brought a smile to Ridley's face, but she gave them a wide berth. There was nothing more deadly in the wilderness than

CHAPTER 4 - RIDLEY

a mother protecting her young.

She managed to sneak past them without mishap and ducked behind a thick stand of ferns and hanging vines. Using that as a shield, she slipped past the last remaining styracosaurus and emerged in the clear. Going forward, the trail was empty, and her home was only a short run away.

It was sad leaving the herd with its fun-loving youngsters behind, however, and she wished she could stay and observe them all day. But her mother didn't care about the wild and its beauty. She only cared about service to the community, leadership, and its burdens, daily chores, and responsibility. *I'd better hurry before she realizes I'm gone.*

Breaking into a sprint, Ridley pushed her body to its limits. Her hair whipped in the breeze like a flag, the dark tresses glinting in the early morning light. Her feet pounded the earth, echoing the beat of her heart, and the blood rushed through her veins with primitive abandon. Not to be outdone, Loki streaked ahead, a grayish blur against the browns and greens of the forest.

As the sun rose above the treetops, Ridley burst into the open with Loki at her side. She stumbled to a halt and paused to catch her breath, both hands braced on her knees. Sweat poured down her skin, and her legs felt like jelly, but she didn't care. "We made it, Loki. We're almost home." Loki yipped and spun in a circle, reflecting her enthusiasm. "Come on, boy. We'd better hurry."

With a grin, she broke into a slow jog. Sneaking into the Zoo wouldn't be easy, but she had her ways. The main trick was getting past the guards. They reported to Ric, her step-grandfather, and he would not hesitate to rat on Ridley.

Besides, she was a little scared of him. Despite his advancing years, Ric still cut an imposing figure, and she did not want him to rake her over the coals. Her grandmother, Olivia, was a different story. She doted on Ridley and spoiled her whenever possible, but even she wouldn't be happy if she found out her only granddaughter was sneaking out of the Zoo at night.

Ridley cut through the field that stretched around for miles, heading toward her home. The Zoo sat in the middle of this vast open space, its walls rising high above the ground. Cobbled together from bits of stone, masonry, and timber, it was a mixture of the old and the new.

As she drew closer, she raised one hand to shield her eyes from the sun and gazed ahead. She wanted to plot her route and hoped the guards were busy with shift change. That would make it easier to sneak in without being detected, but to her utter dismay, the gate was already open, and people milled about at the entrance. "Oh, crap. We're too late!"

The Zoo community was wide awake and bustling with early morning activities. Wagons stood ready to head out to the fields, and what appeared to be a trading party awaited authorization to enter the grounds. Guards thronged the area, and sneaking in would be impossible.

With her heart in her stomach, Ridley weighed her options. She did not want to face her mother's or her grandparents' wrath. For a brief moment, she considered running away. Prime City wasn't that far, and she had plenty of friends and family there: Her step-grandmother Moran, Sir Callum, and his wife, Kat. Their son, Teagan. Paul, Sandi, and their kids. There were lots of people she knew.

Still, none of them would hide her from her mother, and the idea quickly fizzled out, leaving her back at square one until an idea hit her. If she could get close enough, she could blend

CHAPTER 4 - RIDLEY

in with the rest of the crowd and slip inside unnoticed. If someone spotted her, she'd pretend she'd gotten up early and wanted to check out the arriving traders' caravan. Visitors were always a big deal, bringing all sorts of goods, news, stories, and tales to the community.

"Right. This is the plan, Loki," Ridley said, her mind made up. "We sneak inside with the traders and pretend that we belong. Okay?" Loki whined and looked at her with worried eyes. "Yeah, yeah, I know. There's a good chance we'll get caught, but it's our only shot." Determined to try it, Ridley set her sights on the gate. "Let's do this."

Chapter 5 - Jessica

Jessica left Rogue's home and made her way through the crowded market square. She slipped through the stalls and wagons, waving and smiling at all the familiar faces. After spending two weeks on the road with the traders' caravan, they were almost like family.

Initially, she and Bear had gone out on their own. They'd followed Seth's trail as far as they could but lost it a week into the search. Determined to find him or signs of him, they canvassed the area for a further two weeks but came up empty.

Finally, Jessica had to admit defeat. Even her superior tracking skills couldn't cut it, especially after such a long time. She was only sorry she hadn't known about his disappearance earlier, but the alarm was only raised three months after his departure. That was considered the latest date for his return.

Even then, she was unaware of the situation, having gone on an extended trip before visiting friends at Prime City. By the time she returned, two search parties had already returned empty-handed, and a third had gone out. When that one also returned with no information, Rogue begged Jessica to try, and she was only too happy to help.

After their original search delivered nothing, Jessica and Bear visited every community along the way. They inquired at

CHAPTER 5 - JESSICA

each one, looking for evidence that Seth or one of his team had been there. But once again, they came away empty-handed with no new information.

At that point, Jessica allowed herself to accept the inevitable. Seth was gone. Even if he were alive, neither she nor anyone else could find him. He was on his own. That knowledge hit her hard. Rogue and Seth were her best friends, and she owed them everything she had, including her life. With great reluctance, she took the road home, mourning her friend's loss every step of the way.

They joined up with the trading group in Prime City. There was safety in numbers. Comfort too. Jessica soon made friends with the traders, and their warm, friendly natures eased some of the pain in her heart. They were the salt of the earth. Nomads who allowed their spirits free reign, and she was glad they'd formed part of the last leg in her journey.

They could not help her complete the final step, however. Delivering the news, seeing and experiencing Rogue's raw anguish had been almost too much to bear. Nearly as bad as finding out that her friend was dying.

Jessica was not ready to give up on her, though. She was determined to find Rogue the medicine she needed to beat her disease. *I couldn't find Seth, but I sure as hell can fight to save my best friend's life.*

With that goal in mind, she searched for a particular trader. A woman named Eleanor. She spotted the woman's wagon moments later. It was hard to miss. The wheels were painted bright red, and the back was covered with thick white canvas.

Next to it stood a stall made from wooden poles tied together with rope and covered with more white canvas. A painted sign in the front read: Eleanor's Herbs, Tinctures, and Brews. An image of a witch's cauldron completed the picture, a tongue-in-cheek reference to Eleanor's quirky sense of humor.

Jessica grinned when she spotted it and ran to the back of the covered wagon. Rapping on the flap, she called out, "Eleanor. Are you in there?"

At first, silence. Then the wagon rustled, and the flap swept aside. A head topped with dark blonde hair appeared in the opening. Bright blue eyes gazed at Jessica curiously, and the woman said, "Back so soon?"

"I need your help," Jessica added.

"What kind of help?"

"The kind only you can provide," Jessica said, waving a hand at the wagon's interior. "My friend is sick, and she needs medicine. The local doctor doesn't have antibiotics strong enough to treat her."

"What makes you think I do?" Eleanor asked, climbing down the steps.

"Because you're a miracle worker," Jessica said, much to the other woman's amusement.

"A miracle worker? That's refreshing!" Eleanor said with a laugh.

A meow came from inside the wagon, and a gorgeous cat with reddish fur and green eyes slipped through the opening. Long tufts of hair sprang from the tips of its ears, and its whiskers were nothing short of luxurious. It was followed by a second and a third, each as majestic-looking as the last.

Jessica stared at the trio of cats, amazed anew by their presence. She knew about them, of course. She'd even seen them during her time with the traders' caravan, but she'd never gotten this close. They were skittish with strangers and avoided her and Bear at all costs. Now, they were so close she could almost touch them. Cats. An animal from the future brought back with all the other unfortunates flung back in time.

At the sight of their furry faces, Eleanor smiled. "Delilah, Jennifur, Malcolm! Did you come to greet our new visitor?"

Rubbing against Eleanor's legs, the three felines proclaimed their territory, observing Jessica. Evidently, they didn't trust her and wanted her gone, but she didn't mind. Instead, she asked, "Aren't you afraid they'll wander off when you're on the road? Get lost?"

"It was a struggle in the beginning," Eleanor admitted. "Luckily, I've had them from birth and was able to teach them well. They know where their home is and that what's out there is not friendly."

"You are lucky to have such fine companions," Jessica noted.

"Yes, I am," Eleanor said, waving a hand at the wagon. "Come inside where we can talk in private."

"Alright," Jessica agreed with a nod.

She climbed into the wagon, the flap dropping shut behind her. The interior was dim after the bright morning light outside, and Eleanor quickly lit a candle, bathing the space in a golden glow. The flowery scent permeated the air, and Jessica smiled in appreciation. "It smells so nice in here."

"Honeysuckle," Eleanor explained. "Cats love it. It calms them down."

"Interesting," Jessica said, looking around.

"Take a seat, please," Eleanor said, waving to a narrow bench against the far side. Brightly colored cushions decorated the surface, matched by a deep purple carpet on the floor.

Jessica sat down while Eleanor took the seat opposite, her

face expectant. "Tell me about your friend."

"She has tuberculosis," Jessica replied.

"How long?"

"Six months now. She's been taking medication, but it doesn't seem to work."

"Why not?"

"She nearly passed out this morning, and she's coughing blood," Jessica explained. "She looks frail. I'm worried."

"As you should be. It sounds like her disease has become drug-resistant," Eleanor explained.

"What can I do?"

"She'll need multiple types of antibiotics over the course of several months. The main problem is that she'd been taking only one kind of antibiotic this entire time."

"Do you have what she needs?" Jessica asked, holding her breath.

"Not enough. I have a few different courses, but not enough to cure her. You'll need to get more," Eleanor replied with a shake of the head.

"Where can I get that?"

"Vancouver. But it will cost you an arm and a leg," Eleanor said. "I won't be cheap either."

"I don't care about the money, but Vancouver's so far," Jessica said, a frown beading her forehead. Sometimes, she wished she still had all her contacts there. She could've rented a plane and delivered Rogue to their hospital for treatment.

Now, she'd have to travel by river, and it would take weeks. Though she supposed she should be grateful it was even possible. They had the prehistoric landscape to thank for that. It was a lot more water bound than the future world. Rivers were plentiful, as were marshlands and swamps. There was

CHAPTER 5 - JESSICA

an inland sea to contend with as well, making travel across land difficult.

"The medicine I have should buy you enough time to get to Vancouver and back," Eleanor said. "I can also whip up some herbal remedies to ease the symptoms and bolster her immune system."

"Please. Anything you can do," Jessica pleaded.

"Alright. Wait there while I get everything together," Eleanor said, reaching for an ornately carved wooden box.

She opened it, revealing a tray filled with small compartments. Each one contained a bag filled with dried herbs, and she quickly mixed a large pouch and handed it to Jessica. "This is tea. She must steep one teaspoon in hot water and drink it twice daily. It will help bring back her vitality."

Eleanor mixed more herbs into a small pot of fatty ointment until it emitted a pungent smell. "She must rub this on her chest three times a day. It will help her breathe and open her airways."

Next, she handed over several bags containing chalky white pills and another with yellow tablets. "The yellow pills are for pain. She can take them as needed, but the maximum is two tablets four times per day, or she'll risk overdosing. The rest is all the antibiotics I've got left. She must finish each course before starting the next without skipping!"

"Thank you," Jessica said, accepting the armful of medicines. She tucked it all away in her jacket pockets, relieved that she could help Rogue in her time of need. "You don't know how much this means to me."

"Oh, I have a fair idea," Eleanor said slyly. "Which brings me to my payment."

"Of course. How about this?" Jessica asked, removing a

ring from her middle finger. "It's real gold, and that's real diamonds."

Eleanor eyed the ring, then shook her head. "I have something different in mind."

"Like what?"

"A favor," Eleanor said.

"A favor? What favor?" Jessica asked, confused.

"I don't know yet, but when I do, you'll be the first to know," Eleanor said, wagging one finger. "Think of it as a future promise owed."

"That's crazy!" Jessica said. "How do I know you won't ask for something ridiculous when the time comes?"

"You don't," Eleanor said with a shrug. "And I'll expect you to deliver on your promise immediately."

"I don't know. It's too risky," Jessica said.

"Too risky to save the life of your friend?" Eleanor asked, a gleam in her eyes. "You'll never make it to Vancouver and back in time without my medicine."

"I know, damn it," Jessica said, realizing she'd already lost the deal. The moment she'd revealed to Eleanor how desperate she was, she lost any advantage. She lost the trade.

"Tick, tock," Eleanor said, her fingers drumming on the wooden chest.

"Okay, fine. It's a deal," Jessica said, reaching out to shake Eleanor's hand. "You've got a deal."

Jessica climbed out of the wagon and emerged into the early morning sun, feeling like she'd sold her soul to the devil. The hair on the back of her neck rose, and she looked back. Three pairs of feline eyes gleamed at her from the confines of the wagon, and she shuddered. "Shoo, you creepy damn cats!"

She hurried away, her skin crawling. Suddenly, she wasn't

CHAPTER 5 - JESSICA

so sure she liked cats anymore. She had the distinct feeling that her deal with Eleanor would not turn out well for her. But it couldn't be helped. Rogue needed the medicine. *I'll just have to face that bridge when I get to it.*

Chapter 6 - Ridley

Ridley flew across the open field, dodging the deep trenches surrounding the crops. They were filled with sharpened wooden stakes, each as thick as her body, and acted as a deterrent to marauding dinosaurs. Guard towers added another layer of protection, their squat bodies offering advanced warning and shelter in case of an attack.

The system wasn't perfect. There were periodic deaths and losses, and the carnivores weren't the worst offenders. Most of them were scavengers by nature and preferred easy prey. They also tended to stick to their territories unless driven away by a bigger, stronger opponent. Flyers and herbivores searching for a quick meal were an ever-present nuisance. It was astonishing how much damage one herd of triceratops could cause to a field.

Still, it was Ridley's home, and she loved it. To her, the future was just a distant fantasy. A magical place filled with wonders she'd never get to see or experience. She couldn't miss what she'd never had.

Sticking to the shadows and using all available cover, she crossed the open space until she hit the dirt road leading through the gates. A line of people, carts, and wagons thronged the area, waiting for the guards to let them through.

CHAPTER 6 - RIDLEY

It was taking longer than usual. The trading party had arrived during shift change, and it was chaos as the new guards replaced the old.

Ridley took full advantage of the confusion and slipped through the entrance without being noticed by the guards. It wasn't easy, especially with a grown wolf on her heels. Everyone in the Zoo knew Loki, and not everyone viewed him with fondness. But she was used to hiding, and so was Loki. Dropping to her haunches, she signaled to him. "Hide!"

The wolf ducked low, his ears flat against his head, and slipped through the crowd like a ghost. A gray blur, few noticed him, and he avoided open spaces. A couple of horses snorted when he ran between their legs, the only sign of his passing.

Grinning with pride, Ridley followed. She used the trade carts and wagons for cover, hiding her face from the guards and any townspeople. The minute she was inside, she whistled for Loki and headed for the center of town. "Come on, Loki!"

There was no point in heading straight home. It was already too late for that. Her mom would be up, and she would've noticed Ridley's absence. "The only thing I can do now is to putter around for a while, go home, and pretend I got up before dawn because I couldn't sleep. Right, Loki?"

Loki shot her a doubtful look, and she shrugged. "Okay, fine. How about I blame you? I could say you refused to sleep, drove me nuts, and I decided to take you for a walk."

His answer was a deep growl and a headlong rush at a flock of pigeons sitting on the ground not far away. The hapless birds scattered in all directions with offended squawks, their feathers drifting down in a cloud of white and gray.

Like all the other animals, stray dogs, cats, birds, and rodents, they came with the Shift. Some survived, sticking with the humans. Those who ventured into the wilderness were not so lucky, however, becoming snacks for hungry dinosaurs.

As for the Zoo, it went back in time with all of its animal species intact. Survivors looked after the zoo animals, and most of them flourished. A few species, like the penguins and polar bears, died out, unable to handle the heat. The African Buffalo died from a mysterious disease, followed by the wildebeest, hyenas, and most of the big cats and monkeys. The rest remained along with the animals from the kid's petting zoo.

Over time, some smaller dinosaurs were domesticated and kept inside empty Zoo enclosures. Together with the zoo animals, they formed part of the fabric of life—a mixture of the old and new, just like the rest of the community.

As usual, it bustled with life. Smoke rose from the chimneys, roosters crowed, zuniceratops and parksosaurus honked from their enclosures, and workers walked the pebbled pathways, preparing to feed the animals, milk the camels, and gather eggs from the geese and ostriches. Horses neighed, and donkeys brayed from the stables while cows chewed on their cud. It was just another busy day in the compound.

Ridley wandered around, saying hello to familiar faces and enjoying the activity. She spotted Aret, a council member, hurrying past, and said, "Good morning."

Aret looked at her and frowned. "Shouldn't you be at home?"

"I'm just out for a walk with Loki, Ma'am," Ridley said.

Aret wrinkled her nose. "That wolf is a nuisance. Please

CHAPTER 6 - RIDLEY

make sure it behaves."

"Yes, ma'am," Ridley said, wrinkling her nose.

"You behave as well!" Aret added.

"Ugh," Ridley muttered, rolling her eyes. She didn't like Aret. The woman was cold and distant, a workaholic who lived to suck the joy from free-spirited people's lives—a real spoilsport.

Hurrying in the opposite direction, she headed toward the market square. Most of the traders were already there to set up their stalls and unpack their goods. With a grin, she rushed toward them, eager to see what was on display. "Come on, Loki. Let's see what they've got."

It was too early, however. None of the stalls were ready, and after the third person shooed her away, Ridley gave up. "Fine. I'll come back later."

She reluctantly decided it was time to head home and face the music. There was no point in delaying it any longer except to fan her mother's wrath to its fullest extent. "I just wish she'd listen to me. If Dad were here, he'd…."

Ridley trailed off. Her father was not there, and that knowledge was lodged inside her gut like a stone. It never went away, never lightened, and never let her forget. Dashing away hot tears, she reached down to pat Loki. "At least I still have you."

Loki whined and licked her fingers, his presence a bulwark against the grief. She probably would've run away long ago if it wasn't for him. But he was her responsibility and looked to her for his care and safety. It was the one thing her parents had drilled into her head, and she took the task very seriously. "I'll always look after you, Loki. Always."

He nudged her hand with his nose and smiled. His version

of a toothy smile with his lips pulled back and his tongue lolling out of his mouth. The sight lightened her heart, and she walked with a lighter step. No matter what happened, she'd always have Loki.

Moments later, Ridley spotted her home: A small two-bedroom cottage she shared with her parents. The front door was open, and her mother leaned against the doorway with folded arms. Short and petite, she was still beautiful with her dark red hair, golden-brown eyes, and porcelain skin. A few stray hairs and crow's feet added a sense of grace and maturity, not detracting from her looks.

The sight of her mother caused her heart to sink. Next to her, Ridley felt like a lump of clay. Clumsy, unformed, and unshaped with none of the sophistication the other woman bore. It was yet another thing that made her feel inadequate. A palpable sensation that reached out to suffocate Ridley and suck the life and laughter from her bones. On leaden legs, she closed the distance, coming to a halt six feet from the edge of the porch. Staring at her shoes, she refused to meet Rogue's gaze. "Hi, Mom."

"Get your ass inside," her mother replied in clipped tones. She waved a hand at the kitchen table. "We need to talk."

"Mom, I can explain."

"I don't want to hear it. Get inside now," Rogue said.

"Okay," Ridley replied, motioning to Loki. "Stay."

Loki obeyed without complaint, trudging toward the far end of the porch where a thickly woven grass mat and a bowl of water waited.

Ridley walked past him and entered the kitchen. With hunched shoulders, she sat down on the nearest chair and waited for the accusations to fly.

CHAPTER 6 - RIDLEY

Instead, Rogue closed the door behind them with a firm click, shutting out the Zoo and its bustling inhabitants. Silence fell while she poured two cups of coffee and passed one to Ridley.

"Thanks," Ridley mumbled, accepting the cup with reluctance. While the hot brew was precisely what her taste buds craved, she was worried about what was coming next.

Rogue took the chair opposite Ridley, sat down, and fixed her daughter with a stern gaze. "Where were you last night?"

"I... uh, I couldn't sleep, so I got up early for a walk."

"Through the window? You couldn't use the front door?"

"I didn't want to wake you," Ridley said, swallowing hard.

"But you took the time to make your bed and take your backpack and crossbow?" Rogue asked, pointing to the two items lying on the floor by Ridley's feet.

"You know me. I like to be prepared," Ridley said with a shrug.

"I see," Rogue replied, rubbing one hand across her forehead. She sighed, suddenly looking tired. "You know what? I can't do this anymore. I might be old, but I'm not stupid."

"Mom, I swear...."

"I know you're lying, but I don't care. From now on, you can do whatever you want," Rogue said. "You're eighteen, after all. Too old to listen to your mother anymore."

"I... what?" Ridley asked, aghast.

"You heard me. You're a grown-up now and free to do as you wish," Rogue said.

"But I..." Ridley hesitated, unsure of what to say.

"It's what you wanted, right?" Rogue asked. "For me to back off? To let you have your freedom?"

"Yes, but..."

"Well, now you've got your wish," Rogue said, folding her arms.

"My wish? My wish was for you to see me for who I really am," Ridley protested.

"I did see you. I see you now," Rogue said.

"No, you don't," Ridley burst out, suddenly enraged. "You've only ever seen what you wanted to see. Not the real me. The real Ridley!"

"That's not true," Rogue said. "You're my daughter. My child. I love you."

"Then stop trying to control me. Stop trying to turn me into something I'm not," Ridley cried, jumping out of her chair.

"I'm not. I only want what's best for you," Rogue replied, spreading her arms wide. "I don't want you to get hurt."

"But I will get hurt, Mom. I'm supposed to," Ridley protested. "It's part of life, isn't it? Part of growing up."

"I... I..." Rogue stuttered, seemingly at a loss for words.

"Dad understands. He's seen me, the real me. He knows me," Ridley said, pacing back and forth in the tiny kitchen.

"Maybe, but your father's not here," Rogue said.

"No thanks to you!" Ridley yelled, rounding on her mother. Stabbing an accusing finger, she spat out the words that had haunted her for months. "He's gone because of you. It's all your fault."

"How can you say that?" Rogue asked with a gasp, but Ridley spotted the flash of guilt that crossed her features.

"You could've let me look for him. I would've found him. I'm an excellent tracker; you know that."

"You're eighteen years old. You're just a kid," Rogue protested. "You wouldn't last a day out there!"

"I know much more about the outside world than you think,"

CHAPTER 6 - RIDLEY

Ridley said.

"Because you sneak out all the time? Because you run around out there with your little bow and arrows, pretending you're a hunter and tracker?" Rogue asked. "You know nothing."

Ridley stopped midstride and glared at her mother, too angry to reply. *She knew? She knew all this time? All the lectures. All the fights. Was it all for nothing?*

"There are things out there that you've never encountered. Creatures so terrifying, you'd wet yourself if you saw them: Spinosaurus, monster crocodiles, and fish with razor-sharp teeth. Quicksand, bogs, parasites, poisonous insects, and carnivorous plants. You think you're ready to face the outside world? It would grind you up and spit you out in pieces," Rogue cried, her cheeks flushed.

"Like it did with Dad?" Ridley asked, hot tears brimming on her eyelids. "Is he gone? Is that what you wanted to tell me today?"

Rogue hesitated, chewing on her lower lip. "Jessica was here earlier."

"Jessica? She came in with the traders?"

Rogue nodded. "I asked her and Bear to look for Seth. I begged her to find him. I thought if anyone could, it would be her."

"And?"

"There's no sign of him. He's gone, sweetie," Rogue said, her voice quivering. "He's really gone."

"No. He can't be dead. He can't be. It's impossible," Ridley said, shaking her head. The tears brimmed over and spilled down her cheeks—wet tracks of salt and grief.

"I didn't want to believe it either, sweetheart," Rogue said, reaching out to Ridley. "All this time, I held on to hope, but it's been over four months. If he were still alive, he'd be here. You know that."

"No! No, I refuse to believe it. You're lying!" Ridley yelled, pulling away from her mother's touch. She couldn't stand the thought that her father was gone. Dead. The pain was too much. It stabbed into her chest like a thousand hot pokers and seared through her veins. It was easier to deny her mother's words. Easier to hold on to hope.

"Ridley, please listen to me. Your father's gone, but he'll always live on inside you. Just like I will one day when…."

"When what? When you're dead as well?" Ridley asked, pushing past her mother. "I don't care anymore. You're a monster, and I hate you."

"You can't mean that," Rogue said with a pained gasp.

"I do. I hate you!" Ridley yelled, stomping through the doorway.

"Ridley, wait," Rogue cried out, running after her onto the porch. "I have to tell you something."

"I don't want to hear it, Mom. I don't want to hear any of it," Ridley said, waving to Loki. The wolf jumped up and joined her side, the only true friend she had left. "Come on, boy. We're on our own. I'm a grown-up now, right? I can do whatever I want, and what I'm doing is leaving."

"No, please. Ridley, please!" Rogue pleaded, wringing her hands. "Just wait."

"I'm done waiting. Waiting for Dad to come back. Waiting for you to let me live my life the way I want to live it. Just waiting," Ridley said.

With those parting words, she stormed off with Loki sticking close to her side. Her mother called after her, pleading for Ridley to return, but she wasn't having any of it. *He's not dead. I know it. He's out there somewhere, and I'm going to find him.*

Chapter 7 - Seth

Seth sat with his back to the wall, ignoring the water that trickled down its rough surface. It was impossible to avoid the dampness. It permeated every nook and cranny of his prison, a bare concrete room he shared with the rest of his team. What remained of them, at least.

When they set out initially, they were twelve—a sizable number of trackers, hunters, and traders. Well-supplied, armed, and dressed, they were designed to withstand the worst the primordial world could throw at them.

However, they were not prepared for treachery from their fellow man, and that complacency cost them dearly. Caught off guard, they were captured and marched toward their new home.

Now, only eight remained.

Eight out of the original twelve.

Leaning back, Seth stared at the tiny window far above his head. He could still remember that morning in vivid detail. The morning they lost it all:

Their lives. Their freedom. Their future.

***

He woke up just before dawn, summoned to wakefulness by the first rays of light on the horizon. Crawling out of his

CHAPTER 7 - SETH

bedroll, he went to the fire and stirred the coals. When he had a good blaze, he put on a pot of hot water and tossed in a few handfuls of grit. Next, he put the kettle on and prepared to make coffee.

A sixth sense warned him of danger, however, and he stilled. The hair on the back of his neck rose, and he realized he was being watched. The rest of his party either lay in their beds or puttered around with huge yawns splitting their faces. None of them were aware of the danger and wouldn't be much help. Plus, the guard that was supposed to be on watch duty was nowhere to be seen, and Seth feared the worst.

Hunched down low over the fire, he pretended to carry on as usual while his right hand crept toward his gun. From the corners of his eyes, he looked around the clearing, trying not to be too obvious. To the far right, he spotted movement. It was no dinosaur, or the creature would've attacked already. *People. But how many?*

He spotted two more closing in on the camp, but there were probably more. One of his team approached the fire, and Seth tried to warn the man without being too obvious. "Hey, Ronnie. Busy morning."

"Busy?" Ronnie asked with a touch of confusion.

"Uh-huh. Too busy. Lots of new faces," Seth replied, fixing Ronnie with an urgent look. He flashed his eyes from side to side, hoping the man would catch the hint.

He did.

Ronnie's expression tightened, and he casually reached for his gun beside the fire. Seth did the same, but before he could touch his weapon, a rough voice said, "I wouldn't do that if I were you."

The unmistakable cocking of a gun followed, and Seth froze

on the spot. So did Ronnie and the rest of the group.

"Don't make a move. You're surrounded," the same voice said, and several figures emerged from the trees around the clearing.

Seth counted at least eight, all armed with rifles and handguns, dressed in rough gear. A few wore masks, but most were barefaced, their expressions grim and their shoulders tense. They meant business; that much was plain to see.

"What do you want?" Seth asked, turning to face the man who'd spoken.

The man eyed him with displeasure. His hair was cut short, and his jaws were clean-shaven, unlike the rest of his group. His gun shone in the light, well-oiled and cared for, and a pair of old aviator sunglasses rested on his face.

"Are you the leader of this little group of jackasses?" the man asked.

"I am," Seth confirmed with a brisk nod.

"Not anymore," the man said, raising his gun. The butt lashed out, hitting Seth in the temple with a brutal thud. Darkness closed in, and his knees buckled, reality fading to a distant pinprick and then... nothing.

Hours later, he woke up inside his new prison, squeezed into the tiny cell with the rest of his team. All except one.

"Where's Jimmy?" Seth asked.

"Dead," Ronnie said, shaking his head.

"They killed him?"

"Before he could give the alarm, yes," Ronnie replied.

"Alarm?" Seth asked, still a bit befuddled. Then he remembered that Jimmy had taken the last watch the night before.

Seth swallowed hard, feeling the loss deeply. Jimmy had

been Paul and Sandi's oldest child. A bright boy with a broad smile and a good heart. He'd promised the parents, good friends of his, that he'd look after their son. Now, the boy was dead. Killed by a group of thieving marauders.

"Did they bury him, at least?" Seth asked, though he already knew the answer.

Ronnie shook his head. "They left him to the scavengers."

Seth shook his head, staring at his hands. Bile burned at the back of his throat, a direct result of his churning stomach. His head throbbed, and a lump the size of an egg sat on his temple, the skin bruised and swollen. "Shit."

"Shit's a mild way to put it," Ronnie said, his voice dry and humorless.

"Where are we?" Seth asked, looking around. The cell was bare, furnished with nothing but rotting straw and a bucket that stank to high heaven. Flies buzzed around its open lip, and a rat scurried across the floor.

"In hell. That's where we are," another of his team answered. A man named Reed.

Seth eyed him, noting the bruises on his cheek and the split lip. His gaze panned over the rest of the room, cataloging the various wounds that afflicted his friends. Not one seemed to have escaped punishment, each sporting an injury of some kind. Whoever their captors were, they were neither friendly nor gentle.

Turning back to Ronnie, he asked, "Did they say anything? Do you know where we are? What they want with us?"

"No, and as you can see, they don't take kindly to questions," Ronnie said, gesturing to his black eye.

"I noticed," Seth said, mulling over what little information he had. It was pretty obvious that they were in deep trouble.

Unarmed, jammed into a tiny cell with zero intel, far from home, without supplies, food, or water, they were in a proper jam.

He was determined to get them out of it, however. He was the leader, and he was responsible for their lives. He'd get them back home to their families one way or another. To do that, he needed more info, which would take time.

***

Time.

Seth snorted.

That memory was more than four months old now. four months during which they'd accomplished nothing. Nothing but trading their blood, sweat, and tears for scraps of food and water. Barely enough to keep them alive. At night, they shivered in their cell. By day, they worked their fingers to the bone.

That wasn't the worst, however. One element grew to plague them to such an extent that two of the group went mad and committed suicide. That element was water. Despite its innocuous properties, it quickly became the bane of their existence.

The ever-present moisture formed puddles on the floor, caused black mold to grow on the ceiling, and turned their straw beds into a soggy mush. At night, it crept into their bones and leached the warmth from their joints while fungal infections plagued their feet and lungs. It slowly broke down their bodies and their will to resist until nothing remained but dumb acceptance of their circumstances.

Seth shook his head, amazed at their naivety. They'd left the Zoo with such high hopes, saying goodbye to their family and friends with bright smiles and warm hugs. They'd promised to return home soon, having forged new alliances and trade routes to benefit all.

He'd been just as starry-eyed, searching for a place he'd heard about on the grapevine. A community both technologically and medically advanced. He'd hoped they'd have better treatment available for Rogue's illness, something neither the Zoo nor Prime City possessed. Vancouver could've provided the answer, but it was a long trip, and this place was supposed to be much closer.

Now, Seth was sorry he'd been so foolish. Rogue's life depended on him, and he'd let her down by listening to vague rumors. Rumors he was sure had been planted on purpose by the same people who'd captured him.

He didn't know how he was going to escape and get back home. Home to his wife and daughter. But he did know it had to be soon, for he wouldn't last much longer in the hellhole that had become his prison.

A place called the Iron Tower.

Chapter 8 - Rogue

Rogue stumbled after her daughter, begging her to listen. "Ridley, please. Come back. I need to explain. I need to tell you…."

At the edge of the porch, her breath ran out, and she clung to the pillar with both hands. The sun shone bright overhead. Too bright after the shadowy interior of her home, and she could barely make out the shape of her daughter disappearing into the distance. She showed no signs of turning back, despite Rogue's frantic pleas. "Ridley. Please."

Sagging to her knees, Rogue cried. The tears were bitter and intense, an outlet for the extreme agony that filled her heart and robbed her of her breath. In one awful blow, she lost her husband and only child. But the tears were brief, interrupted by the disease that had her by the throat. Harsh and unforgiving, tuberculosis robbed her even of the ability to grieve.

The first cough rumbled up her chest, followed by another and another. They wracked her slender frame until she thought her ribs would crack. Each hack tore into her lungs until bloody sputum stained her lips with crimson. The strength leached from her limbs, and she fell to the ground. *Can't stay here. Not... like this.*

CHAPTER 8 - ROGUE

On her hands and knees, Rogue crawled toward the door. She dragged her body across the wooden floorboards and over the threshold until she found herself inside the kitchen. The dim interior of her home welcomed her back, cool and comforting after the harsh light outside.

Fighting for every inch, she pulled herself toward the nearest chair, but with every cough, she lost a little bit more of her strength. Finally, it ran out, and she slumped to the floor. *No more. Please. No more.*

Her vision dimmed until she could only see the scarred wood beneath her cheek. Stained and polished to a rich golden brown, it told a story. The story of her and Seth starting a family and putting down roots.

A memory flashed to the forefront of her mind, so vivid she could feel, smell, and touch everything anew. It was as if she was there again, eighteen years ago, and maybe she was. Perhaps she was dead, and her soul was reliving a few final moments from her life before it moved on.

***

Rogue drank in the scent of Seth's skin. It was warm and comforting. A mixture of musk, leather, salt, and oil. He held his hands over her eyes, guiding her steps down the cobbled path. The stones were uneven beneath her feet, but she wasn't scared. She trusted him, and she knew he'd never let her fall.

Despite her best efforts to remain serious, she giggled. "What are you doing? Where are we going?"

"I told you. It's a surprise," Seth said. "Don't worry. Only a few more steps."

"Uh huh," Rogue replied, giggling some more. "This is so unlike you. Surprises?"

"What do you mean, unlike me? I can be romantic," Seth

protested.

Rogue snorted. "Yeah, right."

"Ungrateful woman," Seth said with a growl that quickly turned into a laugh. "We're here!"

He whipped his hands away with a flourish, leaving her perplexed and confused. "Um. What is that?"

"That, my dear, is our new home!" Seth cried, his excitement palpable. He pointed toward a structure that she could only assume was meant to be a building of some sort. A cottage, perhaps?

"Err, it's lovely," she said, trying to look as excited as he did.

But Seth picked up on her mood immediately, and his expression fell. "Look, I know it doesn't look like much now, but I'll fix it up. I promise."

Rogue eyed the sagging porch, peeling paint, and ramshackle roof with a mixture of dread and despair. "Do you think you can? I mean, it's a lot of work."

"Don't worry. I'll turn this into the house of your dreams," Seth replied, the excitement back on his face.

"Promise?"

"Promise."

"In that case, I'm in," Rogue said.

"I knew you'd see it my way," Seth yelled. He scooped her up in his arms and swung her around until she squealed for mercy.

"Stop! Stop!"

"Never," he replied with a wicked grin. Slowing down, he planted a kiss on her lips. "You won't be sorry, I promise."

***

The memory faded away, but not the feeling of his lips on hers. He'd kept his promise. Not once during all their years together had she been sorry. Sorry for marrying him or trusting him with her heart and her home.

They'd had their ups and downs, of course. They fought. Horribly, at times. But she'd never regretted a moment of it, and she still didn't. Next to losing Ridley, losing Seth was the worst pain she'd ever felt, but even that wasn't enough to make her wish she'd never met him. *I loved him, and he loved me. We had a good run and raised a beautiful daughter together, but it's over now.*

Darkness crept across Rogue's vision, calling to her with infinite hunger. It wanted her. Broken, tired, and sick, she longed to give in. To surrender to its endless yearning. Maybe she'd even get to see Seth again, waiting for her on the other side, but she couldn't leave. Not yet. Not while Ridley was alone, grieving for a lost father and unaware of the little time her mom had left. *She needs to know. She deserves to know.*

Summoning the last shreds of her strength, Rogue fought against the darkness. She couldn't let it win. Not yet. She had to make sure her daughter was okay first.

As hungry as it was, the dark was also patient and retreated back into its lair. It knew that no matter how hard she fought, it wouldn't change anything. In the end, death always won.

The coughing subsided, and life-giving oxygen filled her lungs. A rush of vitality surged through her veins, enough to grant her a slight reprieve. Voices filled the air, and several pairs of hands tugged at her clothes.

"Rogue? Are you alright?"

"Rogue, please. Answer me."

"Rogue!"

"Thirsty," Rogue replied, her dry tongue touching her even drier lips. She was desperate for a sip of water.

"Hold on. Let me get you something to drink," the voice said.

For a few seconds, the hands disappeared before returning to prop up her head. "Here you go. Careful. Don't choke."

A glass touched her lips, and Rogue swallowed the cool liquid. It flowed across her parched tissues, reviving her senses and washing away the taint of blood on her tongue. The relief was instantaneous, and she ended up downing the entire thing.

"There you go. Better?" the voice asked.

Rogue nodded, recognizing the voice as Jessica's. "You came back?

"I came back with medicine, and it's a good thing I did," Jessica replied. "Can you stand?"

"I think so," Rogue replied.

Together, they got her back on her feet, and Jessica sat her down in the nearest chair. "You rest while I prepare your tea and medicine."

"What is it?" Rogue asked.

"Herbal tea, pain medication, an ointment for your chest, and several courses of different kinds of antibiotics. Enough to give the disease a decent kick in the ass."

"That must've cost a fortune. I can't accept that," Rogue protested.

"You can and you will," Jessica said with a tone that brooked no nonsense. "It's not enough to cure you, but it will last until I return from Vancouver."

"This is too much," Rogue said.

"Just shut up and drink your medicine, okay?" Jessica said, handing her the first dose.

"Fine," Rogue grumbled, but secretly, she was relieved.

CHAPTER 8 - ROGUE

Jessica's actions had bought her the time she needed to win her daughter back, and that was all that mattered. "Jessica. You have to find Ridley."

"Ridley? Why? What happened?" Jessica asked.

"She left, and I don't think she's ever coming back."

"Surely it can't be that bad."

"It is," Rogue said, telling her about the fight.

"Oh, dear. That was one hell of an argument. Didn't I tell you to take it easy on her?" Jessica asked, one hand on her hip.

"I know, and now she's gone," Rogue said. "I've lost her."

"No, you haven't," Jessica said. "I'll talk to her and sort things out. After that, I'm leaving for Vancouver. But first, we have to make a few changes around here."

"Changes?" Rogue asked, suddenly afraid. "What changes?"

"You can't live on your own anymore. Not while you're sick."

"Are you saying I need a babysitter?" Rogue said with an incredulous laugh.

"I'm saying you need help," Jessica said.

"Help? I'm doing just fine on my own, thanks."

"Uh-huh. Doing a bang-up job of it, too," Jessica said.

"I'm fine!" Rogue insisted.

"No, you're not, and I don't want to hear another word about it," Jessica said. "As soon as you've rested, I want you to pack a bag."

"Oh? Where am I going?" Rogue asked with raised eyebrows.

"To your mom's."

"What? No way!" Rogue cried, shaking her head so hard it almost popped off. "I am not staying with my mom."

"Oh, come on. How bad can it be?" Jessica asked.

"She'll smother me to death," Rogue said.

"You mean spoil you rotten?"

"Smother," Rogue said, gripping her neck with both hands while pretending to choke.

"You are such a drama queen," Jessica said, laughing. "I'm not changing my mind, however. Go pack."

"Ugh, fine. Whatever," Rogue said, groaning.

She stood up and dragged her feet toward the bedroom. It was mostly for show, though. Secretly, she was glad Jessica had shown up and bullied her into submission. Her friend was right. She needed help, even if she couldn't admit it out loud.

"Don't make me come back there," Jessica yelled after her.

That prompted a smile from Rogue, the first one she'd had all day. Grabbing a bag, she began to pack.

"Look at it as a vacation," Jessica said once she was finished. "Put up your feet, sit back, relax, and focus on getting better. I'll take care of the rest."

"I'll try, but I make no promises," Rogue said but relented when she saw Jessica's exasperated expression. "Okay, okay. I must admit. A rest sounds kind of nice."

"There, see? I knew you'd come around," Jessica said.

Arm in arm, they set off toward their destination, laughing and chatting like true friends did. Friends who didn't have to impress or pretend. Friends for life.

Chapter 9 - Ridley

Marching away from her home, Ridley fumed under her breath. She couldn't believe her mother was such a coward. Giving up on her dad simply because he was missing. So what if he was missing? That didn't mean he was dead. He was out there in the wilderness, waiting for her to find him. She knew it.

The sound of music and laughter announced the square where the traders had set up shop. She could see the stalls topped with colorful streamers from a distance. The smell of meat roasting on open coals wafted toward her, reminding her that her belly was empty.

Sadly, so were her pockets, but she had a few trinkets stashed away in her backpack. Enough to tide her over until she could figure out a plan. While she didn't know where she was going or what she wanted to do, she did know one thing. She was never going home.

As Ridley approached the market, she couldn't help but feel a sense of relief. Finally, she was away from the suffocating confines of her old life: no more strict curfews or endless rules to follow. From now on, she was free to do as she pleased.

She made her way through the crowded square, the sounds of bartering and haggling filling her ears. As she passed by one stall, a man called out to her. "Hey, you there! Looking for something special? I've got just the thing."

Ridley approached the stall, intrigued but also wary. The man had a sly smile as he pulled out a small, ornate box. "This here is a charm. Guaranteed to bring you luck, no matter where you go."

She eyed the box with wary caution, not a believer in superstition, but she couldn't deny the allure of the man's words. "What is it?"

The man opened the box with a flourish, producing a shimmering scale gleaming against a bed of black velvet. Its iridescent sheen reminded her of a dragonfly's wings, both soulful and fleeting. "This comes from a creature in the ocean far to the east. A terrifying monster bigger than anything you've ever seen before in your life."

"Bigger than a T-rex?" Ridley asked with a doubtful frown.

"Ten times as big!" the man exclaimed, throwing his arms wide. "So big, it makes the trade ships seem puny in comparison.

Ridley stared at him with wide eyes. She'd never seen a trade ship, but it sounded big. Very big. She reached out to touch the scale, but the man slapped her hand away. "Ah ah ah. This is not for the likes of you to trifle with, my dear."

"I can trade for it," Ridley protested, anger flaring in her chest.

"With what?" the man asked with one eyebrow raised high.

Ridley rummaged in her backpack. "I have T-Rex teeth, a utahraptor claw, bambiraptor scales, and dried parksosaurus meat," Ripley offered. "A knife with a handle made from a crocodile tooth. Some silver coins."

The man broke into laughter, guffawing as if she'd told him

the funniest joke on earth. His belly shook and shuddered, his chin jostling with each movement of his head. "That's it? That's all you have?"

Wide-eyed and more than a little shocked, Ridley nodded. "What's wrong with my stuff?"

"Oh, there's nothing wrong with it, my dear," the man said in between more chortling laughter. "It's fine if you need to trade for a meal or a bed, but it's nowhere near enough to pay for this little beauty."

Wiping the tears of laughter from his face, the man snapped the box shut and tucked it away. Snapping his fingers in her face, he added, "Now run along, little girl. You've wasted enough of my time already."

Ridley turned away, fuming at the man's dismissive attitude. She couldn't believe he'd treated her with such disrespect. As she walked away, she couldn't help but think that she needed to devise a plan. If her trinkets were of such poor value, she needed to figure something out soon, or she'd end up on the streets. Besides, she'd need supplies if she planned on looking for her father—expensive supplies.

Lost in thought, she wandered through the market until a commotion caught her eye. A group of people was gathered around a stall, shouting and gesturing at a painted poster. As she approached, she made out the words:

Enter the 10th Annual Vancouver to Chilliwack Endurance Race and win a fortune in prizes.

The word fortune grabbed her attention, and she pushed her way to the front, elbowing people aside until she stood face-to-face with the stall owner, a tall woman with dark-blonde hair and blue eyes. She looked rather exotic with her hair tied in a knot, big gold hoop earrings, and colorful robes, almost like a fortune teller.

Her table was covered with an assortment of pills, dried herbs, ointments, salves, and tinctures. Ridley guessed she was a medicine worker of some kind. Likely an herbalist. *Or a quack.*

"How can I help you, dear?" the woman asked, one hand caressing the ears of a gray cat sitting on the counter.

Loki growled at the cat, baring his canines, and the woman's eyes narrowed with displeasure. "Please control your companion. I will have no fighting at my stall."

"I'm sorry," Ridley said, gesturing to Loki. "Sit!"

Loki glanced at her, clearly unhappy with the command, but he obeyed. Sinking onto his haunches, he eyed the cat with apparent malice. The cat stared right back, secure in its spot on its throne.

"Where were we?" the woman asked, seeming mollified. "My name is Eleanor, and I am at your service."

"I want to know more about the race," Ridley said, gesturing at the poster.

"What for? You are far too young to think about entering," the woman replied.

"I'm eighteen," Ridley protested.

"Mm. The minimum age for entry, but not exactly inspiring of confidence," Eleanor said, quirking an eyebrow.

"That still means I'm old enough," Ridley said. "Please, tell me more."

"It's all there on the poster," Eleanor said, waving a hand at the object.

"If I can get to it," Ridley grumbled, pointing at the crowd before it.

"Hold on. I think I still have a few flyers left," Eleanor said.

CHAPTER 9 - RIDLEY

She rummaged through a couple of boxes before she found it, waving the rough piece of parchment like a flag. "Found it!"

"Let me see," Ridley said, snatching it from her hand. Eleanor frowned, and the cat hissed, but she ignored them both, her eyes glued to the words on the flyer. It read:

Enter the 10th Annual Vancouver to Chilliwack Endurance Race Today! Be the first to cross the finish line in this grueling foot race stretching across 100 miles of rugged terrain, taking only what you can carry on your back, and win a fortune in prizes. More details are below.

Ridley scanned the rest of the details, absorbing the information like a sponge. The race was due to start in one month, and the route spanned from Vancouver to Chilliwack, wherever that was. She'd never heard of it, but she didn't care. *I can always find out.*

The entry requirements were simple. You had to be eighteen or above to enter, of sound mind and body, and pay an entrance fee of ten Vancouver Credits.

In addition, you had to carry your supplies in a backpack and finish the race on foot. The first one across the line won the prize. All finishing contestants would be flown back to Vancouver for the prize-giving ceremony. Relief stations offered safety at night and aid to any who could not complete the race. All contestants entered at their own risk.

The more Ridley read, the more excited she became. The prize was of the sort most people only ever dreamed of. A functioning Jeep with a year's supply of gas, the use of a furnished home in Vancouver for that same period, ten thousand Vancouver Credits, dinner with the Mayor, and access to all of the city's amenities for a year, including the gyms, theaters, and museums.

"Loki, did you see this?" Ridley cried out, excited beyond measure. She flashed the flyer at him, and he responded quizzically. "Imagine what we could do with such a prize? We could live in Vancouver for a year, practically for free, seeing all the sights. And ten thousand credits? That's... that's...."

"That's a lot of credits, kid. More than you could ever imagine, but it won't do you any good," Eleanor answered.

"Why not?" Ridley asked, cocking her head.

"Because you'll never finish the race, let alone win," Eleanor said. "Only the toughest of endurance racers enter these contests, and there's a reason the stakes are so high. Most of them never make it to the finish line."

"I'll make it," Ridley said with determination. "I'll do whatever it takes."

Eleanor looked at her skeptically. "Have you done any training for this? Any at all?"

"No, but I'm very fit. I've spent a lot of time out in the wilderness on my own. I'm tough, and I can hunt and track."

"Maybe, but there's a big difference between endurance running and going for a quick run in the forest. Are you sure you want to do this?"

"I'm sure," Ridley said with a firm nod.

"Alright, kid. I'll give you some advice. Trust no one and nothing. The racers will do anything to come out on top, including sabotage and murder."

Ridley's heart raced with fear and anticipation. She had never been in a race before but knew she could do it. She had to. Winning that prize would set her up for life. *I'll be able to do anything and go anywhere!*

Filled with excitement, Ridley handed the flyer back. "Thanks."

"Keep it," Eleanor said with a wave of her hand. "I'll look out for you during the race."

Ridley turned to leave, gripping the flyer as if it were the most precious thing in the world, and maybe it was. To her, it meant a brand new future filled with possibilities.

"One more thing," Eleanor said, calling her back.

"Yeah?"

"How are you getting there?" Eleanor asked.

"What do you mean?"

"To Vancouver. That's where the race starts. How are you getting there?"

Ridley frowned. That was something she hadn't thought about. "I don't know."

"Well, I guess you're in luck then. We're leaving for Vancouver tomorrow morning," Eleanor said. "You could come with us."

"Do you mean that?" Ridley asked.

"You'd have to speak to the Caravan Master. He's over there," Eleanor said, pointing at a tall man with broad shoulders and a rugged beard. "And you'd have to pay your way. The boats aren't cheap."

"I can do that," Ridley said.

"Off with you then, and good luck," Eleanor said.

Ridley left the woman and her stall, shadowed by Loki. She made a beeline for the Caravan Master, gathering up all of her courage. "Sir? Can I talk to you?" The man ignored her, but she wasn't about to give up and tried again. "Sir? Please, I need to talk to you."

"What is it?" he finally asked, looking at her with little interest.

Ridley stood up straight, determined not to let him intimidate her. "I want to join your caravan to Vancouver for the race," she said, holding out the flyer in her hand.

The Caravan Master gave her a slow appraising look, taking in her young age and slender stature. "And why should I let you come with us?"

"I'm strong, and I can take care of myself. I'll do whatever it takes, and I can pay my way," Ridley replied confidently.

The Caravan Master nodded, seeming to consider her request. "Very well. If you can pay for your fare, you are welcome to join us. The safest way to Vancouver is by boat."

"I understand," Ridley said, grateful for the opportunity.

"Pack your things and meet us at the gates at sunrise. We'll see if you have what it takes," the Caravan Master said before turning and walking away.

Ridley's heart pounded with excitement and nerves. She had taken the first step toward her new future and was determined to succeed. No matter what.

Chapter 10 - Jessica

"Thanks again, Jessica," Olivia said, squeezing her hand. "If you hadn't told me about my daughter's illness, I never would've known." She shot a look of disapproval over her shoulder. "She likes to think she's invincible."

"Mom!" Rogue answered from within the kitchen. Swaddled up in a blanket with a cup of herbal tea, she looked like a caterpillar in a cocoon. Or a giant baby.

"It's my pleasure," Jessica replied with a broad smile. "She needs someone to look after her while I'm gone. Someone to ensure she takes her medication on time and doesn't overexert herself."

"I can take care of myself," Rogue mumbled.

"No, you can't. Stop being so stubborn," Jessica said, rolling her eyes.

"Don't worry. I won't let her out of my sight," Olivia said.

"Neither will I," Ric said, his bushy gray eyebrows pulled into a frown.

Rogue groaned audibly from the other room, and Jessica smothered a laugh. "I'll be back once I've found Ridley, but she might need to stay with me for a few days. Just until everything has settled down."

"Do whatever it takes," Olivia confirmed. "We'll be here

when she's ready to talk to come home."

"Alright. I'll see you later," Jessica said with a wave. Jogging down the steps, she headed straight to the market square. She was sure Ridley would be there. Even if she wanted to leave the Zoo, she couldn't do it alone. She'd need a plan: a plan and help. *I just have to get to her before someone else does.*

She scoured the square for the next twenty minutes, weaving between the many shops and stalls. It was close to noon before she spotted Loki slinking between the legs of the crowd, and she spotted Ridley soon after that.

"Thank heavens, I found you," Jessica said, grabbing Ridley's hand.

Ridley jerked around, her expression hostile until she recognized the other woman. A smile replaced her anger, and she cried, "Jessica? I'm so glad to see you!"

"I'm glad to see you too, sweetheart. I swear you've gotten even taller since the last time I saw you," Jessica said, and it was true.

Ridley had grown at least an inch, and she'd filled out considerably in the weeks Jessica was gone. She looked older and more confident. No longer the shy little girl of yesteryear.

"Now, what's this I hear about you and your mom?" Jessica asked, noting how Ridley stiffened at her mother's mere mention.

"I don't know what you've heard, and I don't care," Ridley said. "I hate her, and I'm never going back."

"Hate is a strong word," Jessica said. "You know she loves you and wants only what's best for you."

"She only cares about herself. She even said my father was dead. Can you believe that?" Ridley asked, looking outraged.

Jessica hesitated. "Sweetie…."

CHAPTER 10 - JESSICA

"Not you, too," Ridley cried. "He's not dead. He's still alive, and I'm going to find him."

"How?" Jessica asked. "On your own? Out there?"

"I have a plan," Ridley said, folding her arms and looking away.

"And I'd like to hear all about it," Jessica said. "But not out here. Let's go home."

"I told you. I'm not going back. Ever," Ridley said.

"Then come home with me," Jessica said. "You need somewhere to stay, right? Or do you plan to camp out in the stables every night?"

Ridley eyed her with a calculating look. "I can stay with you tonight? I don't have to go home?"

"That's what I said," Jessica replied. "Please say yes, because I desperately need a bath and haven't even been home yet."

"Alright, fine," Ridley said, relenting. "I'll spend the night."

"Wonderful," Jessica said with a broad smile. "We can talk, catch up, and maybe sort things out with your mom in the morning."

"Whatever," Ridley mumbled, not looking Jessica in the eyes.

"Seriously, Ridley. You need to work things out. You're family, after all. That's important."

"We'll see," Ridley said, still not meeting her gaze.

Jessica sighed. "Okay, let's go. I'm starving."

"Just wait here. I'll be back right now," Rogue said.

"Where are you going?" Jessica asked.

"To that stall. I need something for Loki. He's got worms," Ridley said.

Jessica recognized the stall in question as Eleanor's and gritted her teeth. She was still unsettled about their earlier trade, feeling like she'd struck a terrible bargain. Still, that didn't mean the woman was bad news, just a bit of a shark. "Alright. I'll wait. Have you got enough to trade?"

"Yes, I do," Ridley said, running off.

She returned a few minutes later, tucking a pouch into her pocket. "Thanks, we can go now. I got what I needed."

"Great. Follow me," Jessica said.

As they walked toward her home, Jessica prodded Ridley about her mother and their fight but got little out of the girl. She debated whether or not to tell her about Rogue's illness but decided against it. *Rather her mom breaks the news. She's got enough on her plate right now with the latest information about her dad.*

Not that Ridley appeared to believe her father was gone. She stubbornly clung to the notion that he was alive and she'd be able to find him given a chance. No matter what Jessica said, she refused to listen.

Finally, Jessica gave up and changed the subject. They talked about traveling, hunting, tracking, and surviving. A topic that quickly drew Ridley from her shell, and she asked a million questions.

Once they reached Jessica's home, she continued to pepper her and Bear on the subject, picking their brains for every tiny detail. The only time they got a reprieve was when they took a bath. It was almost as if she was trying to learn all about the world in the span of a few hours.

That night, around the dinner table, Ridley's mood took a drastic turn. She appeared nervous and pushed her food around with her fork until Jessica lost her patience. "What's wrong? Spit it out."

"Nothing's wrong," Ridley said. "It's just…."

CHAPTER 10 - JESSICA

"Just what?"

"Is it really that bad out there? As bad as everyone says?" Ridley asked.

"Pretty much," Jessica said with a shrug. "I mean, you can survive and even travel if you know what you're doing, but most people don't."

"I do," Ridley said.

"You know more than most, but not enough," Jessica said. "Have you ever faced off against a pack of raptors or a T-rex?"

"A Carnotaurus," Ridley said, referring to the time Seth found her outside the walls.

"Alone," Jessica said with a pointed look.

"Err, no," Ridley admitted.

"Pray you never have to," Jessica said.

Ridley was silent for a while, picking at her food. After several long minutes, she pushed her plate away. "I'm not hungry anymore."

"Something wrong with the food?"

"No, I just don't feel like eating."

"Okay. Want to go to bed?" Jessica asked.

"Can I make us some tea first?" Ridley asked.

"Um, sure," Jessica replied. She wasn't a tea drinker but didn't want to offend Ridley. When Bear looked like he would say no, she kicked him in the shins. "That would be lovely, thanks."

Ridley prepared a bitter herbal concoction sweetened with far too much honey and watched with an eager expression while they drank it.

"Do you like it?" she asked halfway through.

"Delicious," Jessica said, straining not to spit out the nasty brew.

Bear tried and even said thank you but failed to finish the entire cup. Jessica managed to drink all of hers, nearly dying in the process.

"I'm glad you liked it," Ridley said, gathering their cups. She washed the dishes and bid them goodnight with a smile.

"Sleep tight, sweetie," Jessica said, waving after her.

"Night," Bear rumbled, watching her with a thoughtful look.

Jessica sighed and leaned her head against Bear's shoulder. "I hope I can get through to that girl. I really do."

"We'll see," Bear answered.

"Is there something you know that I don't?" Jessica asked, suddenly suspicious.

"Nope, nothing," Bear said, and she relaxed again.

Within seconds, she was fast asleep right there on the couch. Bear carried her to bed, though she hardly registered, unable to keep her eyes open. "Thanks, Babe. Love you."

"Love you too," he replied, tucking her under the covers.

That was the last thing she knew before waking up the next morning feeling groggy and confused. A vicious headache pounded in her temples, and her mouth tasted like stale piss. With a pained groan, she rolled over, surprised to find that it was well past dawn. The bed beside her was empty, and she sat up to look around. "Bear?"

"I'm here," he answered, his bulk filling the doorway. He cradled a cup of coffee between his palms, strong and bitter. Just the way she liked it. He placed it on the bedside table along with two painkillers.

"How did you know?" she asked.

"Because I felt the same way when I woke up," Bear said.

"But why? We didn't drink last night, did we?" Jessica said, one hand shading her eyes.

CHAPTER 10 - JESSICA

"Ridley," Bear replied with a somber look.

"What?" Jessica asked, confused.

"She drugged us."

"You mean...?" Jessica thought it through. "The tea?"

"Yup. I guessed after the first few sips."

"Why didn't you say something?" Jessica cried.

"I wanted to see what her plan was," Bear replied. "Anyway, the dose wasn't strong enough for someone my size, and I didn't finish it. I checked on her this morning, but she was already gone."

"What?" Jessica yelled, scrambling out of bed. "I'd better find her."

"My guess is she's gone with the traders," Bear said.

"Why would she do that?" Jessica said, running around like a headless chicken. She pulled on clean underwear, followed by a vest, t-shirt, and camo pants. Popping the painkillers, she downed the coffee in one go.

"I found this in her room," Bear said, handing her a flyer.

Jessica stared at the parchment, unable to believe her eyes. "An endurance race? Is she crazy?"

"Crazy? No. Young and stupid. Absolutely," Bear replied with a grin.

"Are you enjoying this?" Jessica asked, rounding on him.

"No, but it's kind of funny. No one ever gets one past you, but she did—a teenager. Drugged us good," Bear said with a chuckle.

"I should've known the herbs she got from Eleanor weren't for Loki. Stupid, stupid. What am I going to tell Rogue?" Jessica pulled on her boots. "Maybe I'm lucky. Maybe they haven't left yet."

"Maybe," Bear said with a doubtful shrug.

"Stay here. I'll go check," Jessica said, grabbing her jacket.

She ran outside and sprinted toward the market square. To her horror, it was empty, with no signs of the traders or their belongings. "Shit."

With a sinking feeling in the pit of her stomach, Jessica headed to the gates. They were wide open, and people already worked in the fields, but the road leading away from the town was empty. Judging by the sun, it was past nine already, and the caravan was long gone. "Damn it!"

Stamping her foot, she called to the nearest guard on duty. "When did the traders leave?"

"About two, three hours ago," the guard replied.

"And you didn't notice that Ridley was among them?" she asked.

"The girl with the wolf? Yeah, she was with them," the guard replied.

"And you let her go? A defenseless teenage girl? Your community leader's daughter?" Jessica asked. "Do you know what Rogue will do to you when she finds out? She'll crush you like a bug."

The guard blanched but stood his ground. "I had no choice. She's over eighteen. That makes her an adult."

"An adult? Really? Would you consider your own eighteen-year-old kids to be adults?"

"I don't know, ma'am, but it's not my child who ran away from home, so maybe you shouldn't be talking to me," the guard said, his expression stony.

Jessica blinked, taken aback. He had a point, however, and she realized she was wasting time. With an inward sigh, she turned away from the gate and returned home.

Bear waited for her at the door, their backpacks ready to

CHAPTER 10 - JESSICA

go, along with the rest of their gear and weapons. "I packed for us."

Jessica stared at him, shocked. "How did you know?"

Bear shrugged, his expression benign. "I guessed. I know Ridley. She's gone, right?"

"Yes, she's gone."

"Just like her mother, that one," he said, his voice rumbling from his deep chest. "She just doesn't know it yet."

Jessica realized he was right. Whether she knew it or not, Ridley took after her mom. She was every bit as reckless, stubborn, and adventurous as Rogue had been when she was younger. Luckily, she had her father's instincts and practicality, traits that steadied her. *That doesn't mean I won't wring her neck once I catch up to her.*

Bear handed her a pack, and she slung it over her shoulders. It settled into place with a heavy thud. The sensation was familiar after weeks spent on the road. Too familiar. A few days' rest would've been nice, but that was no longer an option. "Come on. If we hurry, we can still catch up to them."

"What about Rogue? Should we tell her?" Bear asked as they left the house.

"No time. If we don't catch them before they reach the river, we never will," Jessica replied. "I'll leave a message at the gate."

Minutes later, they were through the gates and on the road, setting a punishing pace. There would be no rest for either of them until they found Ridley. The problem was, could they convince her to go back home? *Because if we can't, she'll die in that race, and I'll never be able to face Rogue again.*

Chapter 11 - Ridley

Ridley headed toward the city square well before sunrise, determined not to be late. This was her one chance to get out of town, and she wasn't going to waste it. Besides, she had no idea how long it would take for the herbal sedatives she'd given Jessica and Bear to wear off. Though Eleanor had assured her the stuff was strong, she didn't want to take any chances.

She took the time to raid Jessica's cupboards for supplies, however. The woman was well supplied with anything a person could need for the road, including food, gadgets, weapons, ammunition, and first aid. Everything Ridley needed for the trip to Vancouver and the Chilliwack race.

After thinking it through carefully, Ridley loaded up on sealed bags of nutrient-rich trail mix and strips of salted, dried meat. She also took a canteen with a built-in filter, a bottle of iodine, a first-aid kit, a bedroll, an extra blanket, and a raincoat.

For weapons, she stuck with her crossbow and bolts. It was lightweight and familiar, perfect for hunting and protection from smaller creatures. The hatchet and knife on her belt were valuable tools, useful for everything from chopping wood to butchering meat.

CHAPTER 11 - RIDLEY

She added a length of rope, a compass, a ball of twine, and a fire-starter kit to her bag, leaving just enough room for her clothes and a few toiletries. As an afterthought, she also took a purse full of Vancouver Credits that she found in a drawer.

While she felt guilty for stealing, Ridley reckoned she could pay Jessica back from her winnings when she won the race. There was no doubt in her mind that she'd win. She had to. It was as simple as that.

Besides, they'd forgive her once she found her father and brought him back home. They'd feel sorry for doubting her then, including her mom and everyone who'd ever thought she was just a stupid little girl.

With her supplies packed, she exited the house on silent feet and joined the traders in the market square. They were already awake, packing their things and readying breakfast on smoky fires in the early morning haze.

Guards moved among them, watching as the strangers readied to leave their midst. It was all part of the process, and things proceeded smoothly.

Ridley joined their number, looking for the Caravan Master. She found him not long after that, inspecting the animals used to draw the wagons and carts.

She watched as he ran his hands along a horses' flank before checking its legs and hooves. Satisfied, he moved on to the next animal, and Ridley felt her admiration increase.

"That one has heat in its tendons. Take it easy on the animal, alternate hot and cold compresses, and no heavy loads."

"Yes, Sir," one of the caravan guards replied. He jumped into action, lightening the load on the wagon and redistributing the weight. He also stoked up the fire and put a pot on to boil for a hot compress.

Ridley watched it all with interest, filing the information away like little nuggets of gold. She learned more as she wandered through the camp, watching the people pack away their belongings. There was not a single wasted motion among the lot. Each movement had a purpose, and each task was completed with precision and accuracy. Nothing was left to chance.

"I see you made it," the Caravan Master said, appearing at her side like a ghost.

Ridley jumped, startled. For such a large man, he was light on his feet. Swallowing her fright, she raised her chin and said. "Of course, I came."

"I'd hoped you wouldn't," he said. "Are you sure you want to do this?"

"I'm sure," she said with a firm nod.

"Have you ever been outside the Zoo?"

"I've been to Prime City a few times," Ridley said.

"Alone?"

Ridley hesitated. "No, but I have gone out into the forest a lot. Alone, except for Loki."

The Caravan Master eyed Loki with a deep frown. "I hope the wolf won't be a problem. I won't tolerate any aggression. If he bites one of my people or animals, I'll kill him myself."

"He won't. I promise. He's very well-behaved," Ridley said, patting Loki with one hand. He smiled at her, his tongue lolling from his mouth.

"I'll hold you to that promise," the Caravan Master replied.

Ridley pointed at the camp. "It's all so efficient. Practiced."

"That's because we've been doing this for a long time," the Caravan Master said. "I've been in charge of these people for twelve years, and they are like my family. I won't let anything

CHAPTER 11 - RIDLEY

happen to them."

"I understand," Ridley said.

"Do you? Because if you don't, you'd better learn fast. There's no room for mistakes out in the wild. One slip-up is all it takes, and I don't have the time to babysit you." He waved a hand across the convoy. "There's a reason all of this has lasted so long. It's because we don't allow outsiders to screw things up."

"I won't be a burden. I swear it," Ridley said.

"Hmpf. We'll see about that," the Caravan Master said, returning to his task of overseeing their departure.

Ridley watched him leave with a sense of trepidation. She wasn't good with people, preferring Loki's company over that of most humans. Jessica and Bear were the only exceptions to the rule. She didn't even have friends of her own age.

She was sure things would be okay once they were on the road, though, with the dense primordial forest all around. That was where she belonged and felt most at home. "We'll show them, won't we, Loki?"

Loki yipped in agreement, and she ruffled his fur. "Come on. Let's see what else we can learn about these people. We're going to be stuck with them for a while."

Together, she and Loki wandered around until it was time to leave. At the Caravan Master's command, they got into formation and filed through the gates one wagon at a time.

Ridley hung around the back, hoping to slip out unnoticed, but she was out of luck.

"You there! Stop!" one of the Zoo guards yelled.

"Ah crap," Ridley muttered, turning toward him.

"What do you think you're doing, Miss?" he asked, his cheeks ruddy with the early morning chill.

"I'm leaving," Ridley said, trying her best to look and sound grown up.

"Are you allowed to leave? Where's your mom?" he asked.

"My mom's at home, and I don't need her permission to do anything. I'm eighteen."

"Really?"

"Why would I lie?"

"So you can sneak out like you always do. I know the drill," the guard said.

"I'm not sneaking out. My mom knows I'm leaving," Ridley said.

"You're bluffing," the guard said, his eyes narrowing in his thin face.

Ridley shrugged, acting nonchalant. "You can ask her yourself if you want, but you'd better hurry. These people are in a hurry to get to the river, and they won't appreciate you wasting their time."

The guard hesitated. "You're really eighteen? Swear it."

"I swear."

The guard mulled it over, weighing up his options. While her mother was the head of the council and a community leader, she couldn't keep her daughter locked up if she was of age. Nor did he want to get on the traders' bad side. The last thing anyone needed was for them to boycott the Zoo community. Good trade relations were worth more than some teenager's rebellious streak.

Finally, he nodded. "Fine. You can go, but if I find out you lied to me, there will be hell to pay."

"I understand," Ridley said, holding back a whoop of joy.

The guard moved aside, and she walked through the gate with her head held high. No more sneaking over the wall and

CHAPTER 11 - RIDLEY

hiding from the guards for her. No more lies, secrets, and masks. From now on, she'd live her life the way she wanted live it. Everyone and everything else be damned.

Chapter 12 - Seth

The harsh scrape of iron on concrete alerted Seth that it was time to start the day. He scrambled to his feet, moving as fast as he could despite his aching joints. His muscles screamed in protest, but he managed to straighten up, his head bowed not to look his captors in the eyes. Around him, the rest of the group did the same. It was part of the drill, and it never changed.

The metal door swung open with a screech, and three guards entered the cell armed with spears, knives, and axes. They shouted at Seth and the rest to move, brandishing their weapons and delivering blows to speed things along.

Seth filed out of the room, shuffling on naked feet. The chill morning air cut through his threadbare clothes, finding every tiny rent and tear in the fabric. It stripped the warmth from his bones, and goosebumps pebbled his skin. Shivering, he allowed himself to be marched through the former prison.

The building was big, all gray concrete, barred windows, stained linoleum floors, and smoky lamps. Numerous hallways filled with cells led to a central hub controlled by a guard station. It was operated by armed guards, much like the days it used to be a prison, but now the former inmates ran it.

The strangest thing was that he'd never seen a woman inside

CHAPTER 12 - SETH

the building. Not once. It looked like an all-male community, though he couldn't be absolutely sure, of course.

After four months, he knew the place like the back of his hand. Every week they worked in the laundry, washing clothes and linen by hand before hanging it up to dry in a barren courtyard with four walls and no roof. That was one of the few times he saw the sun, and he often stole a few moments to soak in the warmth and light his body craved.

Afterward, they'd take the dry clothes down, iron them with plates heated in a fire, and pack them away in closets set aside for the purpose.

The rest of the time, they mopped floors, washed windows, cleaned the bathrooms, and emptied the buckets in the latrines.

It was filthy work. Hard work. The kind that made you want to peel off your skin and gouge out your eyeballs while gagging on the stench produced by the hundred-odd men living there.

That day was different, however. For the first time in over four months, they were marched outside into the fields. Seth felt his spirits soar as they stepped into the open air. While his body might be broken, his mind was not, and the lure of the outdoors immediately had him in its grip.

He stared at the blue sky above his head, envying the flyers that soared high above, free to fly wherever they wished. Even the fish in the rivers were free. As free as the T-rex that hunted its prey and the Lambeosaurus that waded through shallow waters in search of weeds. Everything out there was free except him, a prisoner bound in a cage of iron and stone.

"This way," one of the guards said, waving them to an open field surrounded by a rough stone wall with a walkway on top and watchtowers at each corner.

Once they reached the field, the same guard handed each a pickax and instructed: "Your job is to clear this field of stones and to break up the ground ready for plowing."

Seth eyed the pickax, judging the distance between it and the guards. Maybe if he moved fast enough, he could get to them before they could defend themselves. That thought was quickly squashed by the guard's following words, however.

"Don't even think of trying to escape. There are guards in the towers armed with crossbows. They will shoot to kill at the slightest signs of aggression or escape. No matter how small," the guard said. "Consider this your only warning."

The brief surge of hope that had blossomed inside Seth's chest shriveled up and died. Still, it couldn't be eradicated. A tiny seed remained, whispering to him that he was outside. The closest he'd been to freedom since his capture. All he needed was a chance. No matter how small.

"Right. Off to work," the guard shouted. "No slacking off, or it's half-rations tonight."

Seth gripped the pickax and moved into the field. Choosing a spot, he began digging out stones, concrete, and other debris. He dumped the rubbish into a waiting wheelbarrow, which Ronnie wheeled toward the dump site.

At first, the guards were on them like maggots on a carcass. Alert for the tiniest sign of rebellion or laziness. They dealt out blows by the dozen, leaving lumps and bruises in their wake.

But as the day wore on, they got bored and wandered off. Seth and his group were mainly left alone, free to talk among themselves as long as they were careful.

"This is our chance, Ronnie," Seth said, his head held low

CHAPTER 12 - SETH

and his voice barely a whisper.

"Our chance at what?" Ronnie asked, his gaunt face a sickly color.

"Escape," Seth said.

"Escape? You're crazy," Ronnie replied, flashing a look at the towers. "They'll kill us before we make it over the wall."

"I don't mean right now," Seth said. "We need a plan first."

Ronnie snorted. "Good luck with that. Escape is impossible."

"No, it's not," Seth said, looking at the team. "We can't give up now. We have to stay strong."

"Strong?" Reed asked. "Look at us. We're skin and bone."

"Exactly. We need to get out of here before we get even weaker," Seth argued.

"What about out there?" Ronnie said. "We don't have food, weapons, or proper clothes. We don't even have shoes. We wouldn't last a day."

"We stand a better chance out there than in here," Seth said. "Here, you're a dead man. Out there, you might live to see your family again."

The word family fell between them like a stone, and each man grew somber and silent. They all missed their loved ones. It was the one thing that had kept them going thus far: grit, determination, the will to survive, and the hope they'd see their family again.

After a while, Ronnie broke the silence. "All right. I'm in."

Reed sighed. "So am I."

"Me too," Jerry said, a tracker with curly red hair and pale skin.

"Count me in," Billy Barfield said, a man known for his ability to drink copious amounts of beer.

Seth looked at the remaining four, waiting for their answers. The twin brothers, Finn and Liam, looked at each other before nodding. They were hunters—tough men and fighters. Seth was glad they'd decided to try instead of quitting.

That left Boyd and Wallace, both traders. They were good at haggling and negotiations but not so good at surviving.

"At least let us try," Seth prompted. "What's the worst that could happen? We die? We're dead already."

Boyd averted his eyes but said. "I'll try."

Wallace took longer but finally agreed. "Okay."

"Good. It's settled," Seth said with a covert grin.

"What do you want us to do?" Ronnie asked.

"Watch and study. We need information," Seth said.

"Like what exactly?" Ronnie asked.

"The guards. How many are there? What are they like? How do they act? When do they change shifts? When do they eat, drink, or take a piss? Their weapons. The route back to our cell. The number of doors, locks, lights, and people in between. That sort of thing."

"You heard the man. Keep your eyes and ears open," Reed asked.

Murmurs of assent rose around the group, and Seth allowed himself a small smile of satisfaction. While it might not be much, they had hope now. Something to work for. A goal.

Chapter 13 - Jessica

Jessica and Bear wasted no time on the trail. After weeks on the road, they were fit and tough. They set a brutal pace, hardly breaking a sweat. Their backpacks bounced on their shoulders, the skin under the straps calloused by constant chafing. A thick layer of petroleum jelly kept their lips from growing chapped, and a hat kept the sun off their faces.

"How are you feeling?" Jessica asked once they reached the halfway point to the river.

"Hungry," Bear said.

"Me too," Jessica said. They hadn't had time to eat breakfast. Not with Ridley's antics and their rush to leave the Zoo.

"Dried meat?" Bear asked, offering her a strip.

"Thanks," Jessica said, accepting the piece of tough leathery meat with a grimace. She tore off a bite and chewed it without complaint, even though she was sick to death of the stuff.

"A proper breakfast would've been nice," Bear rumbled after a few minutes.

"I know," Jessica said, her stomach rumbling.

"I can just imagine the bacon frying in the pan next to the eggs and sausages," Bear reminisced. "That magnificent sizzle and rich, fatty smell."

Jessica closed her eyes, envisioning the delicious spectacle.

"Don't forget the buttered toast with coffee and fruit juice."

"Flapjacks and syrup," Bear said.

"Flapjacks with fresh strawberries and cream," Jessica said.

"Blueberry muffins."

Saliva flooded Jessica's mouth, her stomach cramped, and she violently shook her head. "Stop! I can't take anymore. When I catch that damned Ridley, I will wring her scrawny neck."

"I'll help," Bear offered with a lopsided grin.

"Oh, please. You couldn't hurt a fly," Jessica said with a snort.

"I've killed stuff before," Bear protested.

"Only in self-defense or to protect the people you care about," Jessica said. "For all your massive size, you have the heart of a teddy bear."

Bear smiled. "Are you calling me your teddy bear?"

Jessica rolled her eyes. "Sure, whatever you want."

"You must've been the mean girl in school," Bear mused.

"I wouldn't know. I never went to school. I was home-schooled," Jessica said. "My dad didn't believe in leaving things up to the system. He taught me how to read, write, think, and reason. He hired tutors who taught me Latin, Greek, mathematics, science, biology, and astronomy. I also had a piano teacher."

"You can play the piano?" Bear asked.

"Badly. My dad quickly figured out I was more at home with a gun in my hand hunting big game and other animals than learning my p's and q's in the drawing room."

"That explains a lot," Bear said with a twinkle in his eyes.

"Yeah, I shot my first deer at the age of six and my first bison at eight. Then the Shift happened, and I ended up here. In

CHAPTER 13 - JESSICA

this world."

"How old were you?"

"Nine."

"How did you adapt?"

Jessica shrugged. "It was scary, but my dad got me through it. He quickly figured out that dinosaurs are just like other animals. They have patterns of behavior. They like to establish territory, form herds, and have hierarchies among themselves. Just like mammals."

"That's true enough," Bear replied.

"He picked up where he left off, hunting dinos instead of other animals. Taking care of problem creatures, protecting traveling parties, and establishing community safety protocols. That sort of thing."

"And he taught you everything he knew," Bear said.

"Pretty much. It's how I got so good at tracking and hunting," Jessica replied.

"You're the best," Bear said.

"You're not so bad yourself," Jessica quipped. "Plus, you've got the strength and stamina of a forty-year-old despite being on the wrong side of sixty."

"Only by two years," Bear protested. He glanced at her. "Do you mind being with someone a decade older than you?"

"Nope. I count myself a lucky girl," Jessica said, winking at him.

"And I'm a lucky guy," he said with an answering wink.

They fell into a companionable silence and focused on their surroundings. It was unlikely they'd chance upon a predator. The road was too busy and noisy for most creatures to be around. As big and fierce as they were, they didn't like fire, and they didn't like people and their guns.

Still, it wasn't impossible either. A small party like her and Bear could look very appetizing to an enterprising hunter. It paid to be careful and never let one's guard down. It was just one more thing her father had drilled into her head before he died.

Her mind flew back to a day filled with blood, disease, and horror. The Red Flux, an unknown disease of prehistoric origins, had struck the citizens of Vancouver. It quickly decimated the population, causing hospitals to burst at the seams until people died on the sidewalks.

Her father was lucky. He got into the hospital but never came out, and she had to witness his last moments in excruciating detail. She'd never forget it, yet she couldn't bear to remember. Her father had been her life, her rock, and his loss still hurt her deeply.

Strangely, the very thing that took her father also introduced her to Rogue. She'd gone on an exploratory mission, looking for other settlements, but her plane crashed in Portland.

Seth and Rogue saw the crash from their vantage point in Prime City and set out to rescue her. In return for their help, she took them to Vancouver and helped broker a deal to provide medicine for the beleaguered citizens of Prime and the Zoo. The two neighboring communities had fallen prey to the Red Flux and needed help. After their encounter with the disease, Vancouver's doctors had developed an effective treatment and could provide the required assistance.

Unsurprisingly, Jessica and Rogue became fast friends, especially since she and Bear hooked up. Moving to the Zoo, she left her old life and friends behind, though she still visited on occasion.

CHAPTER 13 - JESSICA

Her mind drifted back over the years, and she realized she'd been blessed with a life filled with great friends, wonderful adventures, excellent health, and prosperity. *I couldn't have asked for more.*

"We're here," Bear said, breaking into her thoughts.

"What?" Jessica asked, scrambling to catch up.

Bear pointed to a bend in the trail marked by a lightning-struck tree. "There's the marker."

Jessica recognized the spot immediately and sped up to a jog. The river landing was just beyond that bend, and she hoped they were in time to catch the boats. "Come on, Bear. Move your ass."

"Right behind you," he said.

As they rounded the corner, Jessica spotted a long line of boats moving upriver. They were loaded with the traders and their goods, heading up the country toward Vancouver, where they'd trade for goods and refuel. The boats were small, motor-driven, and ideal for carrying small parties upriver.

"Hey! Wait for us!" she yelled, waving her hand. "Wait!"

To her relief, one boat remained at the jetty. A large bearded man oversaw the loading of his belongings. She immediately recognized him as Rupert, the Caravan Master, and rushed toward him. "Rupert, wait!"

He turned toward her with a frown that quickly turned into a smile. "Jessica! Bear! What a pleasure."

"It's good to see you too, Rupert," Jessica said, submitting to a bear hug that nearly broke her ribs. "I'm glad I caught you before you left."

"Let me guess. You missed me so much, you had to come back for more of the Rupert magic," he said, his deep voice rumbling in his chest.

"Thanks, but I have my own magic right here," Jessica said, waving to Bear, and the two men shook hands and slapped each other on the back with much laughter and grunting.

The three of them had become fast friends when they joined the traders after their search for Seth turned up nothing, and she was happy to reunite.

"So, what brings you here?" Rupert asked at last.

"We're looking for a young girl with a wolf," Jessica said.

"Ah, I suspected as much. She's a wily one," Rupert said, touching the side of his nose with one finger. "She bought passage with the Captain over there."

"Bought passage?" Jessica said.

"With Vancouver credits, no less," Rupert said, looking impressed.

"You mean my Vancouver Credits," Jessica said, more than just a little pissed off. "First, she drugs us; then she robs us."

"She did?" Rupert said with a rumbling laugh issuing from his chest. "It seems there's more to her than meets the eye."

"It's not funny, Rupert," Jessica said.

At that moment, she spotted Ridley emerging from one of the cabins on the boat, shadowed by Loki. The girl froze when she saw Jessica and Bear, her posture one of immediate flight.

"Give it up, Ridley. Where are you going to go? Into the river?" Jessica asked, both hands on her hips. When the girl refused to respond, she added, "Please, we just want to talk."

"Talk? I think you mean to tell me to go home," Ridley said, shaking her head. "I'm staying right here."

"Hold on. We're coming onboard," Jessica said, walking up the gangplank.

She crossed the deck, stopping in front of a hostile-looking

CHAPTER 13 - JESSICA

Ridley. "Please come home. You have no idea what you're getting yourself into."

"I know exactly what I'm doing. I'm winning the Chilliwack race and using the prize money to look for my dad."

"That's crazy. You're not trained for that race. You'll die out there," Jessica protested. "Tell her, Bear."

"It's true," Bear said.

"Listen to them, kid," Rupert said, joining them on deck.

"That's just it. I'm not a kid, and I'm tired of everyone telling me what to do," Ridley cried. "My dad's alive. I know it. I feel it in my heart, and he needs me! He needs me, Jessica!"

Jessica stared at Ridley, debating whether to tell her about Rogue's illness, but decided against it. It might push Ridley further away, giving her an added incentive to enter the race. Medicine was expensive, especially the kind her mom needed. "Ridley, please be reasonable."

"I'm doing this with or without you," Ridley said, her mouth set in a stubborn line. "You can help me, or you can leave me alone. Your choice." Folding her arms across her chest, she stared at them.

Jessica shot her a helpless look before turning to Bear. He shrugged. "You heard her. She's not coming back with us, and we can't force her."

"I know that!" Jessica cried, stamping her foot. "So, what am supposed to do about it?"

"Help her," Bear said.

"Are you crazy? It's a suicide mission!" Jessica said.

"If you don't help her, she's dead for sure," Bear said, his logic undeniable.

"Either way, Rogue's going to kill me," Jessica said, looking defeated.

"She'll be more likely to kill you if you let Ridley do this alone."

"He's got a point," Rupert said. "If anyone can help her survive the race, it's you."

"Stay out of this," Jessica said, and Rupert quickly backed off. Bear moved away as well, giving her space. She needed to make up her own mind, or she'd end up resenting the others for their input.

Jessica closed her eyes, tilting her head back for a beat. Finally, she sighed and turned back to Ridley. "Alright. I'll help you."

"Yes! I knew you'd…." Ridley began to say.

Jessica raised a hand, "Hold up. It's on one condition and one condition only."

"What's that?" Ridley asked, her eyes narrowing.

"You do exactly what I say, when, and how I say it. I don't want to hear any buts, excuses, or complaints. Got it?" Jessica said. "This is going to be one of the hardest things you've ever done, and I don't have time for excuses."

"And if I agree, you'll do your best to help me win the race?" Ridley asked.

"I'll do my best to help you survive it," Jessica said.

"Alright. I agree," Ridley said, sticking out her hand.

"Then we've got a deal," Jessica said, shaking on it.

"I take it you're taking the boat now?" Rupert asked.

"Yes, we are, Rupert. I look forward to traveling with you again," Jessica said.

"So do I," Rupert said, smiling through his beard.

"Where's the Captain? We need to make a deal," Jessica said.

"Over there," Rupert said, pointing to a stern gray-haired man watching them from the stern.

CHAPTER 13 - JESSICA

Jessica walked toward him. "Captain. I want to book a passage for myself and my partner to Vancouver, please."

"I don't have any cabins available. The Caravan Master and that girl took my only available space."

"How much did she pay?" Jessica asked.

"Thirty-five credits now, and another thirty-five upon arrival, bed and board for her and the dog."

"Wolf," Ridley said, joining them. "He's a wolf, not a dog."

The Captain shrugged. "Whatever."

"I'll give you a hundred credits for her cabin, bed and board," Jessica said. "She can sleep on the deck."

"What?" Ridley cried out. "That's not fair. I was here first."

"You're one to talk, seeing as you stole money from me," Jessica said with a pointed look.

Ridley shrank back with a guilty look. "I'm sorry about that. I meant to pay you back."

"Uh-huh. Next time, ask," Jessica said. "You're sleeping on the deck with Loki. It'll be good practice for the race."

Ridley groaned.

"Remember what I said," Jessica reminded her. "No excuses."

"Okay, okay, I'll do it," Ridley said, stomping across the deck.

Jessica watched her go with a mixture of amusement and aggravation. While she loved Ridley like her own, the girl was being a massive pain in the ass. *She reminds me so much of her mom, and just like Rogue, she'll be the death of me yet.*

Chapter 14 - Ridley

Ridley jerked awake when a bucketful of ice-cold water hit her in the face. Shock raced through her system, and her nerve endings screamed at the abuse. Flailing about like an octopus, she fought against her invisible assailant, unable to see through the curtain of wet hair that covered her eyes. "What the hell!"

"Rise and shine," a voice she recognized as Jessica's ringing in her ears. "Welcome to your first day of training."

Sputtering with outrage, Ridley wiped the hair from her face and glared at her former friend, now turned foe. "And you couldn't wake me up in a normal way?"

"I tried, but you were fast asleep," Jessica said with a shrug, unrepentant.

"What time is it?" Ridley asked, looking around. It was still dark, with scattered stars and a sickle moon casting the only lights in the sky.

"About four in the morning," Jessica said.

"Four? Why so early?" Ridley said, smothering a colossal yawn.

Jessica didn't answer. Instead, she turned around and walked toward the front of the boat. "Get dressed, then join me. Hurry up."

CHAPTER 14 - RIDLEY

"Fine," Ridley said, reaching for her socks and moccasins. She pulled them on, tied the laces, and grabbed her belt and jacket.

Glaring at Loki, who still lay tucked inside his cozy blanket, she said, "You could've warned me, you know?"

His tail thumped the floorboards, but he didn't move. "Aren't you coming with me? You're supposed to be training as well, aren't you?"

Loki didn't even budge.

"Fine," Ridley said. "Have it your way."

She stomped off in a huff but stopped to relieve herself first. The captain of the boat had been quite innovative. He'd built a cubicle at the back of the boat for privacy with a seat that extended out over the water. There was no need to flush, as everything dropped straight into the water.

Flattened sheets of inner tree bark acted as toilet paper, and a spray bottle filled with vinegar and lemon peels provided a cleaning agent and disinfectant. Afterward, she used the water bottle on the basin to brush her teeth and wash her hands and face. Feeling more like herself, she brushed her hair and tied it back in a smooth ponytail. "There. That should do it."

Squaring her shoulders, Ridley stared at her reflection in the mirror. She attempted a smile but only succeeded in looking wan and sickly. She was too nervous, knowing that whatever Jessica had in store for her wouldn't be a walk in the park.

"Oh, well. Only one way to find out."

She left the washroom and crossed the boat's length, glancing enviously at the cluster of tiny cabins in the middle. She bet they were a lot warmer and more comfortable than her bed, and they didn't have to worry about bugs either.

Still, it didn't help to complain. Nobody cared. Least of all Jessica, who said it was good practice for the race, and Ridley supposed she was right.

Moments later, Loki joined her, and she scratched his head. "This is it, boy. Today is the day it all starts. Are you excited?"

Loki yawned, not nearly as keen as her.

Ridley laughed. "You can at least pretend to be interested. You are coming along on the race, after all."

Loki ignored her, and the moment they reached Jessica, he picked a quiet corner and lay down. That made his disdain for their training clear, and she decided to focus on Jessica instead. "So? What did you have in mind for me today?"

"For starters, you must learn to operate on less sleep," Jessica said.

"Why? The race takes days to complete," Ridley said. "Surely I can sleep at night?"

"Yes, you need to sleep, but the first one across the finish line wins. The other racers have been training for months, and they'll be faster, stronger, and fitter than you."

"So, how do I beat them? I only have a month to train," Ridley said.

"The only way you'll stand a chance is by running longer and harder than the rest. While they're still tucked away in their beds, you must be on the trail, covering those miles."

Ridley absorbed that information. It made sense, though she was starting to wonder what she'd signed up for. Preparing herself for the worst, she asked, "What do I do?"

"Run all day. Don't stop. Eat and drink on the move. Make sure you reach the relief station before dark and sleep there. It's the safest option. Do not get caught outside," Jessica warned, wagging a finger. "However, you must get up before

CHAPTER 14 - RIDLEY

the others. Don't wait for sunrise."

"Isn't that dangerous?" Ridley asked. "Running in the dark?"

"By early morning, most predators will have found their meal already. Also, I'll teach you how to make a torch. After you've eaten breakfast, use the remaining coals to light a torch. The smell of smoke will drive most creatures away. Not all, but most."

"Why is that?" Ridley asked with a frown.

"Forest fires. They're afraid of fire because of forest fires," Jessica explained.

"Oh, I see," Ridley said, understanding immediately. She'd seen the devastation caused by the fires. The blackened corpses, singed trees, and lack of underbrush. While they were a necessary part of nature, ensuring new growth, they were also scary as hell.

"When dawn is still an hour or two away, get up and start running. Use the torch to light your way, and trust Loki. He'll be able to hear and see things you can't. Above all else, trust in him to warn you of danger."

"How long do I have to finish?" Ridley asked.

"Three nights. You should reach the finishing line sometime on the fourth day, depending on your opponents."

"What?" Ridley asked, incredulous.

"That's how long it took last year's contestants, and it might even be less this year," Jessica said.

"Less? How's that possible?"

"It's the 10th annual race. It's special, and the prize is bigger than it's ever been before. You can expect the best of the best to be there, and they'll all be vying for that coveted first spot."

Ridley sat down on the deck with a thump. She hadn't considered that. In fact, she hadn't thought any of it through.

Now, her mind was filled with questions. Questions that needed answers. "How will I know where to go? What route to follow?"

"You will have a map and a compass. Also, there are ten-mile markers along the official trail."

"Official trail?"

"Nobody said you have to follow the exact route. There are shortcuts you can take."

"Short cuts? Isn't that cheating?" Ridley asked.

"Not if you're prepared to accept the consequences. The shortcuts are dangerous, however, and some are downright deadly."

"I see," Ridley said, swallowing hard on the sudden knot in her throat. "What if something happens to me along the way? What if I'm injured or can't finish the race?"

"There will be search parties stationed at each relief station. If you don't show up that night, they will look for you the next day. You can also forfeit the race at any of these stations and will be escorted back to Vancouver."

"Has anyone died yet?"

"Yes, there have been several fatalities over the years. It's the reality of the race," Jessica said, her expression somber. "Why do you think I tried to talk you out of it?"

"Yeah, I get it now," Ridley said.

"And? Have you changed your mind? Are you backing out?" Jessica asked, not bothering to disguise the hopeful tone in her voice.

Ridley thought about it, considering everything that could go wrong in the race. Then there was Loki. She wanted him with her. She needed him at her side. But what if something happened to him? Could she ever forgive herself?

CHAPTER 14 - RIDLEY

"You must be sure about this, Ridley," Jessica cautioned. "There can be no doubt in your mind."

Ridley took a deep breath and tried to steady her nerves. She knew Jessica was right. If she decided to go ahead, she had to be all in. She couldn't hold anything back. Raising her head, she met Jessica's gaze with a level stare. "I'm doing this. I am not giving up."

"Are you certain?"

"Yes," Ridley replied with all the conviction she could muster.

"What about Loki?"

Ridley looked at her canine companion, her heart full to bursting. He stared back at her with his golden-brown eyes, and she knew she couldn't leave him behind. "He's coming with me."

Jessica nodded. "Alright. Despite my feelings on the subject, I'll do my best to prepare you for this race. It's my job to get you both to the finish line in one piece."

"Thank you," Ridley said. "I wouldn't be able to do this without you."

"I know, and that's what kills me," Jessica said, shaking her head.

"Just tell me what to do," Ridley prompted, eager to start now that her mind was made up.

"First, we'll work on your endurance. We'll start with a run in full gear. I want to see what you can do. How long you can keep going."

"Where do I run? On the boat?" Ridley asked.

"That's no good. The deck is too even," Jessica said. "You'll run on the bank alongside the boat."

"Alone?" Ridley asked, suddenly nervous.

"Yes, alone. The same way you'd run the race. Nobody will be there to help you then."

"And Loki?"

"He can stay on the boat for today. I just want you to get used to running, for starters."

"Okay," Ridley said. It was going to be a long day, but she was determined to see it through. She would win the race, no matter what it took.

Chapter 15 - Ridley

The boat edged closer to the embankment, steered by the Captain while the crew stood ready in case of trouble. The first mate tested the water with a long pole, ensuring they didn't hit a hidden sandbank and get stuck.

The Captain gave the signal when he'd gone as far as he dared. "Go ahead."

"Thanks," Jessica said, lowering Ridley into the river.

She cried out as the cold water enveloped her, driving the air from her lungs in a whoosh. "Whoo, it's cold."

Jessica grinned. "Better get used to it."

"Thanks," Ridley replied, her voice laced with sarcasm. She was aware of Rupert's eyes on her, watching with deep amusement. Bear had a similar look on his face while the boat crew eyed her as if she were crazy. *Well. I suppose I am a little crazy.*

She dropped into the water and swam toward the bank, dragging herself up the steep incline. As soon as she was clear of the water, she waved at Jessica. "I'm ready!"

Jessica threw her backpack and weapons onto dry land, the items landing with a dull thump. Ridley slung the pack over her shoulders and grabbed her crossbow. "Thanks!"

"Be careful," Jessica yelled.

"Okay," Ridley said, unsure what else to say.

The boat sheered off from the bank, abandoning her on land, and a shiver ran down her spine. Loki watched her with a mournful look, clearly unhappy with the situation, but she'd commanded him to stay.

Turning away from the boat and Loki, Ridley jogged along the river bank. At first, it wasn't that bad. She was fresh, the breeze was cool, and the sun was warm. Her clothing dried, and the terrain was smooth.

An hour passed, then two. She stopped once to drink water but decided to keep running next time. Once, she had to pee and did it in a stand of reeds.

However, as the day wore on, the terrain grew rough and uneven. She tried to keep a steady pace, but it was near impossible with the irregular footing. Plus, she had to keep one eye on the boat drifting downriver on the current and another on the forest next to her.

Exhaustion set in, and she began to imagine predatory eyes watching her from the dim interior of the trees. Her feet hitting the ground echoed through the quiet space, punctuated by her harsh breathing. Her heart beat too fast, and her brain raced with every step.

Jessica's voice rang in her head, reminding her that she needed to always keep calm and alert. "Panic is the enemy. You can face anything with a clear head."

She tried to focus on those words and quiet her mind, but it was impossible. Her attention kept wandering to the trees and the creatures lurking inside. Monstrous beings ready to pounce at any time.

Not even the familiar figures of Jessica, Bear, and Loki watching her from the boat could calm her down, and she

CHAPTER 15 - RIDLEY

considered flagging them down. *A rest. That's all I need—a short time to gather my thoughts and get back on track.*

Suddenly, a clump of brush to her left rustled, and her heart jumped into her throat. She veered off the path and moved closer to the river, away from the forest. A stand of reeds enveloped her, the tall strands blocking her view. Forging ahead, she hoped to lose whatever was following her.

The reeds scratched at her skin and tugged strands of hair free from her scalp while her feet sank deep into the mud below. She kept moving, her heart pounding in her chest until she burst onto an open stretch of sand.

Breathless, Ridley stopped and turned around, but the reeds had closed behind her, and she couldn't see if she was being followed. She scanned the river and the forested banks, alert to any movement. Nothing seemed out of place, but she couldn't shake the feeling of being watched.

Looking over her shoulder, she noticed the boat had drifted closer. Jessica, Bear, and Loki watched her with concern, and Jessica had her binoculars out.

"Do you see anything?" Ridley yelled.

Jessica scanned the area again before shaking her head. "Nope. Nothing. Probably just the wind."

Ridley sagged with relief, feeling like she'd had a narrow escape. Her breathing was ragged, and she was covered in mud and scratches.

"Are you okay?" Jessica called out. "Have you had enough for the day?"

"No, it's okay. I can carry on," Ridley said, trying to slow her racing heart. She couldn't let her imagination get the better of her. She was on this mission for a reason and had to keep going. *I can't give up every time the going gets tough.*

"Alright, but be careful," Jessica said, and the boat continued its journey upriver.

Gathering her things, Ridley resumed her run. This time, she focused on her breathing and keeping an even pace. The sensation of being watched remained with her for a long time, but she forced herself to ignore it. Either her mind was working against her, or something was out there. If the latter were true, she'd face it when it got to it. Meanwhile, she had a race to train for, and nothing on earth could stop her.

Chapter 16 - Ridley

That night, Ridley barely made the swim back to the boat. After running all day, her legs felt like jelly, and her arms were limp noodles. Her back ached, and her head throbbed. She didn't even have the strength to pull herself up unto the deck, and Bear had to haul her up.

"There you go," he said, plonking her down.

"Thanks," Ridley said, too out of breath to reply. She collapsed onto the floorboards, gasping for air. The sound of her heart pounding in her chest was deafening, and she longed to rest.

Loki disagreed. He bowled her over and licked her face, a ball of wriggling gray fur. She tried to fend him off, but he was everywhere at once. Within seconds, she was covered in wolf slobber and laughing so hard she thought her ribs would crack. "Loki, stop! Please!"

Obedient as ever, he sat back on the deck, his tongue lolling from his jaws. His tail thumped on the wooden floorboards while he waited for her to right herself and wipe the slime from her face. Finally, she leaned forward and wrapped her arms around him. "I missed you too, boy. Next time, you're running with me."

Satisfied, Loki allowed her to get to her feet. Her legs still felt wobbly, and she leaned against Loki to steady herself. Jessica brought her a canteen of water, and she gulped it down gratefully.

"You did well today," Jessica said with a nod of approval. "You managed to keep up with the boat, and you ran the entire day."

"It doesn't feel like I did well," Ridley said. "I feel awful. Like I'm going to pass out or die."

"That's to be expected. Come on. Dinner's ready," Jessica said.

"No, thanks. I'm not hungry," Ridley declined. "I just want to wash up and go to sleep."

"No sleep for you yet, young lady," Jessica said, waving a finger.

"Why not?"

"You need to keep your strength up, which means you must eat," Jessica said.

"But I feel sick," Ridley complained.

"You'll feel better after you've eaten, I promise," Jessica said.

"Alright, I'm coming," Ridley said, reluctantly dragging her tired body across the boat's length.

They sat down to dinner, and the smell of cooked food teased her nostrils. Her stomach cramped, reminding her that the only food she'd eaten that day was a few handfuls of trail mix. The nausea vanished, and she loaded her plate to the brim with freshly cooked fish and greens.

The first bite transported her to heaven, and she groaned with delight. It was the best food she'd ever tasted. She wolfed down half of the plate before coming up for air. "Who made this? It's delicious!"

Jessica pointed at Bear. "You can thank him. He's the chef

tonight and a much better cook than me."

"And you can thank Eddy, our first mate, for the catch of fresh fish," the Captain said, pointing his knife at the man in question.

Eddy ducked his head, a faint blush staining his cheeks. "It wasn't hard. There's fish aplenty in these waters."

"Makes for a hearty meal," Rupert declared.

"It is very good," the Captain agreed.

"It's better than good. It's great," Ridley said, stuffing another forkful into her mouth.

Bear snorted. "Hunger is the best seasoning."

"Huh?" Ridley asked.

"He means that the food tastes so great because you're starving. You could probably eat fried shoe leather right now," Jessica explained.

Ridley stared at her plate. "Honestly, I don't care."

She finished the rest of her food, savoring each bite. Afterward, she licked the oil off her fingers and wiped her mouth. Looking down, she marveled at her bulging stomach, rubbing one hand over the bump. "I'm having a baby. A food baby."

"Oh, God," Jessica said, rolling her eyes. "That must be the worst joke ever."

Ridley stuck her tongue out at Jessica. "You've got no sense of humor."

"Yes, I do," Jessica protested.

"Prove it then. Tell us a joke," Ridley said. "I dare you."

Jessica's eyes narrowed. "Alright. Here's a joke for you: Why did the banana go to the doctor?"

Ridley stared at her, stumped. "Huh?"

"Why?" Bear asked.

"It wasn't peeling well," Jessica finished, chuckling at her joke. Silence reigned over the rest of the group. When she noticed, she pulled up her shoulders. "What? It wasn't peeling well? Get it?"

"Oh, we get it," Rupert said. "It's just not funny."

"Yeah, that was a horrible joke," the Captain added.

"Really?" Jessica said. "Bear?"

"It's even worse than my jokes," Bear said, raising both hands to ward off her glare. "Sorry."

"Ridley? Tell me you got it, at least?" Jessica pleaded.

Ridley stared at her. "What's a banana?"

Jessica blinked. "You don't know what a banana is?"

"No, I don't," Ridley said.

"You forget she's like two seconds old," Rupert said. "She's never seen a banana in her life. They come from the old world."

Jessica threw her hands in the air. "Perfect! Just perfect!"

"I thought it was funny," Eddy, the first mate, said.

"Stop sucking up to the pretty lady, Eddy, and get the crew to wash the dishes," the Captain said. "You can take the first watch tonight."

"Yes, Captain," Eddy acknowledged before he hurried off.

Ridley got to her feet, scraped her plate clean of scraps, and placed it in the kitchen's washbasin. Sticking her hands in the air, she stretched her aching muscles and yawned. "Well, I'm off to bed. See you in the morning."

"Hold up," Jessica said.

"What now?" Ridley asked, her heart sinking.

"Let's clean those cuts and scrapes first," Jessica said, pointing at Ridley's arms. "We don't want you to develop an infection, do we?" Jessica said.

"I guess not," Ridley admitted.

CHAPTER 16 - RIDLEY

Jessica got a small first aid kit and carefully cleaned and bandaged her injuries. "There you go."

Ridley winced when the antiseptic stung her cuts, but she knew it was necessary. "Thanks."

"Next time, I want you to wear a long-sleeved tunic while you run. The leather will prevent all of those scratches from happening again. Now, let's see your feet," Jessica said.

"What for?"

"Your success in the race will depend on your feet. You have to take care of them. Every night, you must treat your feet, wash and dry them, and put on a clean pair of socks," Jessica said.

"How do I treat them?" Ridley asked, peeling off her socks. She winced as Jessica examined her feet, locating several chafe marks and a couple of blisters. "Ouch."

"Like this," Jessica said, showing her how to strap her feet, bandage raw spots, and treat blisters. It wasn't pretty, but it was educational.

"Thanks," Ridley said, flexing her feet. "That feels better."

"You have to look after yourself, sweetheart," Jessica said. "That means eating enough food to fuel your body during the race and staying hydrated. Tomorrow, I want you to practice eating and drinking regularly while running, even if it makes you feel sick. Got it?"

"Okay," Ridley said, barely keeping her eyes open.

"Alright, time for bed," Jessica said, packing away the first aid kit. "We have a long day ahead of us tomorrow."

Ridley nodded, yawning. "Goodnight."

Calling Loki, Ridley made her way to her bed. She stopped at the bathroom first, did her business, then used a clean rag and water to wash the sweat and grime from her body.

Afterward, she pulled on clean clothes: Underwear, socks, a long-sleeved tunic, and pants.

Jessica and Bear still sat around the cooking fire, chatting in low voices. They laughed and joked together, in perfect harmony with each other. It looked like fun, but Ridley was too tired to join in. Her mind was consumed with thoughts of sleep. Wonderful, deep, dreamless sleep.

She climbed into her bedroll, pulled the extra blanket over her head, and promptly fell asleep. Pressed to her back lay Loki, a warm and comforting presence, while underneath her slumbering shape, the boat dipped and rolled in the current—the perfect lullaby.

Chapter 17 - Ridley

A few hours later, Ridley was rudely awakened by a rough hand on her shoulder. She blinked into the darkness, bleary-eyed and confused. A shape loomed above her, indistinguishable in the night. "What the hell? Who is it? Who's there?"

"It's me, sleepyhead," Jessica said. "Time to get up."

"What? Why? It's the middle of the night!" Ridley protested.

"So? We've got work to do," Jessica said, reaching out to shake her again. "Come on. You know the drill."

"Leave me alone," Ridley said, slapping her hand away. She burrowed deeper into the bedroll, clutching her blanket with a desperate fervor. "Come back in the morning."

"Remember your promise, Ridley. You do what I say when I say it," Jessica reminded her. "If you can't handle this, you might as well give up. Let me know what you decide."

Ridley pressed her face into her blanket and listened to Jessica's footsteps receding into the distance. She desperately wanted to stay in her cocoon of warmth and comfort. Her eyelids burned from lack of sleep, and every muscle in her body ached. *Just a little bit longer. Just a few more minutes.*

"Argh, damn it," Ridley cried, throwing the blankets aside. Cold air rushed into her nest, chasing any remnants of sleep away. With a yelp, she jumped to her feet, grabbed her boots and jacket, and chased after Jessica. "I'm here. I'm up, and I'm here."

"Good," Jessica said with an approving nod. She handed Ridley a steaming cup of coffee and pointed to the front of the boat. "Time for a lesson."

"Lesson?" Ridley asked, gratefully accepting the cup. She sipped the hot brew, not surprised to find it was strong and bitter, precisely what she needed.

"Yes, a lesson," Jessica said, leading the way to where a blanket was laid out on the deck. She sat down on the cloth and patted the space next to her.

"A lesson in what?" Ridley asked, sitting down next to her.

"How to navigate by the stars," Jessica said.

"Really? That's so cool," Ridley exclaimed, her interest piqued. She had always been fascinated by the stars but had never known much about them.

Jessica smiled at Ridley's enthusiasm. "It's an important skill to have no matter where you are," she said, gesturing at the sky. "Now, observe. I'm going to show you how to locate the North Star."

Ridley watched as Jessica showed her how to use the Big Dipper to find it. "That's Polaris, the North Star. It's always in the same spot in the sky, which makes it a reliable point of reference."

"That's amazing," Ridley said, filled with wonder.

"It is, isn't it?" Jessica said, smiling. "But it's not the only thing you need to know. Other constellations can help you navigate, depending on where you are and the time of year. Orion, for example, is easy to spot and can guide you to certain landmarks."

Ridley listened intently, soaking up every detail like a

CHAPTER 17 - RIDLEY

sponge. She felt a sense of purpose for the first time since she had found herself on this boat. She had something to learn, something to master. Something that would help her and Loki survive the race.

He'd joined them at some point during the lesson, though he had no interest in learning about the stars or anything else. He only wanted Ridley's companionship, and he curled up tight against her leg. She rested her hand on his head, absently scratching his ears while she listened to Jessica.

As the lesson went on, the sky began to lighten. The stars faded into the background, replaced by dawn's pink and orange hues. A flock of Nyctosaurus flew past overhead, seeking shelter for the day. The flyers were small despite their impressive wingspan, weighing roughly four pounds each, and did not pose a threat.

Instead, she watched as they circled above the forest canopy, their harsh cries cutting through the pre-dawn air before they settled into a giant tree covered in streamers of ivy.

Silence fell, broken only by the splash of fish in the river and the occasional honk or bellow in the distance. Ridley hoped they'd see some dinosaurs drinking water, but the banks were too steep, and she gave up after a while.

When the sun peeked its head above the horizon, Jessica stood up and stretched, her joints cracking in the early morning air. "Alright, that's enough for today. You did well, Ridley."

"Thanks. I enjoyed the lesson," Ridley said, gathering their empty coffee cups and the blanket. "Can I go back to bed now?"

"Haha, very funny," Jessica said. "It's time for the next phase of your training."

"Which is?" Ridley asked, but she wasn't sure she wanted to know.

"How do you feel about a nice long swim?" Jessica asked, her eyes twinkling.

Ridley glanced over the side of the boat. The water was deep green and murky, its depths unfathomable. She knew it was cold too. They were only at the beginning of spring, and the warmth of summer was still a long way off. "You want me to swim in there? How do we know it's safe?"

"It's not," Jessica said. "There are fish in there with teeth as long as my hand, and there's always a chance that a Spinosaurus might be lurking about."

"A Spinosaurus?" Ridley exclaimed. "Are you nuts? I'm not going in there!"

"Relax. There hasn't been one around in years. The river traffic scares them off."

"And the fish?" Ridley asked, watching the river with a doubtful frown.

"They won't bother you. You're too big to be prey, and the boat churns up the water. Chases them away."

"I don't know," Ridley said, still not convinced.

"Listen up," Jessica said, her look earnest. "During the race, you might have to cross rivers like this one. You will be cold, you will be tired, you will be miserable, and you will be scared, but you must learn to push through all of that. To face your fears. That is what I'm trying to teach you."

Ridley sucked in a deep breath, absorbing Jessica's words. The woman was right. She had to be prepared for anything. "Alright. I'll do it."

"The goal is to last an hour. Any longer, and you risk developing hypothermia. I'll time you and tell you when you

CHAPTER 17 - RIDLEY

can come out."

"Only an hour?" Ridley asked. "I'm sure I can do that."

"We'll see about that," Jessica said. "Just remember. If you fall behind or something attacks you, shout out, and I'll throw you a line, but try to hold out as long as possible. Forget your pain; forget when you're tired. Forget everything but winning."

Ridley nodded, a surge of determination running through her veins. "Alright. I'm ready."

"Breakfast first," Jessica said. "Something light but high-calorie, and you'd better dress for the occasion."

Ridley ate a bowl of oatmeal mixed with nuts, dried fruit, and syrup, followed by a glass of water. Next, she removed her shoes and socks, opting to swim barefoot.

She borrowed a pair of tights and a fitted long-sleeved shirt from Jessica. The garments were made from a thin material called polyester which she found fascinating. She was used to simple leather and cotton garments, and the smooth, stretchy material felt strange and alien on her skin. Still, she kind of liked it, flexing her arms and legs until she was frog-jumping all over the boat.

While she prepared for her swim, Jessica haggled with the Captain, and she listened with half an ear. They were all used to negotiating—an expected part of trading. Everyone wanted a good deal and was willing to fight for it.

"I only need you to go slow for an hour," Jessica said, explaining about Ridley's training.

"How slow?" the Captain asked.

"The slowest you can," Jessica said.

"That's ridiculous. The slowest is around a mile or two per hour. We'll never get to Vancouver at that rate," the Captain protested.

"Bullshit. It's only for an hour, and I'll make it worth your while."

"A hundred credits," the Captain said.

"Sixty."

"Ninety."

"Seventy."

"Eighty-five, or forget it."

"Eighty-five, and we will do it again tomorrow."

"Again?" the Captain said.

"She needs the practice.

"Fine. We have a deal," the Captain said, and they shook on it.

Rupert watched the entire scene with great amusement, seemingly unable to believe his eyes. "You're all crazy; you know that?"

"I know," Jessica said.

Ridley shrugged. Other people's opinions had never bothered her much.

"The crew doesn't seem to mind," Rupert said, pointing at Eddy and his two teammates.

They leaned against the side of the boat, watching Ridley as she stretched her lithe body in the skintight swimsuit. They looked like starving hounds at the banquet table, and Ridley immediately stopped what she was doing, her cheeks burning.

"Okay, that's enough," Jessica said, chasing them off. "Haven't you people got work to do?"

Eddy and his chums scattered to the winds, and Jessica waved to Ridley. "Are you ready?"

"As ready as I'll ever be," Ridley replied, dropping her legs over the side while balancing on the edge.

CHAPTER 17 - RIDLEY

The Captain dropped the speed to its lowest, and the boat chugged along at a steady two miles an hour.

Ridley gazed at the water below her feet, more afraid than she'd admit. Even the two miles per hour seemed too fast, and the water's murky depths taunted her with its dark secrets.

"I know you're scared, but remember why you're doing this," Jessica said just before she took the plunge.

Ridley nudged herself off the railing, falling feet first into the river. Before she hit the surface, one thought stood out above all the rest: *I'm doing this for you, Dad. I'm doing this for you.*

Chapter 18 - Ridley

Ridley slipped into the water with barely a splash, the liquid closing around her head. She gazed at the surface, marveling at how the sun cut through the water, coloring everything in an emerald haze. It was beautiful, but the cold demanded her attention, pushing aside other considerations.

Pins and needles stung her arms and legs, the chill cutting into her skin like a knife. She kicked her legs and swam to the surface, the water churning around her. Her head burst into the open, and she sucked in a deep breath of air.

Voices called to her from behind, and she twisted around in time to see the boat moving upriver. If she didn't hurry, she'd get left behind. "Over here, Ridley! Hurry!"

Ridley turned in their direction and began to swim. The water frothed around her form, her legs propelling her forward in a greenish blur. The current fought against her, seeking to hamper her progress, but gradually, she gained on the boat.

Jessica, Bear, and Loki shouted encouragement from the deck, urging her ever onward.

"Come on, Ridley. You can do it!" Jessica cried.

"Faster, faster," Bear yelled while Loki yipped and danced on the deck.

CHAPTER 18 - RIDLEY

Finally, she drew even with them and shot them a thumbs-up.

"Good job," Jessica said. "Now, you must just keep it up for an hour."

Easy peasy, Ridley thought to herself.

Now that she was keeping pace with the boat, she felt confident she could keep going for an hour. While the current was strong and the water cold, it differed from running.

For one, she was not carrying a heavy backpack and weapons. The water kept her from overheating and sweating, and the river had no rough terrain to contend with. Water was water.

Ridley swam on, her arms and legs cutting through the river with smooth, efficient strokes. She felt invigorated, alive, and in the moment. She breathed deeply, feeling the rush of oxygen fill her lungs and fuel her body.

"Thirty minutes," Jessica yelled, waving a hand.

"You're halfway there!"

Ridley grinned with a sense of pride and accomplishment. She was doing something that few people could do or even attempt. She felt like she was pushing herself, proving she could achieve anything she wanted, even winning the race. *I can do this. I know I can.*

But her optimism faded once exhaustion set it. It crept up unnoticed, dragging at her limbs until every kick and push became a battle of wills. Her energy drained away, and the cold seeped into her bones.

Soon, her extremities grew numb until she could hardly feel her arms and legs. Her jaw began to chatter until she had to shut her mouth for fear her teeth would shatter.

Still, she kept pushing, telling herself to go a little further.

To do just a little more. Her ability to overcome pain and discomfort could mean the difference between winning and losing the race.

"Forty-five minutes," Jessica called.

Forty-five minutes. That means only fifteen more, Ridley thought, though her thought processes were slow and sluggish. *I can do it. Just a little bit longer.*

The cold was now all she could feel; every part of her body screamed in agony. Ridley shut her eyes, focusing on the rhythm of her strokes as she swam. The water had become choppy, making it harder to keep her breathing in check.

Taking a deep breath, she dove under the water, hoping to find some relief from the biting cold. But the water was just as cold beneath the surface, and she quickly resurfaced.

"Come on, Ridley! Just a few more minutes!" Jessica shouted from the boat.

Ridley turned her head towards the boat, her arms felt like lead weights. Panic set in as she realized that she might not make it. That she might fail.

Then, she saw something that gave her hope. A flash of silver caught her attention, and she turned to see a school of fish swimming alongside her. They darted and weaved through the water, unencumbered by the cold or the current. Whenever they caught the sun, their scales flashed with rainbow colors.

Ridley watched them, mesmerized by their fluid movements. Instead of being afraid, she felt invigorated and realized she'd come too far to give up now.

With one final burst of energy, Ridley pushed herself alongside the boat. Her limbs ached, and her body trembled with exertion, but she kept going until Jessica whooped with

CHAPTER 18 - RIDLEY

joy. "One hour! You made it!"

The boat slowed as the Captain cut the engine, and a rope dropped over the side attached to a float. "Grab on!"

Ridley latched onto the orange plastic device with grim determination, refusing to let go even when she hit the deck. It was impossible to speak, her entire body wracked with shivers.

A warm tongue licked her face, and a furry face nuzzled her neck. "L... L... Loki. I... I'm... okay, boy."

"Hurry, Bear. Get her to the cabin. We need to get her warm as soon as possible. I underestimated the temperature of the water," Jessica said.

Ridley hardly registered the words, her body clenched into a tight knot. She felt warm hands scoop her up and sweep her through the air. The next moment, she was lying on a bed inside the cabin.

The door closed, and Jessica lit a candle. "We need to get you out of those wet things right now."

"O... Okay," Ridley stuttered.

With calm efficiency, Jessica stripped the wet pants and shirt off her body. She grabbed a towel and dried Ridley's skin with rough strokes to get her blood circulating again. Afterward, she dressed her in warm woolen clothing—pants, a shirt, a thick jersey, socks, and gloves.

Ridley slowly relaxed under her care. The shaking stopped, and her teeth stopped chattering. The feeling returned to her extremities in a rush of hot blood, a sensation so good she almost cried.

"Do you feel better now?" Jessica asked, her voice laced with concern.

"Much better," Ridley said, pointing to the door. "Loki. He's worried. Please, let him in."

"Of course," Jessica said, opening the door.

He jumped onto the bed, straight into Ridley's lap, and showered her with sloppy kisses while she hugged him.

"Come sit by the kitchen stove," Jessica prompted. "I'll stoke the fire and make you something hot to drink."

"Tea. I want tea. Lots of sugar," Ridley said, her voice muffled by Loki's ruff.

"Coming right up," Jessica said.

She hurried out, and Ridley followed as soon as she was able. True to her word, the tiny alcove where the Captain and crew cooked their meals was warm and toasty, heated by the stove.

A hot cup of tea awaited her, and she huddled up in front of the fire to sip on the sweet brew. It tasted like heaven after her ordeal, and she basked in the heat until she thought she would melt into a puddle of goo.

Loki stayed with her the entire time, stuck to her side like a bur, and she soon began to feel tired. Her eyes drooped, and she longed to curl up and sleep.

Jessica noticed, and her expression softened. "The swim was tough on you, sweetie. Why don't you take a nap?"

"Thanks," Ridley said, closing her eyes.

She was ready to drift into a deep sleep when a thought occurred. What if she were out on the trail? Alone? What if she had to cross a river by herself? There wouldn't be anyone to help her then. No Jessica. No Bear. No hot tea and a stoked fire, ready and waiting. She'd have no one to rely on but herself. *I can't sleep. Not now. It's not over. I have to carry on. No matter what.*

Chapter 19 - Ridley

In the days and weeks that followed, Ridley observed a punishing routine that put her through the wringer physically and mentally. She stuck to the strategy laid out by Jessica, sleeping less and running longer.

She lived on the same food she'd be able to carry with her during the race and alternated between running and swimming. They restricted the swimming to thirty-minute intervals, however, not willing to risk another bout of near hypothermia.

Once a week, she was allowed a full day's rest, giving her body time to recuperate. When she was not training, she spent her time planning for the race. She traced the route on an old map Rupert gave her, memorizing it by heart.

Jessica tried to impart as much knowledge as possible, sharing everything she knew about survival. Often, she ran with Ridley, pointing out plants, herbs, and trees that had medicinal or nutritional value. She showed her how to choose a camping spot, build a shelter, find water, and keep hidden. She also taught Ridley basic first aid, navigation, tracking, hunting, and more.

The others pitched in, even the Captain and his crew. Once they overcame their initial skepticism, they began to cheer for

Ridley and help her in any way possible. Between them, they taught her how to catch, gut, and cook fish, read the currents, and predict the weather. Even Rupert imparted some of his hard-won wisdom, telling her stories about his travels with the caravan.

It was a lot to take in, and sometimes Ridley regretted embarking on the entire adventure, but she remained steadfast and determined, pushing herself to the edge. She wasn't doing it for herself. She was doing it for her father.

The worst was the constant hunger, thirst, and exhaustion. It was difficult to think straight when tired. It was even harder to stay alert while running and look out for danger. The likelihood of injuries increased tenfold, and Ridley suffered from her fair share of bruises, falls, cuts, and scrapes.

Her feet took the brunt of it, and she quickly learned what Jessica meant by winning or losing the race because of the condition of her feet. Blisters popped up daily, her skin chafed to the point of peeling off, and her toes cramped until they looked like starfish.

Carrying enough food and water became a challenge. Running all day meant her body burned through a prodigious amount of energy. While the trail mix and dried meat were nutritious and lightweight, it wasn't enough. Even stuffing her face at night didn't help, and the weight kept coming off.

Despite the challenges, Ridley made steady progress. After three and a half weeks on the river, she'd worked through four race cycles, and the results were evident. She was leaner, tougher, faster, and more agile. Her shoulders had broadened from the constant swimming, her skin bore a dusky tan, and she was constantly aware of her surroundings.

Her endurance had increased by leaps and bounds. Her lung

CHAPTER 19 - RIDLEY

capacity too, and her feet had grown tough and calloused. She could tie ten different kinds of knots, track an animal through any terrain, plot her course by stars, spot an incoming storm, build a decent shelter in seconds, and spear a fish with a sharpened stick.

Ridley had never been more prepared in her life, yet she was filled with worry and fear. They'd reached the end of their journey, and her time was up. On the morrow, they'd reach Vancouver, and there would be no more time to train.

That night, she picked at her food, unable to work up an appetite. It didn't take long for everyone to notice, and the conversation died down until all eyes were on her.

"What's wrong?" Jessica asked.

"Do you... do you think I'm ready?" Ridley asked. "For the race, I mean?"

"I think you're as ready as it's possible to be in such a short time," Jessica answered, choosing her words carefully.

"I mean, do you think I can win?" Ridley tried again. "Do I stand a chance?"

Jessica sighed. "Honestly? If you were anybody else, I'd say no. You're not ready."

"Then what's the point? Why did I do all of this if it's for nothing?" Ridley burst out.

"Because you're not just anybody. You're different," Jessica said.

"How am I different?" Ridley asked.

"You have heart, and that makes all the difference," Jessica said. "It's what keeps you going long after any other person would've given up. It's what drives you past your limits. Over and over these past weeks, I've seen you hit a wall, and I thought, this is it. She's done. Only to have you push further, harder, and longer than humanly possible."

Ridley blinked, taken aback. "You mean that?"

"I do," Jessica said. "When you're out there and ready to give up, look inside your heart. It will give you what you need to carry on."

The rest of the group nodded, agreeing with Jessica, and Ridley swallowed on the sudden knot in her throat. She felt lucky to be surrounded by so much love and blinked back the tears that threatened to spill down her cheeks. "Thanks, you guys."

The conversation turned to what she'd need during the race, with food being the primary concern. Her weight loss had not gone unnoticed, and everyone was trying to find a solution.

"Nuts. She needs more nuts in that mix of hers," Rupert said.

"Fat. That was what my mama always said," Eddy added.

"Fat? As in raw fat?" Ridley asked, gagging.

"Dried fat," Eddy said. "Bits of dry fat."

That still didn't sound very appetizing, and Ridley refrained from answering.

"Once we reach Vancouver, we'll go shopping," Jessica said. "You need better shoes. Shoes that will last the distance."

"I like my shoes," Ridley protested, looking at her handmade moccasins.

"Your clothes will have to go too. No seams. Nothing that can chafe," Jessica said, ignoring her comment on her shoes. "You'll need an ointment to prevent and treat chafing."

"A hat," Rupert said. "Don't forget a hat."

"Can the wolf carry a pack?" Eddy asked.

"No, it's against the rules. He can run with her, but he can't help. That's why contestants aren't allowed to use horses,

CHAPTER 19 - RIDLEY

donkeys, or any kind of pack animal."

"Oh, sorry," Eddy said.

"We'll shop around for food options too. See what we can find. I'm sure we can find superior goods in Vancouver. Something better than trail mix and dried dinosaur meat."

"Ugh, I hope so," Ridley said. "If I have to eat more of that stuff, I'm gonna puke."

Jessica laughed. "Don't worry. The worst is over now. At least until the race starts."

"What do you mean?" Ridley asked.

"Starting tomorrow, no more training. Plus, you get to eat lots and lots of starchy food. Think bread, rice, oats, porridge, crackers, that sort of thing. You have to build up solid reserves for the race. Put back some of that weight you've lost."

Ridley smiled. "I can do that."

"I thought you'd like the idea. That and a proper nights' sleep," Jessica said with a grin. "Report for a proper breakfast tomorrow, nice and early. Okay?"

"Yes, ma'am," Ridley said, her eagerness unfeigned.

"She needs socks," Bear said with a grunt.

"Five pairs, at least. The best quality we can find," Jessica agreed.

"Get her salt for the muscle cramps," the Captain suggested.

"Good call," Jessica said.

"What about a gun?" Rupert asked, and all eyes towards Ridley.

"I don't like guns," Ridley said, shaking her head.

"Too heavy. A small gun wouldn't help much, and a big gun would only weigh her down. Plus, there's no time to teach her how to use it," Jessica said. "She's better off relying on stealth and speed."

Ridley nodded, wholeheartedly agreeing. Guns frightened her. They looked strange, felt alien, and smelled terrible. They were from a time she didn't know anything about. A time she didn't belong to.

The conversation continued for a few more minutes until Jessica cleared her throat. "Alright. It's getting late. Time for bed." She fixed Ridley with a stern gaze. "No tossing and turning. No worrying about the race. You need your rest. Got it?"

"Got it," Ridley acknowledged, seeking out her bed. She crawled into her bedroll and snuggled close to Loki. Her eyes drifted shut, slumber tugging at her mind. Jessica needn't have worried. Within seconds, she was fast asleep.

Chapter 20 - Jessica

Jessica stripped off her clothes and climbed into bed next to Bear. He held her tight, enveloping her in his arms. Delicious warmth stole over her limbs, and she heaved a sigh of contentment. It was the best part of her day. The one time when she felt completely and absolutely at ease. Safe, loved, and protected. Cherished.

"Goodnight," Bear said, pressing a kiss to her lips.

"Night, my love," Jessica replied.

With her head resting on his chest, she stared into the darkness, praying for sleep that didn't come. The minutes ticked by, and still, her mind wouldn't allow her surcease, circling the question of Ridley and the race. "Bear? Are you awake?"

"I am now," he said with a sigh.

"Sorry."

"What's wrong?" he asked.

"I'm worried I made a mistake. Did I make a mistake?" Jessica asked.

"You'll have to be a little clearer."

"Did I make a mistake training her for a race that could kill her?" Jessica asked.

Bear was silent for a few moments before he asked, "What

would her chances have been without the training?"

"Zero. Or maybe twenty percent just because she's so damn stubborn," Jessica said.

"And with the training?" Bear asked.

"I think she'll finish. Heck, she might even win. She's a lot tougher than I realized," Jessica said.

"Then what's the problem?" Bear asked.

"The problem is, she could still die. Or get maimed," Jessica said.

"Look. You did the best you could, sweetheart. The rest is up to her," Bear replied. "Her and that wolf."

Jessica sighed. "I suppose you're right."

"Of course I am. I'm always right," Bear said with a chuckle.

Jessica gave him a halfhearted smack. "Stop it."

"Never," Bear replied.

Jessica fell silent for a while, thinking. "It's been a while since I've been home."

"Vancouver?"

"Yup."

"Do you miss it?" Bear asked.

"No, not anymore," Jessica said. "My home is with you now, and I've never been happier. Vancouver can suck it."

Bear chuckled, pulling her close. "Love you too, sweetheart."

***

The following day, Jessica got up an hour early to pack their bags and prepare breakfast. The meal was simple but hearty. Savory oats mixed with butter, salt, and herbs, topped with slivers of dried meat. Coffee and biscuits with gooseberry jam finished off the selection.

It wasn't long before Ridley appeared, freshly washed and dressed. She looked bright-eyed and alert after a whole night's

CHAPTER 20 - JESSICA

sleep, exactly what Jessica wanted. "Sleep well?"

"Very well; thanks for asking," Ridley replied, grabbing the nearest chair. Loki sat down next to her, gazing around with interest. He also looked well-rested and happy, his tail thumping the floor whenever someone talked to him.

"Are you ready for today?" Jessica asked.

"I'm nervous," Ridley admitted with a shaky smile.

"I'm sure you are, but don't worry. I'll be there with you every step of the way."

"You don't know what that means to me," Ridley said.

"Oh, I know," Jessica said with a gentle smile.

Ridley smiled back before turning her attention to Loki, and Jessica watched the two interact while she dished up the food. The bond between them was amazing to see. It was special. They were kindred souls: Wild, free, and adventurous.

Walking over, she handed Ridley two bowls filled with the savory oats she'd made. "I hope you're hungry."

"Starving," Ridley said, placing one bowl on the floor for Loki.

They dug in enthusiastically, not wasting a second, and Jessica smothered a smile. They were like kids, enjoying the small things in life without worrying about the big stuff. For a moment, she envied their innocence.

But that time was long gone for her. In its place, she had something equally as valuable. Confidence. The kind that comes with age, maturity, and experience. It did not care about other people's opinions. It was rooted in a solid sense of self and the knowledge that she owed no one a thing. No one except herself.

With a sigh, Jessica turned away and busied herself with her chores. She handed out the rest of the oatmeal, plated the biscuits, and wiped the stove and kitchen counters.

Finally, she sat down and ate breakfast, savoring the gooseberry jam and biscuits with her coffee. She had a sweet tooth, though she rarely indulged. Today, she did. A long day lay ahead, and she'd need all her energy.

After breakfast, Ridley offered to wash the dishes while the Captain and crew brought them into the river docks. The river couldn't take them all the way to the city, and they'd have to walk about half a mile to the nearest gate. Armed guards in the employ of the city would accompany them, however, ensuring their safety.

Leaning against the railing, Jessica watched as the familiar silhouette of Vancouver drew closer on the horizon. Rupert joined her for a brief moment, trying to catch sight of his caravan. They were long gone, though, and he frowned. "We lost time. They got here before us."

"Yeah, sorry. That's my fault. It's because of all those times Ridley swam, and I paid the Captain to reduce speed."

"It's okay. The caravan can cope without me for a while. I trained them well," Rupert said. "Besides, this was an interesting voyage."

"I'm glad you enjoyed it," Jessica said.

"See you soon," Rupert said, walking toward his cabin.

Jessica returned her attention to her former home, taking in the sights. Ridley joined her not long after and immediately burst into excited chatter. "Is that Vancouver? It's so big! It's huge! Loki, look at that!"

Loki barked and jumped around, egged on by her excitement.

"Whoa, dial down the volume, would you?" Jessica said, laughing.

CHAPTER 20 - JESSICA

"Sorry, it's just... so huge!" Ridley said, jumping up and down. "It's much bigger than the Zoo or Prime City."

"Yes, it is," Jessica said. "So you'd better stick close to me once we're on shore. Promise? The last thing I need is for either of you to get lost."

"I promise," Ridley said. "I won't leave your side."

"Good. Now, fetch your bags. We'll be there soon," Jessica added.

"Okay," Ridley said, skipping across the deck.

"Oh, one more thing," Jessica said, and Ridley paused. "Congratulations. You successfully completed your training."

Ridley's smile was brilliant. "I did, didn't I?"

"Yes. I'm proud of you, and I'm sure your mom would be too if she were here," Jessica added.

Ridley's smile faltered. "But she's not here, is she? And she wouldn't be proud. She'd tell me to go home and behave."

"Ridley...."

"Just leave it, Jessica," Ridley said, walking away with swift strides.

"Damn it," Jessica swore, angry at herself. "Why do I always put my foot in it?"

"What's wrong, sweetheart?" Bear asked, walking over.

"Nothing. I said the wrong thing, that's all," Jessica said.

"To Ridley?"

"Who else?" Jessica said with an angry huff.

He reached out one hand and squeezed her shoulder. "Don't worry. You'll fix it."

"Will I?" Jessica asked. "What happened to that little girl who used to sit on my lap and steal cookies from my plate?"

"She grew up," Bear said. "We all have to grow up sometime."

"I know that. It's just. She and Rogue used to be close. What went wrong between them?" Jessica said, shaking her head.

"I don't know, sweetheart, but I do know they'll sort it out one day," Bear said.

"How?" Jessica asked, allowing him to pull her into his arms. "How do you know that?"

"Because I have faith in both of them. Like I have faith in you," Bear said, holding her close.

Jessica pressed her face into his shoulder, relishing in the feel of his arms wrapped around her. She breathed in his familiar scent and closed her eyes, allowing his steady presence to calm her fears. He was right. Everything would be alright. She just had to believe.

Chapter 21 - Rogue

Rogue looked through her window, eyeing the weather. It looked to be a fine spring day. The sun was up, the sky was blue, and the trees were in bud with leaves so green, it hurt the eyes to look at them. Smiling, she grabbed her favorite book and headed outside. She walked through the kitchen, trying not to disturb her mother, who was busy making lunch.

No such luck.

"Where are you going?" Olivia asked, immediately on high alert.

"I'm going to sit on the porch, Mom," Rogue said, suppressing the urge to roll her eyes.

"In this weather? You'll catch your death," Olivia exclaimed.

"It's not cold at all. The weather's fine," Rogue protested.

"Not with you being sick and all," Olivia said, pointing at her book. "Why don't you read in your room? I'll bring you something to eat."

"If I eat anymore, I'll burst," Rogue said. "Seriously, Mom. I've picked up at least ten pounds since I moved in."

"Good. You were wasting away," Olivia said. "Now you've got some color in your cheeks."

"Whatever. But I'm going outside. I can't stand being cooped up inside all day. You won't even let me attend council meetings anymore."

"We talked about this. Ric used to be the leader of the council before you, and he can stand in for you while you get better."

"No. We didn't talk about it. You decided it for me," Rogue said, still feeling resentful.

"Well, it's for your own good," Olivia said.

Rogue folded her arms and stared her mother down.

"I just want what's best for you, dear. I love you, and I want you to get better," Olivia said, wringing her hands. "Try to understand."

Rogue sighed. "Well, I'm going outside, and that's the end of that."

"At least wear something warm—a jacket. Something," Olivia said.

"I'm fine, Mom. I'm not cold," Rogue said, storming out.

She chose the seat at the farthest end of the porch, an old rocker that made a pleasant creaking sound that was almost hypnotic. She sat down and began to read, enjoying the warmth of the sun and the fresh air.

But her peace was disturbed when her mom came bustling out with a blanket. She insisted on tucking it around Rogue's legs, despite her protestations. A cup of tea and a plate full of oat cookies followed, along with much fussing and exclaiming.

"Stop it, Mom. I'm not an invalid."

"Yes, you are, and I will take care of you, whether you like it or not," Olivia said.

It didn't long for Rogue to become uncomfortably hot, and she tossed aside the blanket with a muttered curse. The tea and biscuits went down like a treat, though. Though she

CHAPTER 21 - ROGUE

complained to her mom, she enjoyed the tasty food and didn't worry about an extra pound or two.

Returning to her book, she tried to focus on the story, but it was impossible. Her mind kept wandering to Ridley and the fight they'd had. Words had been said, words that hurt, but she didn't care. All she cared about was mending the rift between them, but her daughter was being difficult. Days passed. Weeks. Still, she refused to visit. Instead, she chose to stay in Jessica's home, avoiding her mother at all costs.

Or so everyone told her. Everyone except Jessica. She hadn't put in an appearance either. She'd left for Vancouver in search of a cure for Rogue's illness.

After three weeks of being confined to her mother's home and being fed trite stories about her daughter, Rogue was becoming suspicious. Why couldn't she attend the council meeting? Sitting at a table and talking about stuff wasn't precisely tiring. Why couldn't she take a walk or visit anyone? Why hasn't anyone visited her? Surely people would be concerned. *Unless... they're hiding something from me.*

"Screw that. I'm finding out what's going on right now," Rogue said, jumping up from her chair. She tossed the book aside and stormed off the porch.

"Wait! Where are you going?" Olivia cried, rushing after her.

"I'm going to Jessica's house. I want to talk to Ridley."

"You can't. She doesn't want to talk to you," Olivia said, grabbing her hand.

Rogue whirled around. "If that's true, she can tell me that herself."

"No, please. You're not well. This isn't good for you. Think of the strain on your system," Olivia said.

"Mom, stop. Just stop. I don't need to be pampered. I'm a grown woman, and I can take care of myself."

"I know that, but you're my baby. My child. Surely, you understand?" Olivia said. "You're a mother. You know."

"Yes, you're right. I am a mother, and I'm beginning to see where I went wrong. I should've let Ridley go a long time ago. I should've accepted her the way she was, not the way I wanted her to be," Rogue said, turning away from her mother.

"Please, wait. Rogue!" Olivia ran after her, pleading.

Closing her mind, Rogue ignored everything and everyone until she reached Jessica's house. Hammering on the door, she called out. "Ridley? Are you there? I need to talk to you."

When there was no answer, Rogue went inside. There was hardly any crime in the Zoo, and theft was uncommon. Few people bothered locking their doors.

When she stepped inside, she realized it hadn't been lived in for days. Maybe longer. A thick layer of dust coated the furniture and floorboards, dust motes glittering in a stray ray of light.

Whirling about, Rogue fixed her mother with a glare. "Where is my daughter? Where's Ridley?"

"She… she ran away to Vancouver," Olivia burst out. "She joined the traders' caravan and left with them."

"She ran off with the traders?" Rogue asked, shocked to the core. "That was weeks ago. You've been lying to me all this time?"

"I'm sorry. I thought it was for the best. I didn't want to worry you," Olivia said, wringing her hands.

"So you hid it from me? The fact that my daughter's missing?" Rogue said, desperately clinging to the few shreds of composure she had left. She was afraid of what she would do if she lost control.

"She's not missing. Jessica and Bear went after her. They promised they'd keep her safe," Olivia said.

"How do you know that?"

"She left a message with the guards."

"Another thing you hid from me. Is that all? Or is there anything else I should know," Rogue asked, enraged. "The Council Meetings. Do we have a crisis on our hands? Another drought? Disease? A serial killer?"

"No!" her mother said with a gasp. "Nothing like that. I promise."

Feeling betrayed, Rogue found it hard to reply. "How can I believe anything you say anymore?"

"It's the truth. The community is fine. Everything is fine. I only hid the rest from you because I was worried. When Jessica first brought you to me, you were on death's door. You needed time to rest and heal. Tuberculosis is no joke, and this whole thing with Ridley and Seth has been too much for you to handle."

"Death's door? I wasn't that sick," Rogue protested. "I was doing fine."

"Stop being so stubborn. You looked like a stiff breeze could blow you over. If it weren't for Jessica, you'd be dead now. Dead!" Olivia straightened up, a flash of anger crossing her face. "Fine daughter you are, not telling me about your illness in the first place. I'm not a stranger. I'm your mother."

"I know that, but I don't like being fussed over."

"So you'd let yourself die? Alone in your house with your husband gone, your daughter on the run, and nobody the wiser?" Olivia asked. "Don't you realize how stupid that sounds?"

"Are you calling me stupid?" Rogue asked, staring at her mom in shock.

Olivia's mouth worked, and it looked like she might apologize. Then her chin lifted, and the old Olivia, who survived the Shift, helped found a community and started a new life in a world vastly different from her own, emerged. "Yes, you're being stupid, reckless, and selfish, and I will not have it anymore."

Rogue blinked several times, searching for a suitable answer but found none. Instead, laughter bubbled up her throat—irrepressible, unstoppable laughter.

Olivia stared at her, perplexed. "You think this is funny?"

"I do, kinda," Rogue choked out between helpless giggles. "It's been a long time since anyone called me stupid, and I guess I am!"

Olivia's mouth twitched, Rogue's humor infectious. Then she burst out into laughter as well. They continued laughing all the way home, talking about their various foibles now that they were grown.

"Here I was, resenting you for smothering me when I've been wrapping Ridley in cotton wool," Rogue explained.

"I'm sorry," Olivia said. "It was just such a shock when I found out how ill you were. I was afraid of losing you."

"I understand. I've been scared too. I just didn't want to admit it," Rogue said.

"So, you're not mad at me anymore?" Olivia asked as they reached her home.

"No, but I'm going after Ridley. I need to tell her how sorry I am," Rogue said.

"What? You can't. It's too dangerous," Olivia said. "Besides, you're not strong enough. The trip will kill you."

CHAPTER 21 - ROGUE

"Not if I fly," Rogue said.

"Fly? How?"

"Prime City has an airplane. A Cessna. It belongs to Lee Alexander, and he'll be willing to fly me. I know it."

"What about fuel?"

"I can pay, and he can refuel in Vancouver. I've got enough credits saved for that," Rogue explained. In truth, she wasn't at all sure she had enough. The little she had stashed away, she'd saved for Ridley. She wanted to leave her daughter something after her death. Something she could use to explore that great city and live a little. Now she didn't have a choice but to use it.

"But...."

"No buts. I'm going to see my daughter, and no one can stop me," Rogue said, her mind made up. "You can help me or get out of my way."

Olivia hovered around her while she grabbed a backpack and started packing her things. Finally, her mother caved in. "Fine, I'm coming with you. So is Ric."

"You're needed here. Ric, too," Rogue said.

"The community can look after itself for a while. Aret is more than capable, you know that," Olivia said. "That woman is a machine."

"Yeah, she hasn't changed much over the years. She's always been very intense," Rogue agreed.

"So, you'll let us go with you?" Olivia asked.

Rogue sighed, folding a jacket. "Okay, fine. You can accompany me to Prime, and if there's space on the plane, you can come to Vancouver. As long as we leave today."

"Today? Oh, dear. That doesn't give me much time to pack," Olivia cried.

"Pack light. You don't need to take the whole house, Mom. Plus, you need to tell Ric we're leaving."

"I'd better find him right away," Olivia said. "He'll need to organize an escort, talk to the guards, arrange with Aret...."

"The sooner, the better," Rogue said, packing enough clothes and toiletries to last a week. She followed it up with a few necessities for the trail, her medicine, a first-aid kit, and spare ammunition for her gun. Unlike Ridley, she had no objections to carrying one, and she was an excellent shot after all these years. Seth made sure of that.

Stripping off her casual clothes, she dressed in warm, practical clothes and boots. A belt around her waist carried her gun, a knife, and a hatchet. Her rifle went onto her back. Within minutes, the trappings of her life as the community leader fell away, replaced with the guise of a traveler.

An old but familiar sensation took hold of her. The sense of excitement that came before an adventure. It fizzed through her veins and lightened her step. Years of responsibility and duty fell off her shoulders, and she felt young again. Young and free. *No wonder Ridley craved her freedom so much. I've forgotten what it feels like.*

At that moment, Rogue realized she'd fallen into a trap of her own making. When she found out she was pregnant, she thought she had to change. She felt she needed to become the perfect example of motherhood—the kind who did everything right.

When the drought hit, decimating their crops, she stepped up, taking Ric's place as leader. She worked out a rationing system, bartered for food with other communities, planted emergency crops, and sent parties out to forage in the wild.

She did it to save her family. Her community. She wasn't

CHAPTER 21 - ROGUE

sorry she'd done it either, but the role changed her, and she lost herself along the way. No more. She was done pretending to be something she was not. It was time to get back to the real her—the real Rogue. *Vancouver, here I come.*

Chapter 22 - Ridley

Ridley soon forgot about her fight with Jessica when they reached the docks. The Captain navigated the boat until it almost touched the nearest open jetty and shut down the engine. The crew tied down the boat, and everyone lined up to disembark.

She jumped off the boat with a light step, followed by Loki, and looked around. Guards approached, armed with guns. Each wore a black jacket with a golden V embroidered on the chest, and she marveled at their efficiency. They quickly checked everyone's credentials, asked a few pointed questions, and searched the boat. Afterward, they issued visitor passes to everyone, including Ridley.

The only problem was Loki. He was not allowed to roam about the city freely and had to be on a leash. This caused Ridley some consternation, and she had to fashion a rough leash from the rope in her bag. Loki didn't like the contraption and balked at first. After much pleading, he went along with it but made his displeasure known with his stiff posture.

"I'm sorry, boy. It's only for a little while; I promise," Ridley said. Holding the leash tightly, she followed Rupert, Jessica, and Bear.

Together, they walked the short distance toward the en-

CHAPTER 22 - RIDLEY

trance of Vancouver, escorted by a couple of guards. Once inside, Jessica turned to one of the guards and asked, "Do you know when the race starts?"

"The Chilliwack race?" the guard asked.

"That's the one," she said.

"You're in luck. The race starts tomorrow. One more day, and you'd have been too late."

"Tomorrow?" Ridley cried, stunned. "Can people still enter?"

"That I don't know," the guard said. "You'll have to find out at city hall. I do know the official welcoming ceremony is tonight. That's when all of the contestants will be introduced. The tickets cost an arm and a leg, though, so the likes of me won't be there."

Ridley looked at Jessica, silently panicking. "What now?"

"Now we go to city hall," Jessica replied, handing the guards a few credits each. "Thanks for the escort."

"No problem. Do you know where to find the city hall?" the guard asked.

"I do, thanks," Jessica replied. "I used to live here."

"You did? That's great. You'll know your way around then," the guard said. "Good luck!"

He left them to their own devices, and Jessica turned to face the group. "We'd better hurry and get to the city hall before it's too late."

"This is where we part ways," Rupert said. "I have to find my people."

"Of course. We understand," Jessica said. "We'll meet again, I'm sure."

"I look forward to it, and good luck, young Ridley. I wish you and Loki success in the race," Rupert added.

With those parting words, he set off in search of his caravan, and Jessica led the rest of the group hurried toward the city center. According to her, the city hall formed its heart, and they had several miles to cover on foot.

For Ridley, the run was nothing. Her body moved on autopilot while her brain marveled at the sights. She'd hoped they'd have time for a tour, but that ship had sailed.

Besides, she'd have all the time in the world once the race was finished. Time to see it all. From the mountains with their caps of frosted snow to the harbor with its ships, the waves of the ocean, the Strait of Georgia, and the field of wind turbines that powered the city. She'd heard about it all from Jessica and longed to explore the streets—just her and Loki.

In the meantime, she got to enjoy the city's sights. A high wall surrounded the metropolis, manned by guard towers around the clock. Each building boasted an array of defenses. From flares and flashes designed to frighten away curious wildlife to machine-gun turrets.

Lush, green parks dotted the suburbs, filled with people on leisurely strolls. She couldn't believe people had the time to take walks, and she even spotted one man with a dog on a leash. "Pets? People have pets here?

"Not many. Pets are expensive," Jessica said.

Ridley nodded, but she still thought it was wonderful. Nobody she knew at the Zoo or Prime City had an animal companion. It was just her and Loki. and Eleanor with her cats. The other animals at the zoo served a purpose. Even the horses had a job to do.

They passed blocks of apartments with balconies filled with bright flowers, and the windows were covered in lace curtains. The streets were swept, and dumpsters stood on

CHAPTER 22 - RIDLEY

every corner. Passerbys smiled at them, and shops abounded, selling everything under the sun while food stalls sizzled on the sidewalks. It was a place of wonder, and Ridley longed to see more.

She did not have a chance, however. They reached the city hall not long after that and hurried inside. A harassed-looking clerk behind a tiny glass window greeted them with a frown. "Can I help you?"

"Yes, please. I want to enter the Chilliwack race," Ridley said, stepping forward.

"Left it until the last minute, did you?" the woman said, her voice sharp.

"I'm sorry," Ridley said, trying to look contrite. "We just got here by boat."

"Hmph," the woman said, handing her a form. "Please fill in your details, and sign the disclaimer at the bottom."

"What disclaimer?" Ridley asked.

"It's a signed statement freeing the city and its council from any responsibility should you be injured or killed in the race," the woman said, looking bored. "You also confirm that you are of age. You are eighteen, right?"

"Yes, ma'am. I turned eighteen four months ago," Ridley said.

"Good for you. Now, fill in the form."

Ridley obeyed, her hand shaking a little. The whole ordeal was proving to be more stressful than she'd expected. Once she was finished, she handed the form over. "There you go."

"That will be ten credits plus another ten for the late entry. The welcoming ceremony is tonight at six in the city hall. Please be on time, dress smartly, and show the door attendants your entry," the woman said, handing her a folded ticket.

"Thanks," Ridley muttered, handing over the twenty credits.

"What about us?" Jessica asked. "We'd like to attend."

"Twenty credits each. That includes your refreshments," the woman said, not batting an eyelid.

Jessica paid, tucked the tickets into her pocket, and led them back outside. They paused on the sidewalk, and Ridley looked around uncertainly. "Now what?"

"Now, we eat," Jessica said, pointing to a nearby corner cafe.

"But we ate on the boat," Ridley said, still full after the gigantic breakfast of oats and biscuits she'd consumed.

"I know, but you're going to eat again," Jessica said. "As much as you can manage."

"Really?"

"Trust me. Your muscles need to load up on fuel. You'll need it in the days to come. Think of it as saving energy for the race," Jessica said.

Ridley sighed. "I'll try."

"I could eat," Bear said.

"You're always hungry," Jessica said, grinning.

They walked to the cafe, picked a table outside, and sat down. Ridley fingered the blue checkered cloth on the table and admired the watercolors on the white-washed walls. They depicted scenes of the ocean, and her mood grew wistful. "I'd love to see the ocean while we're here."

"There won't be time today, but after the race, I'll take you anywhere you want to go," Jessica said.

"Okay," Ridley said with a bright smile.

Before she could ask what was next, a girl approached and placed three sheets of paper on the table. "How can I help you folks today?"

Jessica picked up one of the sheets and glanced at the

CHAPTER 22 - RIDLEY

selection. "I'd like a coffee with extra cream and a slice of chocolate cake."

"Sure thing," the girl said, making a note on her pad.

"Bear?" Jessica asked.

"A cheeseburger with extra cheese and pickles and a chocolate shake," Bear ordered.

"Ridley?"

"Uh, I don't know," Ridley said, panicking as she stared at the menu. Everything seemed to jump out at her, a jumble of food that sounded equally delicious. She had no idea what to choose, aware of the girl's quizzical gaze.

"It's okay. Can I pick something for you?" Jessica asked.

"Er, sure," Ridley said

"She'll have the same as him, with extra fries," Jessica said. "Throw in a slice of chocolate cake too."

"Coming right up," the girl said, though her eyes widened at the large order.

"What about Loki?" Ridley asked.

"Oh, right," Jessica said. "Can we also have a bowl of water and a couple of burger patties for the wolf? About a pound's worth."

"Raw or cooked," the girl said, her voice faltering.

"He prefers raw," Ridley said with a shrug.

"Okay then. I'll be right back," the girl said, rushing off.

She returned a few minutes later with their drinks and Loki's meal. Ridley handed him the plate, watching with a smile as he devoured the ground beef before lapping up the water. Afterward, he lay his head on his paws and promptly dozed off.

"Now, that's how you do it," Jessica said, stirring sugar and cream into her coffee. "How's the shake?"

Ridley eyed the glass with suspicion. She'd had hot chocolate before but never a milkshake. Her hometown didn't produce ice cream, so she took a tentative sip. As the ice-cold liquid flooded her mouth, her eyes widened. "Oh, my... Loki, you have to try this."

"No!" Jessica cried. "Please, not here. People won't understand."

"Um, okay," Ridley said, taking another sip. She sucked on the straw until her cheeks went hollow, and her eyes closed with delight.

"Good, huh?" Jessica asked with a smirk.

"The best," Ridley agreed.

"Now try your burger," Jessica said as the food arrived.

Ridley took a bite of her burger, and the juicy meat combined with the melted cheese and pickles exploded in her mouth. For a moment, she forgot about the race and everything it entailed.

"This is amazing," she said, taking another bite.

"I told you," Jessica said, grinning.

They ate in comfortable silence, focusing on their food. Ridley savored every bite, taking her time. She wasn't sure how much food she could manage, but Jessica was right. She needed the energy for the race.

The fries were just as good as the burger, though she shared half with Loki before tackling the cake. The rich chocolate was almost too much, but she managed to finish the entire slice.

Afterward, Ridley leaned back in her chair, feeling like she would burst. "That was incredible. I've never eaten so much in my life."

"I'm glad you enjoyed it," Jessica said, picking up the bill.

CHAPTER 22 - RIDLEY

"Ready to go?"

"Sure," Ridley said, standing up. "What's next?"

"Next, we get what you need for the race, and then we're shopping for tonight's ceremony."

"Why?" Ridley asked. "Can't we wear our normal clothes?"

"No, we can't. You heard the woman. Smart attire only," Jessica said.

"Oh," Ridley said, wondering what precisely smart attire was supposed to be.

She soon found out when Jessica picked a shop filled with clothes of the kind Ridley had only seen in ancient magazines. Suits, dresses, coats, and tailored pants filled the racks along with rows of gleaming shoes, handbags, purses, and hats.

"Look for something you like," Jessica said. "I'm going to help Bear pick a suit."

"That's okay," Bear said. "I can take care of myself. There's a tailor further down the road that specializes in my size. I asked around earlier."

"Oh, okay," Jessica said, clearly taken aback.

"You girls carry on and finish your shopping. When you're done, find us a place to sleep," Bear said.

"What about you?" Jessica asked.

"I'll meet you at the ceremony. I'll be waiting at the door," Bear said.

"Why? Where are you going?"

"I want to say hello to some old friends, and we don't have much time to waste," Bear explained.

"Well...."

"Please, sweetheart. I just have a few things to take care of. I'll see you tonight. Promise."

"Alright, see you tonight," Jessica said. "Don't be late."

"I won't," Bear promised, waving over his shoulder.

"That was weird," Ridley said.

"Very. He's up to something. I know it," Jessica said. Shaking her head, she turned to Ridley. "He's right about one thing, though. We don't have time to waste. Let's find you a dress."

Chapter 23 - Ridley

Ridley spent the subsequent half-hour browsing through the racks, trying to find something she liked. It wasn't an easy task. Everything was either too flashy or too revealing. Finally, she picked up a black dress that caught her eye and held it against her body.

"That's a bit too formal," Jessica said. "We don't want to look like we're attending a funeral. How about this one?" She held up a dress in dark blue. It had a fitted silhouette with a high neckline and long sleeves.

"It's beautiful," Ridley said, admiring the intricate lace detail.

"Good, because you're trying it on," Jessica said, leading her to a dressing room.

Ridley tried on the dress, and it fit her like a glove. The material was soft and smooth to the touch. She almost didn't recognize herself in the mirror, feeling like a different person. *Maybe too different. It's not me.*

"You look amazing," Jessica said, grinning.

"Thanks," Ridley said, turning this way and that.

"You don't like it?"

"I like the color, but I don't want to wear a dress," Ridley admitted.

"Okay. Not a problem. Wait right here," Jessica said,

disappearing. She returned with a new outfit minutes later, and Ridley's eyes widened. "It's perfect."

"Try it on," Jessica prompted.

Ridley put on the clothes, fitted black pants and a dark blue silk top with a button-up collar and long sleeves. "I love it."

"You look stunning," Jessica said, pressing one hand to her chest. "All grown up."

"What about you?" Ridley asked.

"Oh, I already found my dress. I also picked out a few more things for us, just in case."

"So, we're done?" Ridley asked, eager to leave the stuffy shop.

"We're done," Jessica said, walking to the till. Minutes later, they stood on the sidewalk with their arms full of parcels wrapped in cloth.

"What now?" Ridley asked, stifling a yawn.

The food she'd eaten lay heavy in her stomach, and she was tired of shopping. The idea of wandering through more rows of pointless, shiny things had her groaning with silent frustration.

Jessica wasn't stupid, however. She quickly picked up on Ridley's mood. "Let's find a boarding house."

"A what?"

"A place to stay for the night. We can store our stuff, and you can take a well-deserved nap while I pick up the last things you'll need for the race."

"Really? I don't have to go with you?" Ridley asked, relieved.

"Nope, we just need to find a decent place to stay."

"What about that one?" Ridley said, pointing to a double-story building on the corner. It was plain, painted deep brown with white windowsills, and a sign above the door

CHAPTER 23 - RIDLEY

read, "Harmony Boarding House."

Jessica studied it. "It looks okay. It's close to the city hall, and this is a good area. Let's give it a shot."

They crossed the street and entered the foyer, glad to find the inside as neat as the outside. A middle-aged woman greeted them with a smile, her appearance identical to the interior of her business. "Good morning, ladies. How can I help you?"

"I'd like to reserve two rooms, please," Jessica said. "One single for my niece and a double for my husband and I."

"Just bed, or would you like dinner and breakfast included?" the woman asked.

"Bed, dinner, and breakfast," Jessica said.

"What about the dog?" the woman asked.

"He's a wo...."

"He stays with her, and I'm willing to pay extra," Jessica interrupted hastily, shooting Ridley a curt look.

"He can sleep on the floor, and he won't be any trouble. I promise," Ridley added, catching the hint. "I'll even take him to the park to do his business."

"Well... alright. I'll make an exception this time," the woman said, handing them a pair of keys. "First floor, first two rooms on the right. Dinner is at eight."

"Understood," Jessica said, turning to Ridley. "Why don't you take our things to our rooms and settle in? I'll fill in the forms and settle up."

"No problem," Ridley said.

She trudged up the stairs, laden with gear and shopping bags. The first room was the double, and she unloaded Jessica and Bear's gear.

The next room was hers. It was small and tasteful, the

furniture plain but of good quality. She immediately liked it. "What do you think, Loki?"

Loki sniffed around, found a comfortable spot on the carpet, and lay down with a deep sigh.

"I feel the same," Ridley said. "A nap would be really nice about now."

Testing out the bed, she found it soft and comfortable. Turning on her side, she dozed off, only to awaken when Jessica knocked.

"What's wrong?" Ridley asked, lifting her head.

"Nothing. I'll be back in time for the ceremony. Make sure you are up and dressed. Until then, enjoy your nap."

"Thanks," Ridley said, yawning.

The door closed with a soft click, and she laid her head back down on the pillow. Thoughts of the ceremony and coming race churned through her mind, but even that wasn't enough to keep sleep at bay. Within minutes, she was fast asleep.

The hours passed slowly while she slept undisturbed. She might even have overslept if it wasn't for Loki. He woke her up around four in the afternoon, whining to get out. Wiping the gunk from her eyes, she sat up. "Do you need to go, boy?"

He yipped, and she took it as a yes.

"Alright, then. Let's take a walk," she said, reaching for his rope harness.

He balked at the sight but submitted when she asked nicely. "Please, boy. Just for a little while."

Ridley left the boarding house and went to a nearby park where Loki did his business in a clump of bushes. When he was done, she headed back but stopped at a roadside food stall. Scratching a few credits from her pocket, she bought a meat pie and a bottle of water. She finished both by the time

CHAPTER 23 - RIDLEY

she reached the boarding house and jogged upstairs to her room.

"There you are," Jessica cried, emerging from her room. "I was beginning to worry."

"I went for a walk," Ridley explained.

"That's okay. Look what I got," Jessica said, waving her inside.

A heap of stuff lay on the floor, a jumble of items that boggled the mind. Ridley stared at it, shocked. "What's all this?"

"This is your gear for the race," Jessica said.

"All of it?"

"The best of it. Take your pick."

"Do we even have time for this?" Ridley asked. "What about the ceremony?"

"Oh, crap! I forgot," Jessica cried. "We can go through this stuff later tonight after dinner. Deal?"

"Deal," Ridley said. "I'll get dressed and meet you downstairs."

"Perfect. Give me ten minutes," Jessica said.

Ridley ran to her room, nervous for an entirely different reason. One that had nothing to do with the race and everything to do with the impression she made at the ceremony. Holding the blue shirt up to her face, she gazed at her reflection in the mirror. *This is it, Mom. This is what you trained me for—looking like I've got it all together. Like I belong at the head of a council table or a fancy do. The question is, do I?*

Chapter 24 - Jessica

Jessica ran up the steps toward the entrance of the city hall, eager to get inside and out of the rain. Even though it was just a fine drizzle, it was accompanied by a chill breeze. The kind that cut to the bone. While it was late spring, they were farther north, and it was colder in this part of the country. She shivered underneath her coat, grateful for its warmth over her flimsy dress.

Ridley was right behind her, dressed in the fitted pants and dark blue shirt they got earlier. A long black coat and boots finished off the look, and she looked lovely in the sophisticated outfit. Lovely, but also achingly young.

Despite Jessica's protestations, she'd insisted on bringing Loki along. The wolf wore the new harness she'd bought for him, and his yellow eyes gazed around with wary caution.

Jessica heaved an inward sigh. Now that the time had come, she wasn't sure she was doing the right thing. Aiding Ridley in her foolhardy venture was rash, but there was nothing she could do to stop it from happening. All that was left to do now was to pray she made it through alive.

At the entrance, she spotted Bear and hurried toward him. As she got closer, she stumbled to a halt. "Oh, my God! Bear? Is that you?"

CHAPTER 24 - JESSICA

He turned toward her with a smooth smile. "In the flesh."

Jessica stared at him, taking it all in. The slicked-back hair, smooth jaws, and fitted suit. It looked like him, but a different him.

"Do you like it?" Bear asked, touching his crisp white collar.

Recovering from her shock, Jessica gripped his hands and leaned in to kiss him. "I love it. You're the most handsome man in the whole of Vancouver."

Smiling, Bear returned her kiss. "You don't look so bad yourself."

"Why thank you," Jessica said, preening a little in her long red dress and knee-high boots.

"You look lovely too, Ridley," Bear added. "Very smart."

"Thanks, Bear, and you look awesome!" Ridley exclaimed, immediately ruining the effect of her outfit.

Jessica shook her head, laughing. "Come on, you two. We'd better not be late."

They trooped inside, pausing to flash their tickets at the door attendant. He pointed them to their seats, and they filed inside, except for Ridley. As a racer, she was expected on stage, and another attendant led her away.

Jessica took her seat next to Bear and waited expectantly. More than anything, she wanted to see who the other contestants were. She was expecting the cream of the crop—the best of the best.

A gigantic banner on the wall next to the stage announced the race, each letter painted in garishly bright colors:

The 10th Annual Vancouver to Chilliwack Lake Endurance Race. A test of bravery, fortitude, and courage.

Standing underneath the banner was a familiar figure, the Mayor of Vancouver, Imogen Finley.

Jessica waved at Imogen, hoping to catch her eye, but failed. Imogen was surrounded by people, talking, laughing, and gesturing. Disappointed, Jessica vowed to look for her after the ceremony.

Not long after that, music announced the start of the proceedings, and a man in a suit took the podium. He droned on for several minutes, thanking everything and everyone who'd made the race possible.

Jessica soon tuned him out. Nothing he said meant anything to her. She perked up when he announced the Mayor and sat upright to see better. In answer to his summons, Imogen ascended the steps of the stage with an elegant gait, her hips swaying beneath her emerald green pantsuit.

The outfit was business-like and sophisticated, complimented by a crisp white shirt and brown leather boots. It wasn't the kind of clothing Jessica would've imagined on the free-spirited Imogen, but much had changed over the years, and the Mayor of Vancouver was both polished and accomplished in her role.

Jessica smothered a smile, however, when she spotted the earrings that decorated Imogen's delicate earlobes. Clunky, oversize, and bright orange, they made a statement. They showed that not everything had changed and that her younger friend's free spirit was still intact. Just hidden below a veneer of professionalism.

Clearing her throat, Imogen spoke into the microphone, her voice smooth and modulated. "Good evening, ladies and gentlemen. Welcome to the 10th annual Vancouver Chilliwack Endurance race!"

Loud applause followed her words, and she waited for it to die down before continuing. "As you all know, this race

CHAPTER 24 - JESSICA

has become a tradition in Vancouver. A race that tests the mettle of even the bravest of athletes. Every year we watch in awe as the contestants vie for victory, and this year promises to be the biggest and most exciting yet. In honor of ten years of excellence, the City of Vancouver has doubled the prize money, and racers have come from far and wide to pit themselves against the dangers of the primordial wilderness."

Wild applause followed her words.

"I want to thank everyone who made this year's event possible, including all of you who are here in support tonight. Now, I'm sure you're all dying to meet the contenders, so without further ado, I present to you," Imogen continued, pausing for dramatic effect, "this year's competitors!"

Imogen stepped aside with a flourish, and the curtain lifted. Twelve athletes stood on the stage, a selection of the world's best. As befitted their reputations, they looked tough, fit, and confident. Ridley stood at the far end, nearly hidden in the shadows, with Loki pressed to her leg.

Running down the list of entries, Imogen introduced each racer by calling out their names and city of origin. Most were from Vancouver, though a few came from other towns Jessica had never even heard of. None were from Prime City or the Zoo, except Ridley.

As Imogen ran down the list, Jessica felt her heart sink. These were not just any competitors. They were hardened athletes with determined expressions on their faces. One man had a shaved head and a neck tattoo, while another with a barrel chest flexed his biceps, earning cheers from the crowd. A dark-eyed woman of exotic origins bowed, revealing a jagged scar on her chest.

Jessica couldn't help but wonder what Ridley had gotten herself into. She turned to Bear, who was watching the racers critically.

"What do you think of them?" she whispered.

Bear shook his head. "They look like they could run circles around us. But don't worry. Ridley can hold her own. She's a survivor."

Jessica nodded, trying to convince herself everything would be okay. Once the cheers died down and everyone had an eyeful of the racers, Imogen stepped forward again. "As you can see, this year's contestants are the cream of the crop, and we can all be assured of a spectacular race."

The room exploded in cheers and wild applause, though Jessica spotted more than a few of the audience pointing at Ridley and whispering with frowns on their faces. She stood out among the rest with her fresh innocent looks and the wolf by her side.

Unperturbed by the noise, Imogen continued. "The race will begin tomorrow morning outside the Northern Gate. Seats and refreshments will be available, and I hope you will all be there to cheer our contestants on as they embark on the first leg of this grueling competition."

She talked more, mentioning minor details, but the ceremony was essentially over. A band in the corner struck up a tune, filling the air with music. People in uniform rushed about, removing chairs and setting out platters of snacks, extra candles, and flutes of champagne.

As the racers filed off stage, Jessica waved at Ridley. "Over here!" Ridley hurried over, looking pale and nervous. "Are you okay?"

"I'm fine," Ridley replied, but Jessica could see her hands

CHAPTER 24 - JESSICA

were shaking as she fiddled with Loki's harness.

"How are you holding up?"

Ridley looked up at her, her eyes bright with fear. "I'm scared."

Jessica put her arm around Ridley's shoulder, squeezing gently. "You can do this, and we're here for you. No matter what."

Ridley leaned into her. "Thanks, Jessica. I appreciate it."

Bear nodded in agreement. "Stay focused, and don't let anyone get in your way."

As the three of them chatted, a figure approached them from the side. It was the woman with the jagged scar on her chest, her expression fierce.

"Hey," she said, her voice low. "I couldn't help but overhear. You're Ridley, right?"

Ridley nodded, looking apprehensive. "Yes, that's me."

The woman raised an eyebrow, scrutinizing Ridley. "You don't look like you belong here. You're too young. You know this isn't just a fun run."

Ridley straightened her back, looking the woman in the eyes. "I know what I signed up for."

"We'll see about that," the woman said, walking away.

"That was Jara," Ridley said in a low tone. "I overheard some of the others talking about her."

"Bad news?" Jessica asked.

"The worst."

"Just give her a wide berth," Jessica said. "Remember what I taught you, and you'll be fine."

"Jessica? As I live and breathe, is that you?" a voice cried.

Jessica turned to greet the newcomer, happy to see it was Imogen. "Yes, it's me!"

Imogen reached out with both arms and pulled Jessica into a warm hug. "It's been years."

"It's been a while," Jessica admitted.

"Why don't you visit more often?" Imogen asked. "Are you too good for us now? Or is it this handsome man who's keeping you busy?"

Jessica flashed a smile at Bear, reaching out to take his hand. "It's his fault. He's got me wrapped around his little finger."

Bear blushed at her words. "It's good to see you too, Imogen."

"And who's this young beauty?" Imogen asked, reaching out to shake Ridley's hand.

"This is Ridley. Seth and Rogue's daughter," Jessica explained.

"Oh, my goodness. I can't believe it!" Imogen cried. "I haven't seen your parents in years, but I'll never forget them. A real firecracker, your mom."

"That she is," Ridley said, her voice dry.

"Ridley entered the race. She's a contestant," Jessica added, not surprised to see a look of astonishment on Imogen's face.

"Are you sure you're ready for this?" Imogen asked, looking at Ridley. "It's a very tough race. We've lost people from time to time."

"I'm ready," Ridley said, raising her chin.

"Well, I wish you the best of luck," Imogen said, smiling. Next, she turned to Jessica, flashing her a look. "I have to go now. Other appointments. But we must talk again soon."

"I look forward to it," Jessica replied.

They hugged again, and Imogen disappeared as quickly as she came. Jessica stared after her, saddened at the brief conversation. She missed her old friend but supposed Imogen

CHAPTER 24 - JESSICA

had other commitments.

"Jessica?" Ridley said, breaking into her thoughts.

"Yes," Jessica said, pushing her disappointment aside.

"Can we go, please? I don't want to be here anymore. Neither does Loki."

"Of course. What was I thinking? This is not the time to party. You need to rest," Jessica said. She offered her arm to Bear. "Sweetheart? Escort us home, please."

"It would be my pleasure," he said with a broad smile.

Bear led them through the crowd and into the night. It had stopped raining, but it was still cold. Luckily, the boarding house was right around the corner. Even better, they were still in time for dinner.

Not everything was working out so well, however. As they walked down the steps of the city hall, Jessica glanced over her shoulder. The woman with the scar on her chest leaned against the side of the door, watching them with narrowed eyes, a smirk on her lips. A shiver ran down Jessica's spine. *That woman is trouble. Real trouble.*

Chapter 25 - Ridley

Ridley was only too happy to leave the ceremony, braving the chilly night air with Loki, Jessica, and Bear. They reached the boarding house in time for dinner, a lucky coincidence. Martha, the owner, ushered them out of the wet and into the warmth of her home.

"Come in! Come in. It's almost time for dinner. It will be served in that room over there, but feel free to change and wash up first," Martha said, wiping her hands on her apron. "I'll get everything ready in the meantime."

"Thank you," Jessica said. "We'll be down shortly."

Ridley ran to her room, followed by Loki. She stripped off her damp clothes and hung them up. Dressed in the blue shirt, pants, and boots, she went back downstairs.

Martha turned to her and said, "I wasn't sure about your dog, but I set out bowls of water and food for him. I hope it will suffice."

Ridley eyed the bowl of rice mixed with scraps of meat and gravy. It was a big portion—more than enough for the hungry wolf.

"Thank you so much," she said, truly touched. She even refrained from correcting Martha and telling her Loki was a wolf. Not dog.

CHAPTER 25 - RIDLEY

"You can sit anywhere you like. I'll be right back," Martha said, rushing off.

Ridley picked a table and chair, sitting down while Loki enjoyed his meal. It wasn't long before Jessica and Bear joined her, looking casual and relaxed in their everyday clothing. They sat down, and the conversation turned to the race and the other contestants.

"So, when you went backstage, what were the other racers like?" Jessica asked. "Besides that Jara woman."

"It's hard to say," Ridley said. "Most of them ignored me, actually, and I didn't try to talk to them."

"Mm, it might be better to avoid them. You don't want them to think of you as a threat," Jessica said.

"Jara sure doesn't," Ridley muttered.

"Stay away from her. She's bad news," Jessica said, remembering how the woman had watched Ridley leave.

"I will," Ridley said.

At that moment, Martha entered the dining room with a trolley loaded with plates. Ridley's mouth watered when she caught a whiff of the delicious smells wafting across the room and her stomach cramped with ferocious hunger.

Martha stopped the trolley next to the table. "I hope you folks are hungry. I made plenty."

"That looks wonderful," Jessica said, smiling. "And I'm sure it tastes just as good."

"Why thank you," Martha said, beaming. "I'll leave you to it. Enjoy."

She left the room, and Ridley reached for a plate. The meal looked fantastic, and she wasted no time digging into the basket filled with soft bread rolls and butter. She scooped up a bowl of salad next, crunching on the crisp lettuce, tomato, and cucumber doused in tangy lemon juice.

Next, she dished up a huge helping of roasted potatoes, grilled chicken, mashed pumpkin, and creamed spinach, shoveling the food into her mouth until the fork scraped against the bottom.

"Room for more?" Jessica asked, fastidiously picking at her salad.

"Oh, yes," Ridley said, going back for seconds. Finally, she could have no more and leaned back in her chair with a groan. "That was amazing, but I think I ate too much."

Bear grunted, busy with his third helping. "Speak for yourself."

"Remember what I said about fueling your body for the race," Jessica added.

"I know, but one more bite, and I'll puke," Ridley said, swallowing a burp.

"It'll pass soon enough," Jessica said.

Martha returned soon after that, pleased that the meal had gone well. She put a tray with biscuits, assorted cheeses, and fruit on the table. "Coffee or tea, anyone?"

"Coffee, thanks," Jessica said, reaching out to nibble on a grape.

"Me too," Bear said, wiping his mouth.

"Tea, thank you," Ridley said.

"Coming right up," Martha said.

"Have some cheese," Jessica prompted once they were alone.

"No thanks. I'm too full," Ridley said, shaking her head.

"Oh, come on. Just one bite," Jessica said.

Ridley sighed and reached for some biscuits, mashing a piece of cheese in the middle. She chewed on the tasty bit, but her heart wasn't in it. Despite Jessica's assertions that she needed to eat as much as possible, she didn't think she'd be able to eat one more mouthful. Swallowing hard, she grimaced. "That's me. I'm done."

"Do you want to go to the room and sort through the stuff I got for the race?" Jessica asked.

"That would be nice," Ridley said, stifling a yawn while thinking Jessica's room was one step closer to her bed.

"Go along," Jessica said. "I'll bring up your tea."

Not waiting to be told twice, Ridley jumped up from her chair and ran upstairs. She entered Jessica's room and eyed the pile of stuff on the floor with trepidation.

Plopping down on the floor, she inspected the new backpack Jessica got her. The pack was light but sturdy, the straps thick and padded. The stitching was dense, and the material was waterproof. It also came with a bedroll and extra blanket tied to the bottom and a canteen in a mesh pocket on the side. Satisfied, she moved on to her next priority: Weaponry.

Not much had changed there. She planned on sticking to her crossbow, ax, and the knife her father had given her years before. She also kept the extra knife tucked into her boot. The only change she allowed was swapping out her worn belt, sheath, and crossbow straps for new ones. It was much harder picking out the rest of her gear. Jessica had gone to great lengths to find the best of the best.

In the end, Ridley stuck to the basics. Overloading her backpack would be a mistake. The lighter her load, the better. Besides, she didn't even know what half of the stuff was. A lot of it looked downright alien.

Jessica walked in halfway through, sat beside her, and helped her pick through the stuff. Together, they packed a length of cord, a tin filled with bandages soaked in tree resin, a first-aid kid, a fire starter kit, a water bowl for Loki, and a compass.

Her running outfit was made from light, breathable material. It would help regulate her body temperature, had no inner seams that could cause chafing, and sported plenty of pockets. It consisted of a pair of tights, a shirt, a jacket, supportive underwear, and cotton socks.

Ridley tried it on, pronounced it perfect, and set it aside for the next day. An identical set with extra underwear and socks went into her bag, along with light gloves, a scarf, a head bandanna, and a hat.

A small toiletry bag carried only the necessities: A hair comb, a toothbrush, tweezers, and scentless soap. A small tube of petroleum jelly went into one pocket to keep her lips from chapping, along with a packet of salt pills for muscle cramps.

The rest of her pockets were stuffed with packets of food, primarily nuts, dried fruit, a jar of honeycomb squares, and wax-covered cheese rounds. Strips of dried meat, fish, and fat rounded off the selection. What they couldn't fit into her pockets went into her backpack along with a spare canteen. Finally, they sat back and surveyed their handiwork.

"I think that's it," Ridley said.

"Yup, I think so," Jessica nodded. "Except for shoes."

"I have shoes," Ridley said, producing a pair of black leather moccasins that laced halfway up her calf. They were relatively new but already worn-in, the leather soft and pliable, and the soles reinforced and padded. They were perfect for running, and she'd bought them along specially for the race.

"Well, I think we're done here," Jessica said.

"Yes, we are," Ridley agreed.

CHAPTER 25 - RIDLEY

"Time to get some sleep," Jessica added. "You need to be as fresh as a daisy tomorrow."

"Can't argue with that," Ridley said, climbing to her feet. "I just need to take care of Loki first."

She waved to the wolf and took him outside for a final bathroom break. He was polite enough to go in a clump of bushes, and she didn't think anyone would be the wiser. Returning to her room, she left him there while she used the bathroom. While a hot shower sounded inviting, she decided to leave it for the morning.

Back in her room, she crawled into bed and tried to sleep, but rest eluded her, and she thought about the ceremony and the other contestants. While she hadn't said much to Jessica and Bear, seeing them had been eye-opening. She'd never felt smaller or more insignificant in her life.

The other racers were older, more experienced, and fitter than her. They carried their scars from previous races with fierce pride and looked down on fresh-faced newbies like her with disdain. None, except for Jara, had even spoken to her.

Now doubt lay heavy on her heart, and she wondered if she was up to the task. Did she even stand a chance? Or was she what everyone thought? An overly-confident teenager with her head in her ass?

As if he sensed her mood, Loki got up on the bed and placed his head on her chest, gazing at her with complete trust and adoration. Ridley stared into his golden-brown eyes, and her doubts receded. While she might not be as good as the others, she had something they didn't. She had a reason to win. A reason more important than anything else in the world. Her father.

Shaking off her fears, Ridley turned onto her side and

snuggled close to Loki's side. He always knew exactly what she needed when she needed it. He was her best friend, and together they'd win the race. "Sleep tight, boy. Tomorrow, we'll show the world what we're made of."

Chapter 26 - Ridley

Ridley was up before dawn, unable to sleep any further. Now that the race day had dawned, she wanted to get it over with. No more worrying. No more thinking, planning, or training. Just the race.

She ran across the hall to the bathroom, eager to get started. After using the toilet, she brushed her teeth, jumped into the shower, washed her hair and body with scentless soap, and oiled her skin.

Afterward, she got dressed in the outfit they'd chosen. The clothes differed from her regular leather pants and tunic, but she liked them. The tights were thick, warm, and comfortable. The long-sleeved shirt, too. Even the sports bra was alien, made from some weird stretchy material, but she liked how it smoothed out her curves and granted extra support.

The pure cotton socks went on like a dream, perfectly encapsulated by her moccasins. That was the only part of her outfit she was familiar with, and she was glad for them. This was not the time to try and wear brand-new shoes. It would only lead to blisters.

She smoothed her hair back into a tight knot, put on her cap, and tied the bandanna around her neck. A pair of fingerless gloves provided warmth and protection to her hands without sacrificing performance.

Looping her belt through the pants, she let the knife and ax settle into familiar places on her hips. She slipped on her jacket and filled the pockets with food, her empty stomach cramping in anticipation of a hearty breakfast. They'd asked Martha to serve them early because of the race, and she'd obliged.

Finally, Ridley checked her backpack, ensuring that everything was in order. Loki seemed equally interested in her stuff, shoving his nose inside. He sniffed at the packet of dried meat and licked his chops. She pushed him away with a laugh and closed the pack. "No, Loki. Not now."

Getting to her feet, she gathered up her gear and ran downstairs. It was dark outside, but a lantern glowed in the foyer, and another shone from the dining room. The smell of eggs and bacon filled the air, and her mouth flooded with saliva. "Martha?"

"In here, dear," Martha replied. "I hope you brought your appetite?"

"I sure did," Ridley said, glancing at the stairs. "Jessica? Bear? Are you guys up yet?"

A door opened, and Jessica appeared at the top of the flight. "Yes, yes. We're coming."

Satisfied, Ridley walked into the dining room and looked around. Martha bustled around, putting the finishing touches on the food. When she spotted Ridley, she waved at the spread. "Help yourself to coffee and juice, dear. The food is almost ready."

"Thanks," Ridley said, pouring a glass of orange juice.

She sat down at the nearest table, dumping her gear on the floor. Martha bought Loki a bowl of water and another

CHAPTER 26 - RIDLEY

filled with cooked ground meat and rice. He gulped it down while Ridley watched with bemusement, wondering how he managed to pack it away. "Eat up, boy. Today's a big day for us."

Bear and Jessica joined her soon after that, dressed warmly against the chill. They didn't have any gear since they planned to return to the boarding house after the race began, and Ridley realized she'd never asked what was next for the couple. "What happens after I start the race? Are you guys waiting for me here until I get back?"

Jessica exchanged a smile with Bear. "Not quite. We have a surprise for you."

"What is it?" Ridley asked, jumping around in her seat.

"When you cross that finish line, we'll be there to cheer you on," Jessica said.

"What?" Ridley cried. "How's that possible?"

"I've arranged transport for us to Chilliwack. We leave tomorrow," Bear said. "That's where I disappeared to yesterday."

"That's why you left us at the shop?" Ridley said, surprised and thankful.

"Yup. Now we'll be there at the end, whether you win or not," Jessica said.

Tears pricked Ridley's eyelids, and her voice roughened. "I don't know what to say. You guys are the best."

"Don't say anything. Just make sure you cross that line in one piece. Winner or not. Promise?" Jessica said.

"Promise," Ridley said, thinking she couldn't have asked for better friends. They'd been at her side through thick and thin, and she vowed not to disappoint them.

Just when she thought things couldn't look any better, Martha announced, "The food is ready. Help yourselves."

"Finally," Ridley said, pushing back her chair with a loud scrape. She almost ran to the table and dished a heaping plate of bacon, eggs, sausages, and a few slices of freshly baked bread.

"Are you sure you have enough?" Jessica asked with an amused look.

"Oh, this is just the beginning," Ridley said, smearing a thick layer of butter and fig jam over the bread. She took a big bite, savoring the buttery sweetness on her tongue. A strip of crispy bacon added an edge of salt, and she almost melted into a puddle of goo.

"Well, enjoy it while you can," Jessica said with a shake of the head. "After this meal, you can only eat what you have in your pack."

"Oh, my! Is that really true?" Martha asked, overhearing the conversation.

"I'm afraid so," Jessica replied.

"Can't she forage or hunt along the way?" Martha said.

"It'll slow her down too much," Jessica said.

"What about the relief stations? Don't they help the racers?" Martha said, looking more worried by the second.

"They provide water, shelter for the night, and medical treatment. They also send out search parties for missing runners, but nothing else."

"That's ridiculous," Martha said, rounding on Ridley. "Are you sure you want to do this? It's terribly dangerous. and you're still so young."

"I know, but I trained for this. I have to win," Ridley said, squaring her shoulders.

"But why?"

"I need the prize money to look for my father," Ridley

CHAPTER 26 - RIDLEY

explained.

"Where is he?"

"He went missing a few months ago."

"Months?" Martha said, looking doubtful.

"I know what you're going to say, but he's still alive. I know it," Ridley rushed to say. "I have to find him."

"Oh, I'm so sorry, dear. What an awful thing to go through," Martha exclaimed. "I wish you the best of luck, and I'll pack you some food."

"Um, thanks, but I don't have a lot of space in my pack," Ridley said.

"I'll keep it small and light," Martha promised.

"Thanks," Jessica said, flashing the woman a smile. As Martha walked away, she added, "Remind me to give that woman a huge tip."

"Uh-huh," Ridley said, nodding through a mouthful of eggs and bacon. The bacon was the best. They had pigs at the Zoo. Ancestors of the original warthogs that populated one of the pens. They were wild, though. Their meat was not as fatty or succulent as the domesticated pigs of Vancouver.

After a second big plate of bacon, pancakes, and syrup, Ridley finished off the meal with another glass of juice and a fruit salad. Swallowing a burp, she pushed away her empty plates and bowls. "That's it for me. I can't have another bite."

"You've picked up some weight, at least," Jessica nodded approvingly.

"I have?" Ridley asked. Looking down at her bloated stomach, she grinned. "Guess I have."

"It's not real weight, mostly water, and glucose," Jessica said. "It'll disappear after the first day, but your muscles are fueled, and your reserves are topped up. That's the best we can ask for."

"I suppose," Ridley said, shifting in her chair. Privately, she wondered if she'd even be able to run with such a full stomach. *Oh, well. Guess we'll find out soon enough.*

The thought that the race was around the corner caused her stomach to churn, and she suddenly regretted eating so much for breakfast, even if it was for a good reason. "I don't feel so well."

"Mm, you look a bit pale. Nauseous?" Jessica asked.

"A little," Ridley admitted.

"Nerves, probably. Just close your eyes, breathe through your nose, and try to relax," Jessica said.

"Okay," Ridley said, leaning back in her chair. With her eyes closed, she listened to the low hum of Jessica and Bear's conversation—the clink of cutlery on glass sounded in the background, and her nostrils flared with the aroma of fresh coffee mingled with burnt toast.

It didn't take long for her anxiety to lessen. Her mind drifted away, and her muscles relaxed, melting into the chair. One hand dropped down to rest on Loki's head, and she absently scratched his ears and ruffled his fur. It was a rare moment of peace, and a smile grew on her lips. *This is the life's all about—the little things.*

Finally, Jessica and Bear announced that they finished, and Martha cleared the table. They thanked her for the meal and promised to return in time for dinner.

"We just need to make a few final arrangements before leaving for Chilliwack tomorrow," Jessica explained. "I'd also like to see Imogen again. If she's not too busy."

"I'll be sad to see you go, but you're welcome back anytime. The good ones always are," Martha added with a wink.

CHAPTER 26 - RIDLEY

"You are a rare gem yourself," Jessica replied warmly.

"Why, thank you, dear," Martha said, blushing deep red. She gathered the last few plates and hurried toward the kitchen.

"Ready to go, Ridley?" Jessica asked.

"I guess so," Ridley replied, shaking herself awake. She gathered her gear and glanced through the blinds on the window. The sun was up, streaking the sky with orange, purple, and red. A sense of urgency took hold, and the last bit of sleepy fog fled her brain.

At that moment, Martha came running with a parcel in her hands. "Ridley!"

"Yes?"

"I've got something for you."

"What is it?" Ridley asked, eyeing the foil packet with interest.

"It's a roast beef and cheese sandwich. I'm sure it'll fit in your bag, and you can have it for supper tonight," Martha explained. "It's not that warm yet, so it should last until nightfall without going sour on you."

"Thank you," Ridley said, tucking the parcel into a side pocket.

"And this is a tonic to give you energy. My secret recipe," Martha said, handing over a bottle filled with a thick pinkish liquid. "You just take a sip whenever you need a boost."

Ridley eyed the strange liquid with trepidation but tucked it into her pocket. *Whatever helps me win this race.*

On impulse, she pulled Martha into a hug, gratified to see tears shimmering in the woman's eyes. She'd met so many new people on her trip. Rupert, Martha, Imogen. She'd made enemies, too, thinking back to her encounter with Jara, but she wouldn't let that get her down. *Not now. Not today. Today,*

I'm running my heart out.

Chapter 27 - Ridley

Ridley and Loki burst through the boarding house's door and into the open with eager steps. Loaded and ready for action, they ran down the stairs and into the street, headed for the park. The minute they reached it, Loki disappeared into a clump of bushes to relieve himself while she waited on the curb.

Jessica and Bear followed their headlong rush at a more sedate pace, confident they'd reach their destination on time. She watched them with a mixture of curiosity and impatience, wondering how they could be so calm. Unflappable. That's the word. "Come on, guys. We're going to be late."

"No, we're not. The race starts at nine," Jessica said.

"But I have to be there earlier," Ridley pointed out.

"Earlier. Not at the break of dawn," Jessica said, rolling her eyes.

"Relax, girly," Bear said, his voice gruff with amusement.

"Ugh, whatever," Ridley said, unable to contain her excitement. She ran ahead with Loki, skipping and jumping like a kid. "Race you there!"

"Conserve your energy," Jessica yelled after her.

"I'll try!" Ridley replied but didn't bother.

Luckily, they reached the Northern Gate before she could

break a sweat, her body warmed up and ready to go. Jogging toward the guarded exit, she waited for Bear and Jessica to catch up while eyeing the proceedings beyond.

It looked like a different world. It was as if the gates were a portal to another universe. Inside the city walls, all was calm. People came and went in an orderly fashion, kept in check by the guards and the rules set in place. Inside hundreds of homes, people prepared to go to work, and kids set off for school. Boats left the harbor, farmers tilled their fields, and the turbines pushed electricity into the city's battery banks. All was as it should be.

But outside, it looked like a kid had dropped a giant box of tinsel, glitter, and balloons into an open field, and it exploded into a riot of colors. People waving flags milled about. Their excitement was evident in their shining eyes and heightened voices, the atmosphere abuzz. A mixture of workers, guards, and helpers added to the crush, rushing to get everything set up and ready for the race.

"Oh, wow. I wasn't expecting this," Ridley said, staring at the scene wide-eyed.

"Mm, the race has become even more popular than I thought," Jessica said, looking impressed.

"Hmph," Bear said, his only contribution to the conversation.

"Well, we'd better get in there," Jessica said, moving toward the nearest waiting guard. "We'd like to join the festivities, please."

"Passes," he replied, his face impassive.

Jessica handed over her visitor's pass, followed by Bear and Ridley. The guard scanned the passes before eyeing the trio of visitors with narrow eyes. He honed in on Ridley and shook

CHAPTER 27 - RIDLEY

his head. "No weapons allowed beyond this point."

"I'm a racer," Ridley protested.

The guard snorted. "Yeah, right. You're far too young to be a contestant."

"I am; I swear it," Ridley said. "This is my running gear."

"No weapons beyond this point," the guard repeated, obstinate.

"I can show you her entry," Jessica offered, digging the piece of paper out of her pocket.

The guard stared at the slip with disbelief. "You entered the race? A little girl like you?"

"Yes, I did, and I'm not a little girl. I'm eighteen," Ridley said, lifting her chin.

"You're crazy, you know that?" the guard replied.

"I'm not crazy. I trained for this," Ridley said, refusing to give ground.

"Your parents are crazy, too," he added, looking at Bear and Jessica. "You're actually allowing this? She could die out there!"

"They're n…." Ridley began, but Jessica quickly cut her off.

"I'm sorry, but can we go now? I don't want her to be late. After last night's welcoming ceremony, everyone expects her," Jessica said with smooth confidence. "Especially Imogen Finley."

"Imogen Finley?" the guard repeated.

"The Mayor," Jessica said. "She's a personal friend."

The guard blanched but quickly hid his dismay. Handing back Ridley's race entry, he pointed at a white-topped tent and said, "All contestants are to report at that pavilion over there."

"Thanks," Ridley said, trying not to show the guard how

pissed off she was. Jessica had it right. There was no point picking a fight so close to her goal.

"Spectators can sit on the grandstands or stand on the sidelines of the track. There are food stalls, games, and shops over there. Understand?" the guard continued.

"Understood," Jessica said.

"Do not go beyond the borders of the field. The city of Vancouver will not be held accountable for the safety of anyone who disobeys that rule. Got it?"

"Got it," Jessica said.

"Enjoy your day," the guard said, effectively dismissing them.

"Come on, Ridley," Jessica said. "Let's get you sorted out."

Ridley walked through the gates and into the festive world beyond with a sense of awe. It was so different from anything she'd ever seen. The Zoo and Prime had their own festivities at particular times of the year. Nothing quite like this, however.

The grandstands were festooned with color, a red ribbon marked the start of the race, and a smooth track of packed earth led into the distant forest. A stage with a microphone stood ready to receive the Mayor, and a photographer was busy setting up his gear. A band rigged up their speakers on a separate stand, and a drone whizzed overhead.

"Is that a...." she asked.

"Drone, yes," Jessica said. "I haven't seen one in a while."

"What are they for?"

"Mostly reconnaissance. You send it ahead to map any unfamiliar territory and look for predators." Jessica glanced at her. "I used them to look for prey when I went hunting. This time, they're being used to track your progress through

CHAPTER 27 - RIDLEY

the race."

Ridley's lips formed a soundless oh of astonishment. There was so much she had to learn and experience. So much left to see. For a moment, she felt like a child setting foot inside a magical world filled with awesome gadgets. Booths dotted the field, offering everything from games to sketch artists, tattooists, printed t-shirts, body piercings, and hair dyeing.

That wasn't all.

There was plenty to keep the kids occupied as well. A couple of girls painted pictures on the children's faces, the proceeds going to the Vancouver Orphanage. Clowns made balloon animals for kids while stalls sold their weight in candyfloss, popcorn, toffee apples, fudge, sweets, and brownies. That night would see many a parent pulling out their hair while the children worked off a massive sugar high, but for the moment, all was bliss.

When Ridley spotted a familiar figure, she said, "Isn't that Rupert?"

Jessica looked in the direction she pointed and smiled. "Yes, that's him. I should've known he'd be here emptying people's pockets."

"Can't blame him," Bear said, angling in Rupert's direction. "He has many mouths to feed and a reputation to uphold."

"True. This race is a big deal, after all," Jessica said, looking around. "Look how many people are out already, and it's only going to get busier as the day goes on."

"Is this going to be here all day?" Ridley asked, looking at the activity.

"Most likely," Jessica said. "Though, they'll probably move everyone inside before nightfall. The pubs will do a roaring trade tonight. I heard they even organized a parade through the streets this afternoon."

"A parade?" Ridley said, wishing momentarily that she was a spectator and not a competitor.

"Don't worry," Jessica said, picking up on her mood. "There will be an even bigger celebration after the race."

Ridley smiled. "Perfect."

"Still planning on winning?" Jessica asked.

"Of course. That's why I'm here," Ridley said.

"Then you'll be the center of attention. You might even have your own parade," Jessica said.

"My own parade?" Ridley repeated with a frown. She wasn't sure she liked that idea. Anonymous fun, yes. Being in the spotlight, no. But it was for a good cause, so she guessed she'd have to suck it up.

"Hi, Rupert," Bear said, greeting the Caravan Master with a shake of the hand and a slap on the back.

"Good to see you again, Bear," Rupert said, replying in kind. "Jessica, Ridley. Always a pleasure."

"Same here," Jessica said, granting him a warm smile.

"Hey," Ridley said, though her focus wasn't on the Caravan Master. Instead, she stared at the tent where all the competitors were gathered. They stood around drinking bottled water, talking, and nodding.

"Nervous, Ridley?" Rupert asked.

"Nope," Ridley said, her lips popping on the p.

"Uh-huh, and I'm the Queen of Sheba," Rupert replied with a rumble of laughter.

"The Queen of what?" Ridley asked, momentarily distracted.

"Oh, sorry. I forgot you're a Post-Shifter," Rupert said.

"A what?"

CHAPTER 27 - RIDLEY

"Post-Shifter. You were born after the Shift and know nothing of the old world," Rupert explained. "We're Pre-Shifters."

"Oh, okay," Ridley said, losing interest once more. She didn't care about the future. Not like the oldsters did. They had actual memories of that time. She didn't, and it just didn't feel real to her.

"Are you ready for this?" Rupert asked, suddenly serious.

Ridley blinked at him before answering with utter sincerity. "More ready than I've ever been in my life."

"Then I wish you good luck and good fortune, my dear," Rupert said, pulling her into a bear hug.

"Thank you," Ridley said, her voice muffled by his fur coat.

"I'll be rooting for you," Rupert said, releasing her from his grip. Waving at his caravan, he added, "We all will."

Ridley nodded, too filled with emotion to answer. The day had been a roller-coaster of feelings and emotions, and she didn't know how to cope. Tears burned her lids, and her throat swelled.

"Alright. Let's get you settled in with the other racers," Jessica said, putting one arm around her shoulders.

"Uh-huh," Ridley said, turning toward the white tent that occupied such a large space in her mind.

"Are you okay?" Jessica asked while they walked, giving them ample time to reach the structure.

"I'm alright. Just nervous," Ridley replied.

"When the time comes, forget about everything except your goal, and you'll do just fine," Jessica replied. "You have a big heart, Ridley. You only need to realize it."

Ridley hoped Jessica was right. She hoped she had as much guts as the other woman seemed to think because if she didn't, she might as well give up right there and then.

Chapter 28 - Ridley

Ridley stepped into the tent, pausing to allow her eyes to adjust to the dim lighting. The low hum of conversation died the moment she walked inside, and all eyes turned to her. Frozen to the spot, she panicked, uncertain of herself, but Jessica didn't bat an eyelid. Casting around, she spotted an open table and led her toward it.

"Come on. Let's check your gear for the last time," Jessica said, sitting down. She waved a hand at the other chair. "Have a seat and relax."

Ridley obeyed, though she didn't know how she was supposed to relax with a dozen sets of eyes on her. Most of them were cold and unfeeling.

"Remember what I said. Forget everything and focus on your goal," Jessica said. "It will all fall into place; I promise."

They went through her things individually, and the rest of the room faded away. Engrossed, she hardly noticed when a dark-skinned woman sat beside her until she spoke.

"Nice gear," the woman said.

"Huh?" Ridley said, startled.

"Sorry to scare you," the woman added, raising both hands in the air. "I come in peace."

"Peace?" Ridley asked, taken aback.

"You're Ridley, right?"

"That's me."

"I'm Maya. Nice to meet you," the woman said, reaching out with one hand.

"Nice to meet you too," Ridley replied, taking the proffered hand. Maya's grip was cool but firm, and she wore a faint smile on her lips. While she wasn't exactly friendly, she wasn't combative either.

"I just wanted to welcome you to the group. I know some of us might not seem very welcoming. We're a close-knit community that doesn't take kindly to strangers."

"Community? Aren't you competing against each other?" Ridley asked.

"Yes, we are, but most of us have been doing this for a while now, and we know each other," Maya explained. "There's not exactly a ton of endurance runners around, and not many races either."

"Oh, I get it," Ridley said. "That makes sense."

"You're new. Plus, you're young, and some of us are worried about you."

"Worried about me?" Ridley asked, incredulous.

"You're young and inexperienced. This is a dangerous race, and we're scared something might happen to you."

"We? Who's we?" Jessica interjected.

"Myself and a few others," Maya said. "I can't speak for everybody, of course."

"Of course," Jessica said, throwing a glance at Jara.

The woman stood in the far corner, talking to a tall, rangy man with sandy hair and watery blue eyes.

Maya followed her gaze and frowned. "Do not trust Jara. She is cruel and will stop at nothing to win."

CHAPTER 28 - RIDLEY

"We gathered as much," Jessica said. "Who's the guy?"

"That's Zeke. I don't trust him much. Especially since he and Jara began hanging out together."

"A couple?" Jessica asked.

"More like ill-begotten friends. He follows her around like a puppy and does anything she says," Maya said. "I'd be careful of them if I was you."

"I see, thanks," Jessica said with a nod.

"The rest of us are just here to race. We're not here to cheat or hurt people. We want to win, but we'll fight fair."

"Well, there's no need for you or anyone else to worry about me. I'll be just fine," Ridley replied, faking a sense of confidence she didn't truly feel. It was a trick she'd learned from Jessica, noticing how the woman commanded respect simply by her attitude.

Maya inclined her head. "Good luck to you, then. I'll see you at the starting line."

"Good luck to you, too," Ridley said, watching Maya return to her companions.

"Do you think she was sincere?" she asked Jessica.

"I think so, but it's best not to trust her anyway. Better safe than sorry," Jessica said.

"Yeah, I thought so," Ridley said, Jessica's words in line with her thoughts.

Suddenly, a group of people entered the tent, one of them the Mayor, Imogen. Ridley glanced at the sun outside. She put the time at around eight in the morning. "Do you think the race is starting soon?"

"The race? Yes, I'm sure it is."

"About time," Ridley said, shifting in her seat. She was becoming impatient, and so was Loki. He kept nudging her with his nose and looking outside. "Hold on, boy. Just a little bit longer."

Imogen spotted Jessica and walked over with her arms extended. "Jessica, it's good to see you again. We didn't get much chance to talk last night."

"No, we didn't, but you're a busy lady," Jessica said, and the two hugged with the affection of old friends.

"Unfortunately, today is no exception, but I hope to see you tomorrow?" Imogen asked. "I have a gap in my schedule."

"I'm leaving tomorrow morning for Chilliwack. I want to be there when Ridley crosses the finishing line," Jessica said.

"Of course. How thoughtless of me. How about afterward? When the race is over?" Imogen asked. "Things should settle down by then, and we can meet up for a chat."

"Sounds good to me. I'll arrange it when we get back from Chilliwack," Jessica said.

"Please do. I've missed you, and I want to hear all the latest news," Imogen said, flashing them a warm smile. "And good luck with the race, Ridley. I wish you the best."

"Thank you," Ridley said, smiling back. She liked Imogen. It was impossible not to. The woman had charm and personality, but most of all, sincerity. She acted like she genuinely cared.

Stepping onto a stand, Imogen took a microphone and cleared her throat, waiting for silence to fall. Once everyone was quiet, she spoke with smooth precision, her tone brisk. "Good morning, everyone. I trust you are feeling well and in the mood for running. If not, now's your chance to bow out."

She looked around expectantly, but no one spoke up, and she continued. "Excellent. It seems we have a full house today." She glanced at a list in her hands. "Please ensure that you have a copy of the rules, a map of the route, and understand what

CHAPTER 28 - RIDLEY

is expected of you. You can get these copies from my assistant and direct any questions to him."

Ridley glanced at the assistant, glad for the map and the rules. The last thing she needed was an accidental disqualification for doing something wrong. *I'd better make sure I know what I'm doing and where to go.*

"The race starts at nine—forty-eight minutes from now. Please, make sure you are ready to go on time. There's an ablution hut, a dressing room next to it, and refreshments are available there."

Imogen pointed out all the various points of interest before finishing her speech. "Thank you again for entering the 10th Annual Vancouver to Chilliwack Endurance Race, and I wish you all the best of luck!"

Muted cheers and clapping of hands broke out while she handed over the microphone. With a smile and a wave, she exited the tent and left to attend to the rest of her duties.

Imogen left her assistant behind, and the racers soon mobbed him as each clamored for a copy of the map. They knew the rules, but the map was an essential race component.

Waiting patiently for her turn, Ridley stood in line. She was almost at the front when the hair on the back of her neck rose, and she whirled around. "Jara."

The woman smiled, standing right behind Ridley. "I see you're still here. I thought you would've given up by now."

"Why would I do that?" Ridley asked.

"Because you must know it's a waste of time. You can't possibly win. Why risk your life for nothing?" Jara asked.

"That's for me to decide," Ridley said.

Jara shrugged. "Of course. I'm just looking out for you."

"I'm sure you are," Ridley said.

Shoving past Ridley, Jara snatched a map from the race assistant's hand. She turned away but paused to flash a mocking smile. "Watch yourself out there. We wouldn't want you or your dog to get hurt, now would we?"

She marched away, followed by her friend, Zeke. He glanced at Ridley with his pale blue eyes, seeming to dismiss her instantly. Still, something about him worried Ridley, and she vowed to keep an eye on them both.

"And Loki's a wolf! Not a dog," Ridley yelled after them. "Why is that so hard to understand?"

"Forget it," Jessica prompted. "Don't mind them. Keep your head in the game."

"Yeah, I know," Ridley said, pushing the nasty duo from her mind for the moment. Collecting a map, she studied it for the next thirty minutes until she'd memorized the route.

"Watch out for these bits," Jessica said, pointing to a few sections. She gave Ridley more information about each, giving her more specific details. "And avoid the shortcuts. They're not worth it."

Ridley nodded. "Alright."

"Just remember what I taught you. Sleep less and run longer," Jessica said. "Look out for the five-mile markers. They'll show you where to go."

"I will," Ridley said, mentally preparing herself for the ordeal ahead.

Suddenly, a voice interrupted their conversation. "Miss? May I speak with you for a moment?"

Ridley looked up into a strange face. The face of a man in his mid-thirties with nondescript looks, wearing a woolen suit with a long coat. "Can I help you?"

"I'm Allen Scott from the Vancouver Times, and I'm inter-

CHAPTER 28 - RIDLEY

viewing each of the competitors for an article this year," he said, taking a notepad and pen from his coat pocket. "May I ask you a few questions?"

"Uh, sure. Go ahead," Ridley said, standing up.

"You're Ridley, right? From the er... the Zoo?" he said.

"Yes, I am. How do you know that?" Ridley said, nervous despite herself.

"Your entry form," Allen Scott said. "The Mayor granted me access to your forms."

"Okay," Ridley said, unsure how she felt about that.

The man pointed at Loki. "Is that your dog?"

"Wolf. He's a wolf," Ridley said, bristling. "And his name is Loki."

"Loki? That's an interesting name," Allen Scott said, making a few notes on his pad. "Is he running the race with you?"

"Yes, he will," Ridley said, patting Loki's head.

"If I may ask, why did you enter this race? It's tough and dangerous," Allen Scott asked.

"Why not? If they can run it, so can I," Ridley said, pointing at the other racers.

"They're a lot more experienced than you are," the man said. "Older too. To date, you're the youngest entrant ever."

Ridley shrugged. "Then I'll be the youngest winner ever."

"You're very confident," Allen Scott said. "Is that because you've got an ace up your sleeve?"

"No, I just know I have what it takes to win," Ridley replied.

"I guess we'll find out," Allen Scott said, a smile tugging at his lips. "Good luck."

"Thanks," Ridley said, shouldering her gear.

The race assistant waved everyone toward the starting line and announced that the race was about to begin.

"Come on, Ridley," Jessica said. "It's time."

Ridley nodded. "I'm ready. Let's go."

***

Allen Scott watched Ridley walk away, shadowed by her wolf, Loki. To the onlookers, she looked like a pretty girl who was in over her head, filled with the brash confidence of youth, and doomed to fail. Or worse, die.

There was something about her, however. Something that told him there was a story in her. A story that could make him famous. All he needed to do, was find it, which meant tracking down all her friends and associates.

Chapter 29 - Ridley

Ridley walked toward the starting line, her stomach a churning mess of nerves and anxiety. Loki walked next to her, so close that his fur brushed against her leg. She was glad for his presence. He steadied and calmed her down. A few feet from the start, she stopped and turned to Jessica. "Thank you for getting me this far."

"No problem, kiddo, but the rest is up to you now," Jessica said, squeezing her arm. "Make me proud."

"I will."

Ridley turned back to the starting line and took the only empty spot left. To her relief, she found herself standing between Maya and another woman while Jara and Zeke were several positions away.

"Ready for this?" Maya asked, flashing her a smile.

"Yup," Ridley said, smiling back.

"Good luck," Maya added.

"Same to you," Ridley said.

She turned her attention to the front, adjusted her clothing, and smoothed an errant strand of air from her face. Satisfied, she dropped into a crouch and looked at Loki. "When I say run, you run, boy."

He nudged her with his nose and smiled, his tongue lolling

from his jaws. Ridley grinned. Despite her fears, she loved to run, and the race was no exception. *Show them who you are.*

The spectators were no exception. They crowded the sidelines, waving colored flags and cheering for their favorite racers. Music blared from the band on stage, and the guards were hard put to keep everyone in line.

Ridley could feel their excitement, and it fueled her own. She took a deep breath and waited for the starting signal. When it came, she pushed off with all her might and sprinted down the track. Her backpack and crossbow bounced on her shoulders, and her boots raised puffs of dust with every step.

Running at top speed, she relished the thrill of the chase. Her blood fizzed through her veins, and the breeze whipped her cheeks into a rosy blush. Her muscles warmed and lengthened, her ligaments stretched, and her joints grew lubricated.

Loki ran with her, enjoying it every bit as much as her. His lean body, streamlined and trim, flew across the earth like a bow from an arrow. His yellow eyes were fixed ahead, and his ears held flat against his skull.

A sudden blow sent Ridley veering off track, and she almost fell. Stumbling over her own feet, she fought for balance, looking up in time to see Jara laughing at her over her shoulder. "Try to keep up!"

Gritting her teeth, Ridley righted herself and continued running, determined not to let the woman get her down. "Screw you, Jara!"

Loki growled at the woman, his eyes blazing with anger. Now that they'd left the city with its rules and constraints, his true nature had free reign. Recognizing that, Ridley put her hand on his head, trying to calm him down. "It's okay, boy.

CHAPTER 29 - RIDLEY

Let's focus on the race."

She picked up her pace again, her heart pounding with adrenaline. Jara's taunts were like fuel to her fire. She could feel her legs moving faster and faster, her breath coming in short bursts. The wind rushed past, whipping tendrils of hair into her face.

The rough track curved around a bend, and the crowd faded from view. The sounds of cheering and music vanished into the distance. The other contestants slowed, stopping their headlong rush to the finish line. With Vancouver fading into the distance, they stopped performing for the crowd and embraced the wisdom of their training. One by one, they settled into a steady jog. The kind that ate up the distance without cutting into their reserves.

Understanding their logic, Ridley did the same. Whistling for Loki, she commanded him to stay at her side. If she had to pace herself, so did he.

One mile turned into two.

Two into three.

Three into four.

The fifth was marked by colored streamers flashing from overhead branches. The five-mile markers. They were there to keep the racers on track and to count off the distance.

The contestants drew apart, losing sight of one another. The rough track they'd followed bled into the forest until it disappeared completely.

Vancouver and its promise of safety were left far behind, part of a world that held no sway in the wilderness. Out here, it was kill or be killed, and only the strongest, wiliest, or fastest survived.

The other racers veered off individually, each following

their own path. Soon, Ridley found herself alone, running through a forest she'd never seen before. It looked different from the region around the Zoo.

The trees were spaced far apart, their slim trunks reaching high up into the sky. The sun filtered through the sparse canopy, casting dappled sunlight onto the ground below. A thin layer of dead leaves covered the hard-packed earth, but shoots of green peeked shot up in defiance of winter past.

Weaving between the trees, Ridley stayed alert. She knew that danger lurked around every bend and couldn't afford to let her guard down. She kept her senses sharp, listening for any sounds that might indicate someone or something was following her. Predators weren't the only danger. The other contestants couldn't be trusted either.

Loki stayed by her side, his ears pricked and his nose twitching as he took in the unfamiliar scents of the forest. Ridley trusted his instincts, knowing he would warn her of potential threats.

As she ran, she couldn't help but wonder what lay ahead. The race had begun, and she was no longer sure where it would lead her, but she was determined to see it through no matter what obstacles she might face.

Suddenly, Ridley heard a rustling in the bushes ahead. Her heart racing, she stopped in her tracks and reached for her crossbow. She had no idea what was lurking ahead but was ready for anything.

Loki growled, his hackles rising, which put her on edge. Swallowing hard, she whispered, "Careful, boy."

A small, bird-like creature hopped into sight as she aimed her crossbow at the rustling bushes. It had a long beak filled with teeth, front legs folded back against its sides, lean hind

CHAPTER 29 - RIDLEY

legs, and a long tail. It cocked its head at Ridley and Loki, eyeing them with predatory intent.

Recognizing the beast in an instant, Ridley swore under her breath. "Shit, it's a Tweetweeraptor. Back away slowly, Loki. Come on."

The raptor's actual name was a Buitreraptor, but Ridley called it a Tweetwee because it reminded her of the birds she'd seen in old books and films. Though it lacked feathers, it had the same looks and mannerisms.

Bird-like or not, they were vicious and opportunistic, attacking anything they perceived as weaker. They also operated in packs and worked together to bring down their prey—her worst nightmare in unfamiliar terrain.

Ridley eased away from the Buitreraptor, placing each foot with care. Her eyes flashed around, looking for the rest of the raptor's pack. There were bound to be more; it was just a question of how many.

Loki followed her retreat, his lips pulled back from his teeth in a vicious growl. The raptor followed, bobbing its head up and down while its feet danced across the ground. Sunlight gleamed on its leathery skin, moss green fading to brown in patches.

Loki was not amused by the raptor's display. A flurry of ferocious barks ripped free from his chest, and he lunged at the creature. It screeched and jumped to the side, narrowly missing decapitation. Snapping at Loki, it scored a glancing blow and drew first blood. With a yelp, Loki retreated to Ridley's side.

She was ready for the raptor, however, her crossbow loaded and aimed. A bolt slammed into the creature's chest, and it slumped to the ground, blood trickling from the wound.

A flash from the side warned her of incoming danger, and she reached for another bolt. Four more raptors jumped out of a bank of bushes, their tails lashing the air. They hissed, exposing twin rows of teeth and a whole lot of nastiness.

"Damn Tweetwees," Ridley yelled, letting off another bolt. It slammed into the nearest raptor's hind leg, crippling the dinosaur. Loki pounced on it with a growl and snapped its neck, his hackles raised.

Ridley knocked a third bolt and shouted at the raptors. "Get lost, you stupid Tweetwees!"

The nearest beast attacked, sprinting across the open space. Ridley waited for it to get close, her body tensed, and her crossbow raised. The creature pounced, its beak extended and its clawed hind legs reaching to impale her. She pulled the trigger on the crossbow, and the bolt punched into the raptor's throat at point-blank range. The barbed metal head exploded through the back in a spray of gristle and bone, killing the raptor instantly.

The remaining raptors hissed and tittered, backing away on uncertain legs. Hunters of opportunity, they had little backbone and zero courage.

Loki advanced on them with a snarl, his nose writhing above his exposed canines. The raptors took one look, turned tail, and fled with Loki on their heels. Squawking like frightened chickens, they disappeared into the forest.

Ridley grinned at the spectacle. "Stupid Tweetwee birds. They won't try that again in a hurry."

She checked the bodies and made sure they were dead. In death, the Buitreraptors didn't seem very threatening. Barely a meter high, they were small and lightweight. They were nasty customers, however.

CHAPTER 29 - RIDLEY

When Loki returned, she patted his head. "Good boy. What a good boy! You sure showed those dumb raptors." But she quickly sobered when she saw the blood on his flank. "You're hurt. Let me have a look."

Loki waited patiently while she examined the cut. Luckily, the wound was shallow, and she quickly disinfected it with a salve from her first-aid kit.

Afterward, Ridley poured him a bowl of water, took a few swigs from her canteen, and straightened up. "Come on, boy. Let's go. We've lost enough time already."

She checked her map, chose a landmark, and set off at a steady jog. With her eyes on her selected milestone, she kept moving in the right direction. Every five miles, she'd spot the mile markers and know she was on the right track. The colorful streamers were a pleasant reminder that she wasn't alone and that there were people ahead waiting for her at the relief station.

The hours wore on, and still, Ridley ran. Periodically, she slowed down to eat or drink. Twice she stopped to relieve herself, feeding and watering Loki simultaneously. Other than that, she kept running.

It was late afternoon before she crossed her first stream. It was shallow, and she made it across without wetting her gear. Loki stopped to quench his thirst, but she carried on, knowing he'd catch up.

The second stream was deeper, and Ridley had to wade through the hip-deep water. Halfway across, something brushed against her leg, and Ridley gasped. She glanced down, seeing nothing but the murky depths below. It was probably just a fish, but the thought of something lurking beneath the surface gave her the chills.

Running the last few yards, she burst onto the bank, sopping wet from the waist down. She wouldn't allow it to slow her down, however. Picking up the pace, she gave it her all despite the exhaustion that tugged at her limbs.

The first hint of panic set in when she realized she hadn't seen any mile markers since crossing the first stream. Like Hansel's bread crumbs, they'd disappeared, and she could not know if she was still on the right track.

Stumbling to a halt, Ridley checked her map and compass. On paper, everything seemed fine, which added to her confusion. Where were the damned mile markers? Was she lost?

Turning this way and that, she tried to determine which way to go. The relief station had to be close, but indecision weighed her down. "What do I do, Loki? Where do we go?"

But Loki had no answers, and she realized she had to take responsibility for herself and her companion. A final look at the compass assured her she was on the right track; she simply had to trust her abilities. "Come on, boy. Let's move."

Ridley broke into a run, setting a punishing pace. The hour was late, and it would be dark soon. She had to get to the relief station soon or risk spending the night in the forest—a prospect she did not relish.

Her mind switched off, and her body moved of its own volition. Mile after mile passed, still without any signs of the mile markers. Either she was well and truly lost, or something else was happening. Trusting her gut, Ridley kept moving.

The sun dropped toward the horizon, lower and lower. Gray crept into the air, and the moon began its assent into the heavens. A chill breeze picked up, stirring the dead leaves on the forest floor. It whipped around her body and swirled

CHAPTER 29 - RIDLEY

around her limbs.

She began to shiver from the cold and the exhaustion that had set into her bones. Still, she ran, pushing her body to its limits. She had to keep going until she found shelter. If she stopped now, she might not be able to get going again.

Loki kept pace, faring much better than she did. He was fitter and leaner than her, a creature made for running. "Way to go, boy," she managed to huff between deep gasps for oxygen.

The terrain dipped into a hollow, and Ridley leaned backward as she descended. Falling was easy when going downhill, and she did not want to break a leg or sprain an ankle.

At the bottom, a small stream cut through the forest floor, and she paused to splash cold water on her face. She jumped across and pushed her tired body up the hill, drawing on her last reserves.

Heaving for breath, Ridley topped out on the rise. She dragged her aching body upright, determined not to give up, but a wave of dizziness hit out of nowhere. Her belly heaved, and she bent over as the contents of her stomach rushed up her throat. It splattered onto the ground, and she hacked until the sickness passed.

Finally, she was able to straighten up and wipe her mouth. She reached for her canteen, hoping to rinse her mouth, but froze when she heard a familiar sound: A deep grunt followed by a low bellow. More bellows sounded, a chorus of mournful notes that shivered down her spine.

Ridley turned to look, sure she recognized the distinctive calls. They belonged to her favorite dinosaur, the Triceratops. She'd spent many an afternoon watching the herbivores from a hidden perch. To her, they were magnificent.

Standing atop the hill, she watched as the herd approached. The trees shook and shuddered under the onslaught of their five-and-a-half-ton bodies. The foliage parted, revealing a herd numbering at least thirty. They were done with the day's grazing and were on their way to their nightly resting place.

Awed, Ridley watched as they lumbered past her lofty perch, so close she could smell their musky scent. Their massive heads swayed with each ponderous step, crowned by a bony frill and their most distinctive feature, the trio of horns that sprouted from their skulls.

They crossed the tiny stream and stomped across an open stretch of ground one by one before disappearing into the distant trees. As quickly as they arrived, they were gone again, the mysterious behemoths of the forest. "Now that was something, wasn't it, Loki? The kind of thing you tell your grandkids about. Or your grand pups. Are you going to have grand pups one day?"

Loki gazed after the Triceratops, his demeanor as somber as hers. "I'll take that as a yes," Ridley said. "Come on, boy. We're not out of the woods yet."

Revitalized by her encounter with the Triceratops, she pushed ahead. Loki stuck to her side like a shadow, and together, they ran down the hill and crossed a clearing. The sun was almost completely gone, and panic said in. The night was almost upon her, and still, there was no sign of the mile markers or the relief camp. *Damn it. I'm lost.*

Tears pricked her eyelids, burning like acid, and fear churned in her breast. She needed to find the relief camp. It wasn't safe out in the open. She was tired and hungry. Loki was hurt. They needed protection and shelter.

But there was no use in crying over spilled milk. They were

CHAPTER 29 - RIDLEY

lost, and there was nothing she could do about it except find a suitable spot to shelter for the night. *Fire. We need fire.*

Suddenly, Loki alerted her to another presence in the forest, Something else besides them. Slowing down, she watched him with care. His ears were pricked, and his posture had changed, but he didn't seem scared, just alert. "What is it, boy?"

Loki barked and cut across the ground at an angle. Ridley followed, pushing her aching body onward. They cut through a clump of bushes and emerged into an open clearing. That was when she heard it. Voices. People. *The camp!* "Oh, thank you, thank you! We made it, Loki. We're here."

With a spurt of desperate energy, Ridley sprinted toward the site. Her feet thudded into the ground with a dull beat, carrying her toward the safety of a chain-link fence guarded by armed men.

She dashed through the entrance with Loki on her heels, her breathing ragged and harsh. She was exhausted to the point of collapse but didn't care. The only thing that mattered was that she'd made it. She'd finished the first leg of the race.

Chapter 30 - Ridley

Ridley nodded to the guards at the entrance of the camp. They nodded back but didn't say anything, and she continued onward. A relief worker spotted her and hurried over, wearing a reflective yellow vest. He stared at her with amazement. "You're Ridley, right? The girl with the wolf?"

"Uh-huh," Ridley said with a nod, her throat dry. She nodded to Loki. "This is the wolf."

"He's something, isn't he?" the worker said, eyeing Loki with wary caution.

She might've found his instinctive fear amusing if she wasn't so exhausted. Not everyone felt about wolves the way she did. Most were frightened of the big canine, unnerved by his intense yellow gaze. "He's something, all right."

"We thought you got lost. It's almost dark, and none of the other racers have seen you since the start of the race," the worker said.

"I thought I was lost too. I haven't seen any mile markers in ages, and I thought I was off course," Ridley added.

"No mile markers? That's strange. We put them up all over the place. You should've seen them on your way in," the worker said.

"Not a single one," Ridley said.

CHAPTER 30 - RIDLEY

"Are you sure you looked properly?" the relief worker said.

"Pretty sure," Ridley mumbled, but she was too tired to argue further.

"Well, you made it. That's something, at least," the worker added.

"Huh," Ridley said, not caring about the man's words until he mentioned water. Her canteen was bone-dry, and her tongue felt like a stick of wood. She'd given the last of her water to Loki an hour back.

"I bet you're thirsty," the worker said, leading her toward a white tent with a red cross on the side. Inside, he plucked a bottle of water from a cooler and handed it over.

"Thanks," Ridley said, gulping it down. The precious fluid flowed across her parched tissues, a sensation that was the closest to bliss she'd ever gotten. She handed back the empty bottle. "May I have another one?"

"Of course. Help yourself," the worker said, watching with interest as she removed Loki's bowl from her backpack and filled it.

While the wolf quenched his thirst, she tucked two more bottles away.

"All better?" the worker asked.

"Much better, thanks," Ridley replied.

"Do you need any medical assistance?" the worker asked, looking her up and down.

"No, we're fine," Ridley said. "It's just a couple of scratches from a Buitreraptor pack."

"Raptors?" the worker said. "You ran into raptors? We didn't know there were any in the area."

"Well, they're not going to stick around much longer. We killed three of them."

"Three? That's impressive," the worker said, leading her toward the nearest fire.

"Not really. They're pretty small, and I'm good with a crossbow," Ridley said with a shrug.

"Maybe, but still. I wouldn't take one on myself. You must be pretty brave," the relief worker said, admiration on his face. "But where are my manners? I bet you're cold and tired."

"Exhausted, actually," Ridley admitted, following him to a central fire. She faltered when she spotted several figures sitting around the blaze. It was the other contestants, and they stared at her like she'd grown a second head.

Feeling self-conscious, she chose a seat on a tree stump as far away from the rest as possible. Dumping her gear on the ground, she drank a few more sips of water and looked around.

Without trying to be too obvious about it, she counted the racers. That led to a devastating realization. Despite running her heart out that day, she'd come in last. Dead last. Ridley's mood plummeted into her shoes. *I can't believe it. I'm the last one here. How embarrassing.*

Her cheeks burned, hot blood flooding her veins. To top it off, Jara picked up on her discomfort and said, "Glad to see you finally made it. We thought you got lost out there." She smirked, exchanging a triumphant look with her buddy Zeke who laughed out loud. A couple of others joined in, and a chorus of chuckles surrounded the fire.

"Ah, well. Better late than never," Jara added.

"Knock it off, Jara. She did better than any of us could've done on our first day," Maya said, earning a look of gratitude from Ridley.

"Shove off, Maya. She doesn't need a champion. She's big

enough to fight her own battles, right?" Jara said, throwing Ridley a pointed look.

Ridley ignored the woman, glancing at the other racers. Only two met her eyes: Maya and the blonde woman who stood next to her at the starting line that morning.

Maya flashed her a smile.

The blonde nodded.

The rest disregarded her, and Ridley got the message loud and clear. She was the outsider. The one who didn't belong. Grabbing her stuff, she moved away from them, seeking shelter at one of the other fires that burned in the camp.

After a visit to the restrooms, she washed her hands and pulled a strip of dried meat out of her backpack. "Here you go, Loki. Eat up."

Loki snapped up the strip and devoured it within seconds. Sitting back on his haunches, he begged for more. "Hungry, huh? So am I."

She pulled out the beef sandwich Martha had packed her that morning and unwrapped it. The sandwich was squashed, but she didn't care and bit into the thick bread with a groan of delight. Demolishing half, she gave the other half to Loki and ate a handful of dried cranberries and apricots. Afterward, they each chewed on another strip of dried meat and drank the bottled water she'd gotten from the relief worker.

"That's much better," Ridley said, rubbing her full stomach. "How about you, boy?"

Loki licked his chops with a look of satisfaction and curled up next to the fire. Within seconds, he was fast asleep, and she longed to follow his example but still had a few chores to perform.

She stripped off her mocassins and treated her feet for

blisters and chafe marks. Afterward, she readied her bed and blanket beside the fire and pulled out her race map. Studying the route, she spotted a shortcut and honed in on it.

When a relief worker passed, she called, "Excuse me, miss. Can you tell me anything about this route over here?"

The woman glanced at the map and blanched. "That's Deadman's Gully."

"Do you know anything about it?"

"Not much. Only that two contestants have died going that way. It's said to be dangerous."

"But it's shorter than the main trail?" Ridley pressed.

"Fourteen miles shorter, and it cuts through the rocky hills ahead instead of over them."

"Because of the gully? This one here?" Ridley said.

"That's what they say," the woman said with a shrug. "I don't know much more than that."

"Thanks," Ridley said, offering the woman a faint smile.

"You're not thinking of going that way, are you?" the relief worker asked with a frown.

"No, of course not. It sounds too dangerous," Ridley said, tucking the map away.

The woman nodded and left, and Ridley crawled into her bedroll, hugging Loki close to her side. Her mind ran circles around the idea of taking the shortcut. Her brain told her it was too dangerous. Too risky. But her heart thought otherwise. She'd lose the race if she didn't take the shorter route. She wasn't as fast or fit as the others.

But what did it matter? Even if she got to the relief camp first, that didn't mean she'd win. Unless... unless she used the shortcut to get ahead of the other racers, bypass the relief camp, and spend the night in the wild. She'd have a headstart

CHAPTER 30 - RIDLEY

the next day. Enough to give her an edge.

"Too dangerous!" her brain screamed.

"You've done it before," her heart said, remembering the times she'd snuck out of the Zoo overnight.

"It's not the same. You don't know the area or the patterns of the wildlife."

"Yes, it is. You've trained for this. You can do this."

"It's suicide. What about Loki?"

Still undecided, she fell asleep.

The following day, Ridley woke up several hours before the other racers. Moving silently, she slipped out of her bedroll and went to the women's restrooms. There, she did her business, washed her hands and face, brushed her teeth, and combed her hair. Smoothing it back into a ponytail, she put on a set of clean underwear and socks.

Next came breakfast, a quick meal of dried fish, fruit, and nuts. She poured Loki a bowl of water and topped up her canteen. At the last moment, she grabbed an extra water bottle and tucked it into her bag with the rest of her gear.

Finally, she stoked up the coals and built a torch using a long thick piece of wood and the bandages soaked in tree resin that she carried in a packet. With the fire to light her way, she crept out of the camp while the other racers slept unawares. After a slight hesitation, she turned toward the shortcut. Dangerous or not, she had to try to win.

Consequences be damned.

***

The only people who noticed her departure were the guards and a few relief workers. The woman she'd questioned told them about her interest in the shortcut, and the guards confirmed she'd taken the alternate route. They all wondered if she'd ever be seen alive again. Her or her wolf.

The story quickly spread from camp to camp, carried over the radio waves by relief workers or guards to the next. Allen Scott, the journalist, caught wind of it and decided to do some digging. He retraced Ridley's steps, talking to Martha, the boarding home's owner, and Rupert, the Caravan Master of a small trade group. He just missed Bear and Jessica, who departed for Chilliwack that same day.

His sensationalized article hit the press within hours, and greedy readers lapped it up. The girl and her wolf became an overnight smash hit.

Chapter 31 - Jessica

The Jeep bounced across the rough track that wound through the forest, and Jessica clung to the handle above the window. Each jounce and jostle sent vibrations up her spine and into her skull until a throbbing headache took up residence between her temples.

They'd been on the road for a solid three hours, departing from Vancouver following breakfast that morning. Although it wasn't that far, traveling through the wilderness was much slower. The roads were terrible, and the wildlife was an ever-present hazard.

After paying their bill that morning, Martha bid them a tearful farewell. She also handed them a huge packed lunch, determined not to let them go hungry. Jessica glanced at the picnic basket with a fond smile. She was going to miss Martha. Her cooking too. She felt sad for leaving her old home behind so soon. A few days of catching up and seeing the sights would've been delightful, but she needed to get to Chilliwack.

It was the race's second day, and she'd kept tabs on Ridley's progress. The girl had made it through her first day, reaching the relief camp in last place but also one piece. That was a relief. She'd set out early this morning, just like Jessica had taught her. However, she had not listened to Jessica's advice about the shortcuts, taking the route through Deadman's Gulch.

"Why did she do that? Why did she go through the gully?" Jessica asked for the hundredth time.

"I don't know," Bear said, also for the hundredth time.

"Stupid, stupid," Jessica cried, worry gnawing at her gut.

"I know, but there's nothing we can do but trust that she'll make it through," Bear said. "We'll reach Chilliwack soon, and then we can find out how she's doing."

"I know. I'm just so worried," Jessica said, gazing outward.

Bear squeezed her hand in silent reassurance, and she leaned against his side. The forest rose tall on either side of the dirt road, its interior a hidden mystery.

Minutes later, they reached a bridge. The concrete and metal structure stretched across a deep river, its blue water sparkling in the sunlight.

The Jeep slowed, navigating the bridge with careful precision. It was old, the sides crumbling, and the steel girders rusted and sagging.

Jessica clung to the seat, more scared than she'd ever been in her life. She wasn't fond of heights, and swaying above the river wasn't her idea of fun.

Suddenly, a gigantic head burst out of the river and rose into the air until it towered above the Jeep. Water streamed down in sheets, drenching Jessica and the other occupants of the Jeep. "Oh, my God! Is that a...."

"Alamosaurus," Bear replied, his eyes wide with shock.

Craning her neck, she stared at the long-necked dinosaur that loomed several stories above them, chewing on a mouthful of algae. It peered at the truck briefly before turning away

CHAPTER 31 - JESSICA

and lumbering toward the river bank.

Each step caused waves of water to surge through the river, flooding the banks and annoying the other herbivores attempting to get a drink of water.

Gaping at the spectacle, Jessica spotted more dinosaurs lining the river, drinking, bathing, and eating the rich plants that grew in the shallows.

There was a herd of Ankylosaurus with their knobby tails and spikey backs. Lambeosaurus with their duck-like bills, eating water lilies and weeds. Styracosaurus with their crested heads and horns sprouting from their snout and cheeks. Similar to the Triceratops, they were almost as impressive, though smaller.

There were several smaller herbivores too. Zuniceratops, frilled and horned like their cousins, the Triceratops, gamboled in the shallows. Parksosaurus and Stegoceras fought for space with the larger dinos, and a flock of Pteranodons fished in a clump of rocky pools with their pelican-like beaks.

"It's… it's…."

"It's amazing," Bear said, saying what Jessica could not.

She nodded, though amazing couldn't begin to describe the sight of so many different dinosaurs lining the banks of the deep blue river. At the same time, the sun shone down with golden benevolence, and dragonflies as large as her hand flitted about like iridescent gemstones.

For several long moments, no one moved. Not Jessica, Bear, or the driver. A spell lay over them—a spell woven from the magnificence of the primordial world in all of its raw power and beauty.

Finally, the driver of the Jeep regained his composure and drove across the bridge at a low speed. It would not do to scare or startle the dinosaurs, resulting in a stampede. That would be suicide.

After what felt like an eternity, they were across, and the river with its creatures was left behind. In time, the memory would fade, but the emotions it evoked would not. It would linger, leaving a permanent impression in the hearts of those who witnessed it.

Chapter 32 - Rogue

Rogue leaned back in her chair and squeezed her eyes shut. The Cessna 182 shook and shuddered when it hit an air pocket, and she clutched the armrests until her knuckles turned white. Her breath sawed in and out of her lungs, and her anxiety levels shot through the roof.

This was not what she'd envisioned when she first thought of flying to Vancouver. She'd imagined a short and restful flight through blue skies and white clouds, the warm spring sunshine filling the cabin.

Instead, she was rocketing through stormy skies in a tin can held together with blue wire and duct tape. Thunder rumbled through the air, followed by flashes of lightning in the distance.

"Don't worry!" Lee yelled across his shoulder when they hit another air pocket. "This is normal. Just a patch of bad weather."

"Normal?" Rogue muttered with disbelief. "Normal, my ass."

"It's okay, dear. It won't be long now," Olivia said, patting her forearm. "We're almost there."

"Man, I hope so," Rogue said, muffling a cough. It was one of many brought on by the stress of the trip. While the journey to Prime had been uneventful, it took a toll on her reserves, and she felt drained.

"Are you okay?" Olivia asked.

"I will be as soon as I find Ridley," Rogue said.

"You mustn't push yourself too hard," Olivia said. "You're still weak."

"I don't care," Rogue said.

"You should," Ric said sharply. "Despite our reservations, we came all this way to help and support you. Don't be so difficult."

Rogue suppressed an eye roll. Ric liked to preach on occasion. It was one of his less attractive qualities. He was right, however. They'd dropped everything to accompany her on this journey, and they deserved her respect for that. "I'm sorry."

The plane shook again, the engine making a high-pitched sound that grated on her nerves. "Oh, God. We're going to die."

"We're not going to die," Olivia said, patting her hand. "Try to relax. Think of something nice."

"Something nice?" Rogue said, her mind winging back over the past day and a half.

Seeing her friends at Prime City had been nice, though it had been a short visit at best. She'd spent the night with Moran and her husband Bruce, and catching up with them had been pleasant. Retired from the council and the Watch, they spent their days catching up to all sorts of mischief.

Rogue was five when the Shift happened, throwing her millions of years into the past. Separated from her parents, she would've died if a group of survivors hadn't found her and taken her to Prime City.

CHAPTER 32 - ROGUE

There she ended up on the streets, orphaned and alone. It was Moran, a fighter and a street thief, who found her and taught her how to survive. Following in her footsteps, Rogue grew into a headstrong and rebellious young woman.

Years later, she was reunited with her birth mother, Olivia, who'd found refuge at the Zoo. Her father was still in the future, however. Lost to them forever.

Then there was Lee Alexander, the plane's owner and pilot. Like Jessica, he was originally from Vancouver. He'd settled in Prime after meeting and falling in love with Patti. Patti was Moran's right-hand woman, helping her lead first the Rebel Army and then the Prime Council.

Moran, Bruce, Olivia, Ric, Patti, and Lee formed part of her past. They made up the very fabric of her existence. There were others. So many people she'd met over the years. Some were still alive; some weren't. Seth... Now she wondered who was the next to go. *Probably me.*

It was a morbid thought, but Rogue was a realist. There was no point in beating around the bush. While the medicine Jessica got her was working, there were no guarantees. *Hell, it doesn't even have to be the tuberculosis that kills me. It could be this stupid plane.*

She shook her head, trying not to envision herself plummeting to the ground and exploding in a great ball of flame. It would be quick, at least. Unlike the disease that chiseled away at her will to live. Breaking off tiny pieces each day until nothing was left but a misshapen lump.

Thankfully, Lee interrupted with a happy announcement, drawing her thoughts away from her misery. "We're here, folks. Get ready to land!"

He spoke into this microphone, requesting and receiving

permission to land on the Vancouver Airstrip. The plane angled toward its destination, the wings dipping through the clouds toward the earth.

Relieved but still afraid, Rogue sucked in her breath when the plane began its final descent. It shook and shuddered as it dropped, each moment raising a question mark in her mind. Would the rusted piece of crap that Lee called a plane make it safely to the runway?

The seconds ticked by while she waited and prayed. Finally, the wheels touched the tarmac, bouncing across the surface like a rubber ball. The plane slowed as Lee eased back on the throttle. He tapped the brakes, and the wheels screeched before stopping in front of the hangar.

Lee flashed them a triumphant grin. "We made it, folks. Safe and sound!"

"You call that a safe landing?" Rogue cried.

"You're still in one piece, right?"

"I guess so," Rogue replied, standing on wobbly legs. She looked through the window, surprised to see a car waiting for them. "Who's that?"

"I radioed ahead and made a few arrangements," Lee explained. "We're staying at the Blue Water Guest House tonight, usually reserved for diplomats and officials from other communities."

"How? Who?" Rogue asked, stunned.

"Imogen. I told her who was visiting, and she was happy to make the necessary arrangements," Lee explained. "Plus, she made an appointment to visit you at the guest house this afternoon."

Rogue's eyes widened in surprise. Imogen was one of the few friends she had in Vancouver. They'd met during Rogue's first trip to the city. Imogen's keen mind and sharp wit had made an impression on Rogue, and they had kept in touch ever since.

Still, it had been years since they last saw each other, and she was touched by the reception they got. A lump formed in her throat. "I don't know what to say."

"Just thank her when you see her," Olivia said, giving her a reassuring smile.

The group stepped out of the plane, the chilly air whipping around them. Rogue pulled her coat tighter around her body, feeling the cold seep through her clothes. Her body shivered with a mixture of exhaustion and cold. The flight had taken a lot out of her, and she wished she could crawl into bed and sleep for a week, but Ridley came first. *I have to find my daughter.*

They made their way to the waiting car, Rogue feeling more and more grateful for the support of her friends. The car was a sleek black sedan, the driver waiting patiently for them to get in. Olivia helped Rogue into the backseat, and they settled in for the drive to the guest house.

As they made their way through the city, Rogue couldn't help but think of the last time she was in Vancouver. It was right before she found out she was pregnant with Ridley.

They'd attended Imogen's induction ceremony as the Mayor and concluded a successful trade deal between the cities of Prime, Vancouver, and the Zoo.

Afterward, she and Seth spent the day together, exploring the city and discussing their hopes and dreams for the future. It was a bittersweet memory, knowing she'd never have the opportunity again. Despite Ridley's belief that he was still alive, Rogue couldn't hold on to the same hope. It was too hard.

As she rode through the city again, Rogue felt a sense of nostalgia mixed with a twinge of sadness. She missed Seth terribly, and the thought of never seeing him again was almost too much to bear. But she pushed those thoughts aside, knowing she had to focus on Ridley. "When can I see Imogen? I need to find Ridley as soon as possible, and I'm sure she can help."

"She said she'd visit us as soon as possible," Lee said. "We just have to be patient. In the meantime, we can settle in at the Guest House, and a doctor is coming to look at you."

"A doctor?" Rogue said with a frown. "That's not why I'm here. I'm here to find Ridley before she does something stupid like enter that race."

"And I'm sure Imogen will help us," Lee said. "Seeing a doctor while you wait can't hurt."

"Please, dear. If nothing else, it will help to pass the time," Olivia said. "Besides, I'm sure Ric and Lee can make some inquiries the moment we've settled in."

"Promise?" Rogue said.

"Of course," Ric said. "Anything for our granddaughter."

"Thank you," Rogue said, feeling a little better. Even so, she'd only be able to relax once she'd seen Imogen and knew where Ridley was and what she was up to.

"Remember, dear. She's not alone. Jessica and Bear are with her."

That thought did much to allay Rogue's fears, and she settled back into her seat with a sigh. As the car pulled up to the Blue Water Guest House, Rogue felt a sense of relief wash over her. It was a beautiful old building with a red brick facade and large, arched windows. The driver helped them out of the

CHAPTER 32 - ROGUE

car, and they made their way inside.

The interior was just as impressive as the exterior, with a grand staircase leading to the guest rooms. The reception area was empty, but a bell sat on the counter, waiting to be rung.

Lee stepped forward and rang the bell, and a moment later, a young woman appeared from a door at the back. She smiled at them warmly. "Welcome to the Blue Water Guest House. How can I help you?"

"We have a reservation," Lee said. "For Rogue and company."

"Yes, of course. You'll be staying in the Presidential Suite and adjacent rooms, as requested."

"Thank you," Lee said, smiling back at her.

The young woman handed them keys and some papers to sign, which they quickly did. As they made their way up the grand staircase, Rogue couldn't help but feel grateful for the unexpected hospitality.

The Presidential Suite was everything Rogue had imagined and more. It was a spacious room with a four-poster bed, a sitting area with plush armchairs, and a balcony overlooking the ocean. The walls were adorned with elegant paintings, and the carpet was soft underfoot.

Rogue sank onto the bed, feeling the weariness of the past few days catching up with her. Olivia sat down beside her, rubbing her back soothingly. "Rest, dear. We'll take care of everything."

Rogue nodded, feeling her eyes grow heavy. "Thank you," she whispered before drifting off to sleep.

The sound of a knock on the door jolted Rogue awake. She sat up, rubbing her eyes. Olivia was already at the entrance, welcoming Imogen into the room.

Rogue couldn't help but smile at the sight of her old friend. She looked just as Rogue remembered her: sharp, witty, and ready for anything.

"Rogue!" Imogen exclaimed, rushing over to embrace her. "It's so good to see you again."

"You too," Rogue said.

Imogen pulled back, taking a good look at Rogue. "You look exhausted. What happened?"

"It's Ridley," Rogue said, feeling a lump form in her throat. "We had a terrible fight, and she ran away from home. I have to find her before it's too late."

Imogen's expression sobered. "Ran away? I don't understand."

"She left the Zoo and joined a trade caravan headed here," Rogue explained. "I have to find her before she gets into any trouble."

"I'm afraid you're too late," Imogen said.

"Too late? What do you mean I'm too late?" Rogue asked, her stomach dropping. "Where is she? What happened to her?"

"As far as I know, she's safe, For the moment, at least," Imogen said. "She entered the Vancouver Chilliwack Endurance Race."

"What? No! You have to stop her," Rogue cried.

"I can't," Imogen said. "The race started yesterday morning."

"Yesterday morning?" Rogue repeated, feeling faint. She sat down on the bed with a thump, her legs giving way. "She's been out there for more than a day and a night? Alone?"

"Technically, she's not alone. She's got that wolf of hers, Loki," Imogen said. "Plus, she stayed at the first aid station last night."

CHAPTER 32 - ROGUE

"I can't believe it; I can't believe she'd do this. Why?" Rogue said, hardly hearing what Imogen said. All she knew was that her only child was lost in the woods. Woods that were filled with vicious monsters ready to tear her daughter to pieces.

"I don't know why she wanted to run the race. I didn't ask, but Jessica seemed to believe she could do it," Imogen said.

"Jessica?" Rogue said, whirling to face Imogen. "Jessica allowed her to do this?"

"Well, I wouldn't say allowed," Imogen protested. "Ridley is eighteen, isn't she?"

"Yes, but she's not prepared for a race like this. It's too dangerous!"

"Maybe so, but it's her choice. She entered, and she's running," Imogen said. "All you can do now is be at the finish line."

"Over my dead body," Rogue said, rounding on the hapless Mayor. Stabbing a finger in the air, she said, "I want you to pull her out of the race. Now!"

"I can't do that," Imogen protested.

"Yes, you can."

"Rogue, please. Think about it. She's overage. This is her choice. Her decision."

"No, it's not. She's just a child. A spoiled, rebellious brat who doesn't know what's good for her," Rogue said. "Pull her out of the race."

"No," Imogen said, shaking her head.

"What do you mean, no?"

"You heard me," Imogen said, raising her chin.

Rogue gaped at her friend, shocked. "I can't believe this. Even you're turning against me."

"No one is turning against you, Rogue. You're not thinking

clearly," Imogen said.

"She's right," Olivia said, placing a gentle hand on Rogue's arm. "If you do this… if you pull her from the race, she'll never forgive you."

"I don't care!"

"Yes, you do," Olivia said. "Isn't that why you're here? To make peace?"

"I can't let her do this," Rogue said, her voice small.

"You have to let her make her own choices and live her own life," Olivia said gently. "And you have to love her, no matter what those choices are."

Rogue felt a tear roll down her cheek. "I do love her. That's why I can't let her do this."

Olivia hugged her tightly. "Then love her enough to let her make her own mistakes."

Rogue nodded, feeling a heaviness in her chest. She knew Olivia was right. She had to trust that Ridley was strong enough to handle whatever came her way. She had to believe in her daughter.

"Okay," she said, wiping her tears. "Okay, I won't stop her."

"That's the spirit," Imogen said.

"But I need to be there at the finish line. I need to make sure she's okay."

Imogen smiled, relieved. "Of course. I'll make the arrangements. A truck will take you to Chilliwack the day after tomorrow. You'll be there when she finishes the race."

"Thank you," Rogue said, feeling a weight lift off her shoulders.

"Be ready to leave at dawn," Imogen said.

"I'll be ready."

"In the meantime, I'll keep you updated on Ridley's progress.

CHAPTER 32 - ROGUE

We receive regular news via radio, and I'll ensure you are informed."

Rogue nodded. "Thanks."

"But you have to do something for me in return," Imogen said.

"What?"

"I want you to rest, and I'm sending that doctor up straight away," Imogen said. "You must get better. For your sake and Ridley's. Deal?"

"Deal," Rogue said, knowing her friend was right. As much as she wanted to jump into a truck and look for her daughter, she had to be patient. She had to have faith in Ridley and her abilities. *It's what Seth would've wanted.*

Chapter 33 - Ridley

Ridley hacked at the thick foliage with her ax, clearing a path for her and Loki. Each step was a battle, and she rued her decision to take the shortcut. While the other contestants were running on their merry way, she was reduced to a snail's pace.

Sweat ran down the sides of her face and dripped down her chin. Her shirt was soaked, and salt crystals had formed along her collar. This resulted in chafing, and the skin was raw to the touch, burning like fire with every move she made.

Flies, gnats, and mosquitoes buzzed around her face, delighting in her misery. They fed off her blood, sweat, and tears, parasites sucking on her life essence.

Loki had it just as bad. His thick fur trapped the heat close to his skin, and the humid air made it worse. He panted heavily in an effort to cool down, breaking off only to snap at the annoying insects that sought to crawl into his eyes, ears, and nose. "I'm sorry, boy. Only a little bit further. I promise."

Ridley renewed her efforts, vowing to get them through the strangling vines. But with every hack and slash, she expended more energy, sapping her strength and vitality.

Finally, she stopped and dropped to her haunches, heaving for breath. It was only the third day, and already she wanted

CHAPTER 33 - RIDLEY

to give up the fight. But Ridley wasn't a quitter. She had come too far and trained too hard to let nature defeat her. "Short break. That's all we need. A short break."

Ridley pulled out her canteen and took several long pulls. The liquid was stale and lukewarm, but it quenched her thirst. She poured Loki a bowl, too, waiting while he lapped up the precious fluid.

Once he was finished, she packed the bowl and canteen away, straightening up with a grimace. She gritted her teeth and continued, hacking her way through the jungle with renewed vigor.

As she swung her ax, however, she noticed something strange. The vines in front of her were moving. She paused, one hand in the air and her heart in her throat. "What the hell?"

A pair of yellow-slitted eyes blinked at her, and a head rose from the writhing wall until it was level with her face. It hissed at her, its jaws opening wide to reveal twin rows of sharp teeth.

Ridley stared at the snake-like creature with shock. She'd heard about them, but she'd never seen one. They were the ancestors of modern-day snakes, a primordial version that still sported a pair of tiny hindlegs. As thick as her forearm, the creature blended in with its environment, its scales different shades of green and brown.

Loki growled at the snake, jumping to her defense. The creature hissed at the wolf, rearing back in readiness to strike. "No!"

Without hesitation, Ridley struck at the creature with her ax, catching it with a glancing blow. The creature recoiled, hissing and spitting. Ridley's heart pounded as she raised her ax again, ready to fight with everything she had.

The creature lunged at her, its jaws snapping shut inches from her face. Ridley's ax came down, connecting with the creature's neck this time.

Blood sprayed from the wound, coating her face and arms with a crimson mist. The snake squirmed and writhed on the ground, bleeding out into the carpet of moss underfoot.

Loki was by her side, a low growl rumbling in his throat. Ridley put a steadying hand on his back. "Don't worry, boy. It can't hurt us anymore."

Loki whined, rubbing his muzzle against her arm. Ridley ruffled his ears. "Tonight, we feast."

Loki whined softly at her, his tail wagging as if to agree.

Working fast, she gutted the snake and cut off its head. She wrapped it in a piece of cloth and tucked it away in her bag. Satisfied, she stood, shaking off her fatigue. "You okay to go on, boy?"

Loki yipped, and she gave him a nod. "Good. Let's keep going."

Ridley cleaned and put away her knife, washed the blood from her hands and face, and stood up. Ax in hand, she continued on her way, followed by Loki.

They continued like that for the next hour, cutting through the foliage. She saw no more creatures, but she knew they were there. Faint rustles, trills, calls, and hisses echoed throughout the canopy.

Finally, the trees gave way to the foot of a mountain that blocked the way forward. Ridley stood at the base, staring up at the sheer wall of rock that rose before overhead. This was the reason she'd taken the shortcut. According to her map, a narrow gully cut through the base and emerged on the

CHAPTER 33 - RIDLEY

other side. Instead of going over, she'd go through. The only problem was she didn't see any signs of a gully. "Shit."

Ridley pulled the crumpled map from her pocket and studied it. The gully was marked with an x, but she couldn't see it. "It has to be here somewhere. I'm sure of it."

Replacing the map, she waved to Loki. "Come on, boy."

They searched up and down the mountain's base for the next twenty minutes but found nothing. Despair set in, and Ridley slumped onto the nearest rock. "Why can't I find it? Where is it?"

Loki whined and nudged her hand, trying to comfort her. She patted him on the head, but tears were close to the surface. Going back was not an option. She might as well quit the race, then.

Suddenly, Ridley heard a whistling noise and frowned. *Whistling? Here? That's impossible.*

Getting to her feet, she followed the sound. The rock appeared as solid as ever, and she wondered if she was going crazy. But when a cool breeze touched her face, she started. "Did you feel that, Loki? There's an opening nearby. There must be."

Running her hands across the rock wall, she moved sideways until her hand discovered an edge. Behind it was an open space, and she cried out with relief. "Loki! Over here!"

Running through the mountain's base was a rough passage filled with brush and stones. It was pretty narrow in places, but she thought she could squeeze through. "Come on, boy. We have to hurry. We've lost too much time already."

Biting her lip, she scrambled into the gully, Loki on her heels. She carefully picked her way through the brush, avoiding the piles of loose rock that littered the bottom. The last thing she needed now was a sprained ankle.

Loki ran ahead, eager to escape the narrow passage, and Ridley didn't blame him. The towering rock walls on either side hemmed her in, creating a suffocating atmosphere. Sucking in a deep breath, she forged onward, determined to make the best of a bad situation. *I am never taking a shortcut again.*

Suddenly, Loki was back by her side, growling, his hackles raised. She paused to listen, her senses on high alert. "What is it, boy?"

At first, she heard and saw nothing, despite scanning every inch of the gully. But she knew she was being watched when a trickle of rocks rained down from above, dislodged by some creature.

Her right hand crept toward the ax in her belt, and she drew it with barely a sound. The crossbow wouldn't be much use in such a confined space. With her weapon held ready, she backed away further down the gully. The sooner she was through, the better.

One step. Two steps. Three.

Ridley kept moving, slow but steady. Doing her best not to appear threatening to whatever watched her from the heights above. She had her suspicions. Streaks of white on the rock walls spoke of excrement. Probably from a type of pterosaur.

The flying beasts came in all shapes and sizes. From the gigantic Quetzalcoatlus to the tiny Nyctosaurus. Judging by the size of the gully, she guessed these would be of the smaller variety. That didn't make them any less dangerous, and she hoped they let her pass through their territory without attacking.

A few more steps. A scramble down a shallow slope. A

CHAPTER 33 - RIDLEY

maneuver between two stunted trees. Each movement made with excruciating care.

Ridley swallowed hard, her mouth as dry as sand. Sweat burned her eyelids, and an itch had formed between her shoulder blade. Please, don't attack. We mean you no harm.

Another trickle of rocks rained down, and a shadow flitted overhead, momentarily blocking the light. Harsh caws echoed through the space, bouncing from one wall to the other until they drilled into her ears with painful intensity.

The sound of flapping wings caused her eyes to widen, and Ridley looked up in time to see a pterosaur diving straight for her, claws and beak extended. There were more behind it, their winged shapes filling the narrow space. "Loki, run!"

Her warning came too late.

A blur of feathers and beaks descended on her, ripping and tearing at her flesh. A hank of hair was plucked from her scalp, and she screamed. "No! Stop!"

The ferocious creatures took no heed, continuing their vicious attack. Beaks stabbed at her head, neck, and shoulders. Claws tore at her arms and clothes while leathery wings beat about her head.

Blood poured from her wounds, and the smell of copper pennies filled her nostrils. She hacked at them with her ax, but there were too many. The creatures were everywhere, a whirlwind of death.

A flurry of vicious growls cut through the din, and Loki launched into the attack. He tore into the nearest flyer's wing, tearing the thin membrane to shreds. He snapped at another and crushed its head with a meaty crunch of bone and brain.

Taking heart, Ridley threw herself into the fray. A lucky blow with the ax cut through a pterosaur's body and hacked into another's chest. Blood misted the air, followed by pained squawks.

Baring his teeth, Loki pounced on another pterosaur as it sought to flee. Bearing it to the ground, he snapped the unfortunate creature's neck before jumping and catching another by the wing tip. Unable to fly away, the beast flapped in vain until Ridley finished it off with a backhand blow.

The remaining fliers shrieked with rage. They flew away, only to circle about overhead, and she knew they weren't finished. There were at least a dozen more of the creatures, too many to count, and she knew they had no choice but to run. "Go, Loki! Go!"

Loki streaked for the exit at the far side of the gully. A slender strip of blue sky beckoned to her with its promise of safety and succor.

Setting her sights on her goal, Ridley ran for her life. The passage was only a few yards away, but the rocky terrain hampered her progress, and she cursed every step of the way.

Another pterosaur dropped from above, the beat of its wings the only warning she got. Risking a backhanded slash, she felt the ax blade connect with a smack. The flyer shrieked and veered off, its claws brushing the top of her head.

Ridley yelped and quickly looked over her shoulders—more pterosaurs dove in for the kill, swooping overhead.

With a final burst of speed, she closed the distance, leaping over rocks and swerving around clumps of brush. Loki urged her on, his frantic barks ringing in her ears.

Another pair of claws raked across her shoulders, and she almost fell. Stumbling the last few feet, she burst into the open. The walls on either side fell away, and the brush thinned until she stood on a grassy slope.

CHAPTER 33 - RIDLEY

Whirling around, Ridley watched the pterosaurs wheeling about inside the gully. Their harsh cries caused her to wince, but they made no move to leave the safety of the walls. They returned to their nests one by one, leaving their dead and dying on the earth below.

With a sob of relief, Ridley fell to her knees. She reached for Loki and clung to his comforting form. He licked the blood and tears from her face, helping the only way he knew how.

Once she could calm down, she inspected him for injuries but found nothing except for a few shallow scratches. He'd gotten off lightly, unlike her.

She was covered in cuts, none deep, but they were everywhere. Wincing, she probed the worst of them, a gash in her upper arm that leaked a steady stream of blood.

Pulling a bandage from her backpack, she wrapped it around her arm as tightly as she dared. It would have to do until she reached the relief camp. Her plan of bypassing it and sleeping in the open had failed. Wounded and reeking of blood, she'd be a sitting duck for any predators in the vicinity. It had all been for nothing. She'd gambled on the shortcut and lost.

Filled with despair, Ridley got to her feet. "Come on, boy. Let's get out of here. We're sleeping at the camp tonight."

Chapter 34 - Ridley

Ridley stumbled into camp as darkness fell, her energy spent. The wound on her arm leaked blood in a steady stream, and she almost collapsed. Two relief workers rushed forward to assist her, and they half-dragged and half-carried her to the medical tent. They deposited her on the nearest stretcher and stripped her gear from her back.

Loki stuck to her side the entire time, not letting her out of his sight. He was just as tired and out of it as she was, the injury on his flank weeping blood.

"What the hell happened to you?" the medic on duty asked, grabbing a pair of gloves.

"Deadman's Gully," Ridley whispered, too tired to speak up. "Flyers attacked me."

"What possessed you to take that route? Everybody knows it's dangerous," the medic said. "Even the most seasoned racers giver it a miss."

"Yes, I know," Ridley replied, his recriminations further sapping her strength. The last thing she wanted or needed was a speech.

"You know? If you knew, you wouldn't be here covered in blood, worn out, and dehydrated," the medic said, handing her a bottle of water.

CHAPTER 34 - RIDLEY

"I'll be fine," Ridley said. "I just need some food, water, and rest."

"You need a lot more than that," he said, examining her injuries. "Stitches for starters."

"Stitches?"

"That's right. Now let me get a good look at you," the medic said, removing her jacket. He cut off her sleeve with scissors and tossed it aside.

"Hey, that shirt was new," Ridley protested.

"Not anymore," he said. "Now sit still and don't move."

Ridley obeyed, having no choice in the matter. She winced as he poked and prodded her wounds, disinfecting and bandaging the cuts. Afterward, he stitched up the deep slash on her shoulder and another on her scalp.

"The shoulder injury will leave a scar," he pronounced once finished.

Ridley shrugged. She didn't care about such things. Scars were just a reminder of the adventures you'd had. Stories told in blood. That was what her father said, anyway, and it made sense.

"This is a broad-spectrum antibiotic," the medic said, jabbing a needle into her upper arm.

"Thanks," she muttered, rubbing the sore spot afterward.

He turned away, rummaging in a drawer before returning with two plastic bags. Waving the first in her face, he said, "This is for pain. Take as needed, but no more than two tablets three times a day. Got it?"

"Yes, I've got it," Ridley said, taking the bag.

"And these are the rest of the antibiotics. Take one tablet twice a day until the course is finished. Do not skip or miss a tablet; you must take them all. Okay?"

"Yes, doc," Ridley said, tucking the medicine into her pocket. The medic's cutting tone was starting to grate on her nerves, and she wanted nothing more than to be done with him.

"Now, I suggest you get some food and rest. I'll arrange for your transport back to Vancouver in the morning."

"What? Why?" Ridley said, perking up.

"You're injured, dehydrated, and exhausted. You can't continue with the race. Not without risking your life," he said.

"I'm not giving up. I'm going on with the race," Ridley said, gritting her teeth against the pain in her shoulder.

The medic sighed, clearly exasperated. "Why are you so eager to throw your life away? Where are your parents? How can they allow this?"

"I'm old enough to make my own decisions, no matter what they are," Ridley said. "And I'm doing this for my father. He's missing, and I need the prize money to put together a proper search party."

The medic frowned. "How long has he been missing?"

"Four months. He left on a trade expedition and never returned," Ridley said.

"Four months? In that case, he's dead, and you're a fool," the medic said.

"Then I'm a fool, but I'm not giving up. You can either help me or leave me alone," Ridley said.

"I already helped you. There's nothing more I can do. If you really want to throw your life away, go ahead," the medic said. "It would be a waste of good stitches, however."

Ridley flashed him a sullen look. "Can you at least treat Loki's wounds too? I don't want him to get an infection."

"Only if you promise to think about what I said," the medic

CHAPTER 34 - RIDLEY

said.

Ridley hesitated, mulling it over.

"Please. Would your father have wanted you to risk your life for his?" the medic asked.

"Fine," Ridley said, his words hitting hard. "I'll think about it."

"Good," the medic said with an approving nod. "Let me know in the morning."

"Alright, thanks," Ridley said, grateful for his assistance even if he was an ass. She called Loki over and held him still while the medic checked him over. He had a few small cuts and abrasions, nothing serious except for the slash on his flank. A dab of disinfectant and a shot of antibiotics did the trick, and Loki was ready to go.

"Look after yourself," the medic said, watching with a critical gaze as she climbed off the stretcher. Grabbing her bag, she waved to Loki. "Come on, boy."

Ridley made her way to the nearest fire on legs that felt like jelly. She dumped her bag, sat beside the blaze, and stretched her hands to the flames. The heat was pleasant after the chill of the night, and her muscles slowly relaxed as warmth crept through her body.

Swallowing a yawn, she popped two painkillers and half the water the medic had given her. The rest of the water went to Loki while she removed the snake carcass from her bag. The meat was still good, and she fashioned a spit out of a couple of forked branches and a stick. The meat sizzled over the coals, the smell causing her mouth to water.

"At least we'll get a decent meal tonight," she told Loki. He sniffed the air and whined, every bit as impatient as she was. "Soon, boy. Soon."

While she waited for her food to cook, she visited the restrooms, washed up, treated her feet, and fetched more water from the medic tent. On her way back to the fire, she encountered Jara, the last person she wanted to see. She tried to step around the woman but found her path blocked.

"What do you want, Jara?" she asked.

"You made it again," Jara said. "Through Deadman's Gully, no less."

"Yeah, so?"

"I didn't think you had it in you."

"I guess you underestimated me."

"I guess so. It'll take more than a few missing mile markers to stop you," Jara said.

"That was you?" Ridley asked, her suspicions confirmed.

"Maybe," Jara said with a shrug.

"Is that the only way you can win? Through cheating?" Ridley asked.

"I don't need to cheat to win," Jara sneered.

"Oh? Then prove it," Ridley said, flashing Jara a challenging look.

Jara stared at her for a few seconds before she nodded. "Fine. Fair and square it is. If only to show you how easy it is for me to beat you."

"We'll see," Ridley said, watching as Jara stalked off into the night.

"That was brave," another voice said, appearing from the darkness.

"Maya?"

Maya nodded. "It's me."

"Do you think she'll play fair?" Ridley asked.

"I think so, yes."

CHAPTER 34 - RIDLEY

"Why?"

"You stood up to her. She respected that. Strength is the only thing Jara respects."

"I see," Ridley said, staring after Jara's receding figure. As much as she disliked the woman, there was also something different about her. Something hard but vulnerable.

"Are you okay?" Maya asked. "Do you need anything?"

"No, thanks. I'm okay," Ridley said.

"Okay, well. See you," Maya said.

Ridley returned to the fire in time to remove the snake from the coals. The skin was charred on the outside, but the flesh was tender and juicy. It was the first time she'd eaten a snake, and it reminded her a little of fish. Very flaky. "Do you like it, Loki?"

Loki didn't bother to answer, crunching through his portion at the speed of light. Soon, the snake was gone, leaving nothing but a picked-over carcass.

Ridley licked her fingers clean. "Time for bed, boy. We need our sleep."

Before she could lie down, however, a relief worker approached her. The young woman smiled at her, her eyes bright with curiosity. "Did you really go through Deadman's Gully?"

"Uh-huh," Ridley replied, trying not to yawn.

"You're so brave," the woman breathed.

"Or stupid," Ridley muttered, not feeling brave after her ordeal.

The woman produced a sheet of printed paper and a pen. "Will you autograph this for me?"

"What?" Ridley asked, eyeing the paper with suspicion.

"It's your story. Right there on the front page," the woman

replied.

"My story?" Ridley repeated, reaching for the paper. She read the header, surprised and shocked simultaneously: The Girl and the Wolf.

"The girl and the wolf?"

"That's you," the relief worker said.

"Me?" Ridley said, scanning the article.

Ridley, a young girl, tackles one of the most dangerous races on earth, accompanied only by her faithful companion, a wolf named Loki. Determined to win the prize, she's vowed to use the money to find and rescue her beloved father, Seth, who has been missing for several months. Originally from a small community in the South, she has traveled all this way on a hope and a dream—a dream to restore her family. Driven by bold determination and courage, she braved Deadman's Gully, a deadly shortcut avoided by all but the most desperate. Can this young woman survive the race? Does she have what it takes to win? Only time will tell.

"How do they know that stuff about my father?" Ridley exclaimed. "And Deadman's Gully?"

"I don't know about your father, but race information is exchanged daily via radio and drones."

"Ugh, it reads like a bad novel," Ridley said, shaking her head.

"No, it doesn't. It's wonderful," the woman said. "You're famous!"

Ridley snorted. "Famous, my ass. Half-dead is more like it."

She scanned the rest of the article, amused and horrified at once. It was more of the same, but one comment caught her attention.

"Ridley is not just any young girl. She's special, and I'd be happy to share my knowledge with anyone who visits our

CHAPTER 34 - RIDLEY

trade caravan in the Vancouver Market Square. " Rupert, Trader and Caravan Master.

"That son of a bitch," Ridley muttered, unable to believe her eyes. Still, she supposed she couldn't blame him. He had people to take care of—a family. If she was going to blame someone, it would be Allen Scott, the journalist who wrote the schmaltzy piece.

"Please autograph it for me," the relief worker pleaded.

"Er, sure. What's your name?"

"Emily."

Ridley signed the paper, her handwriting spidery and skew. Her arm hurt too much to make it look nice, but the girl appeared satisfied with the results.

"Good night, and thank you," Emily said. "I hope you win, and I hope you find your father one day."

"Thank you," Ridley said, crawling into her bed. She snuggled against Loki's warm form and remembered her promise to her father. His absence was like a thorn in her heart, a constant pain that wouldn't disappear. I have to win. I have to find him.

One thing was for sure. She had no intention of forfeiting the race or keeping her promise to the medic. In the morning, while it was still dark, she'd grab her things and slip out of the camp. And this time, she wouldn't let anything stop her from crossing the finish line.

Chapter 35 - Rogue

Rogue leaned against the balcony of the presidential suite at the Blue Water Guest House. It was around eight in the evening, and darkness had settled on the land. A chill wind cut through the air, the kind that sucked the heat from your bones, leaving you a shivering husk.

It didn't bother her, however. She'd just had a long hot shower and was dressed in flannel pajamas, a thick robe, and woolen slippers. A cup of hot chocolate warmed her innards, and soon she'd retire to a soft bed covered by a feather duvet and pillows.

Spread out below lay the city of Vancouver. Its lights twinkled like a thousand stars, mirroring the heavens above. The salty tang in the air spoke of the ocean, its vast blue depths stretching across the far horizon.

None of that occupied Rogue's thoughts, though. All she could think about was her daughter, running through the wilderness with only a crossbow for protection and a wolf for company.

Rogue had no way of knowing if Ridley was safe. She didn't know if she'd reached the relief camp at the end of the second day or if she was lost in the wilderness. Possibly hurt… or worse. She anxiously awaited an update from Imogen and didn't think she could last much longer.

When the door to the suite opened, admitting Olivia, Rogue whirled around and ran toward her mother. "And? Is she safe? Did she reach the relief camp? Tell me, please!"

"Calm down, dear," Olivia said, closing the door behind her. "You'll make yourself sick. You heard what the doctor said. Absolutely no stress."

"I don't care about that," Rogue insisted. "Just tell me about Ridley."

"She's safe," Olivia said.

"Oh, thank God," Rogue said, sagging with relief.

"She reached the second relief camp about an hour ago," Olivia added, a slight hitch in her voice.

Rogue noticed and straightened up. "Mom? What's wrong?"

"Nothing, dear. As I said, Ridley is safe and sound," Olivia said, looking away. "How about we celebrate with some hot chocolate and cookies?"

"Cut the crap, Mom. What aren't you telling me?" Rogue asked.

"Nothing. Everything is fine," Olivia said with a smile.

"I don't believe you. You're holding something back," Rogue said, advancing on her. "Either you tell me, or I'll march downstairs and find out myself."

"Okay, fine. I'll tell you, but you must promise to keep calm," Olivia said.

"Keep calm? Just spit it out," Rogue yelled, anger welling up inside her chest.

"Ridley took the shortcut through Deadman's Gully, and she got attacked by flyers," Olivia said.

"What?" Rogue cried, anxiety taking the place of anger. She

sucked in a deep breath, worry permeating every part of her being. "How bad is it?"

"She's cut up and bruised. Exhausted, of course, and she needs stitches on her arm and head," Olivia said.

"I can't believe this is happening," Rogue whispered, sinking down onto the nearest chair. "My poor baby. I must go to her straight away."

"It's already dark outside. You can't leave now," Olivia protested.

"Yes, I can," Rogue insisted, jumping back to her feet. "Start packing. I'm telling reception to contact Imogen right now. She must send a car or a truck around."

"This is ridiculous," Olivia said. "She's already arranged for transport to Chilliwack tomorrow morning."

"Tomorrow will be too late," Rogue said, running to the door. "I need to be with Ridley now."

"It's too dangerous to travel at night. Be reasonable, please," Olivia pleaded. "Ridley is fine. She's not hurt that badly, and she's receiving treatment as we speak."

"How do you know she's not hurt that badly?" Rogue cried, rounding on her mother. "You can't know for sure because you're not there."

"Rogue, please," Olivia began.

"I don't want to hear it, Mom. I have to…." Rogue gasped for air, a sudden wave of dizziness knocking her flat. She stumbled, trying to catch her breath, but it felt like a vice was constricting her chest.

"Rogue? Are you okay?" Olivia asked, rushing forward.

"I… I… can't breathe," Rogue said, reaching for her mother. Her heart was pounding so fast she thought it might burst through her rib cage. She felt dizzy, and the world spun

CHAPTER 35 - ROGUE

around her.

Suddenly, she was falling. The ground rushed up to greet her, and she found herself lying on the plush carpet. For a second, she marveled at how soft the fibers were against her cheek, her thoughts confused and chaotic.

"Rogue! Speak to me!" Olivia said, tapping Rogue on the cheek.

But to Rogue, her voice came from far away, echoing across a chasm that widened with each passing second. "M... Mom," she said, attempting to form a sentence, but her speech was slurred.

"Hold on, Rogue," Olivia said. "I'll be right back. I'm getting help."

Olivia rushed from the room, calling for Lee and Ric. "Ambulance! I need an ambulance. Rogue's ill. She collapsed."

Did I? Rogue wondered, faintly amused. *I don't feel ill, but Ridley is hurt. She needs me. I must go to her.*

But her muscles refused to cooperate, and her eyes dimmed as less and less oxygen reached her brain. The world faded away, replaced by a growing shadow.

The darkness was warm and comforting, and Rogue felt herself enveloped in its embrace. She tried to fight it, to cling to consciousness, but the pain in her chest was too great, and she was too weak to resist. So she let go, sinking into the darkness as it claimed her completely.

When she opened her eyes, Rogue was no longer in the hotel room. Instead, she was standing on a white sandy beach, the warm sun beating down on her skin. The ocean stretched out before her, a never-ending expanse of crystal blue water. But there was something strange about this place, something she couldn't quite put her finger on.

Then she saw a figure walking towards her, and her heart leaped into her throat. It was Seth, her husband, looking just like the last time Rogue had seen him.

Seth smiled at her, his bright green eyes shining with joy. "Rogue. You're here."

"Seth? Is it really you?" Rogue cried, running toward him.

"It's me, my love," Seth said, opening his arms.

Rogue threw herself into his embrace, tears streaming down her face. She had missed him so much, and the thought of being reunited with him was overwhelming. "I can't believe it," she whispered, burying her face in his chest. "I thought you were gone forever."

Seth held her tightly, stroking her hair. "I'll always be with you, my love. You know that."

Rogue breathed in his scent, feeling a sense of peace. "Is this real, or am I just imagining you?"

"Does it matter? I don't have to be real, do I? Just real to you," Seth asked.

"Am I dead?" Rogue asked, looking around.

Seth shook his head. "Not yet. But you will be soon if you don't go back."

"Why can't I stay with you?" Rogue pleaded, not wanting to leave Seth's side again, even if he was just a figment of her imagination.

"Because you have more to do in this world, Rogue," Seth said, his voice gentle. "You have a daughter who needs you, a family who loves you, and a life you've yet to live."

"But what if I can't do it? What if I'm not strong enough?" Rogue asked, feeling a weight settling in her chest.

Seth cupped her face in his hands, his gaze intense. "You are strong enough, Rogue. You've always been strong enough.

CHAPTER 35 - ROGUE

You just need to believe it."

Rogue took a deep breath, feeling a sudden surge of determination. "I'll go back," she said, pulling away from Seth's embrace. "For Ridley and myself."

Seth smiled at her, his eyes warm. "I knew you would."

As Rogue turned to leave, a thought occurred to her. "Wait, Seth. Can I see you again?"

Seth's smile grew wider. "Of course, my love. Whenever you need me, I'll be here."

Rogue nodded, feeling a sense of peace settle over her. She turned away from him and started to run, her feet sinking into the warm sand. The sun beat down on her back, and the sound of the ocean filled her ears. She ran until she was out of breath, until her legs ached, until she felt like she couldn't run anymore.

Then she was back in the hotel room, her mother and the paramedics hovering over her. Rogue gasped for air. She felt like she had been underwater for hours, like she had been holding her breath for too long.

"Rogue? Can you hear me?" Olivia asked, her voice strained.

Rogue nodded weakly, her eyes fluttering closed. She was back in the real world, but she knew that Seth was with her, watching over her. She felt a newfound sense of strength and determination, knowing that she couldn't give up now. She had to be strong for Ridley, her family, and herself.

"I'm okay," she whispered, her voice hoarse. "I'm going to be okay."

"Yes, you will. I'll take good care of you," Olivia said. "I promise."

"What about Ridley?"

"She'll be fine. She's strong. Just like you," Olivia said.

"But...."

"No buts. You need to take care of yourself now. Ridley has her own life, and it's time for you to let her go."

Rogue nodded, realizing it was true. She couldn't protect Ridley from everything. She had to make her own decisions now—her own mistakes.

The paramedics helped her onto a stretcher and wheeled her out of the room and into the ambulance.

As they drove to the hospital, Rogue closed her eyes and thought of Seth, feeling his presence with her even though he wasn't physically there. It felt like the past few months' grief fell away, easing the pain inside her heart. While he was still missing and probably dead, he wasn't gone. *He'll always be with me. Always.*

Chapter 36 - Ridley

As planned, Ridley woke early the following day. While it was still dark, she slipped out of bed, grabbed her gear, and left the camp without a backward glance. She was afraid the medic would try and stop her, and she wasn't about to let him take away her one shot at winning. What did he know anyway?

It was the third day of the race. She stood a chance at taking the lead by leaving long before the rest. She might win if she could keep going, skip the next relief camp, and strike out early on the fourth day. The question was, could she do it?

Ridley wasn't sure. The few hours of sleep she'd gotten wasn't enough to leave her fully rested. Her eyes burned, her brain was foggy, and her reactions were slow. To top it off, every muscle in her body ached, and the various injuries inflicted by the flyers stung with each movement.

Navigating in the dark wasn't easy either. The moment she left the camp's protection, she was on her own, and the darkness descended like a shroud. She'd left the camp without making a torch and rued that decision with each tentative step. Neither the moon nor the stars were much help, their silver light covered by a thick bank of clouds.

Finally, Ridley conceded defeat and stopped. "Loki, you'll have to help me. I can't see a thing." Removing a length of rope from her bag, she fashioned a rough harness for the wolf. He accepted the lead with some coaxing, having gotten used to it in Vancouver. With her hand on the rope, she said, "Lead the way, boy. But be careful."

Loki forged ahead, weaving a pattern through the trees and brush. He chose the flattest ground, skirting any dips and hollows. She followed, trusting in his senses to lead them safely.

The forest was grim and foreboding, the tree trunks like the pillars of some ancient sacrificial temple. Monsters lurked in the shadows, their teeth bared at the sight of her vulnerable flesh, or so her restless mind imagined. Nocturnal whoops and calls caused her to flinch, the slightest rustle in the bushes setting her teeth on edge. With her hand clutching the handle of her ax, she kept moving. *Just a little bit longer. Keep going.*

But the darkness seemed neverending. The constant barrage on her senses was exhausting. It sapped her strength and drained her will to keep going. She began to question her motives, her reasons, and her determination. *Why am I doing this? Is it really that important? Maybe I should give up.*

As if he sensed her wavering resolve, Loki nipped her hand, causing her to yelp. "Ow, what was that for?"

He nudged her with his nose, and she rubbed the sore spot with her other hand. "Okay, I get it. I'm acting like a crybaby."

He pulled on the rope, and Ridley continued walking. Step by step, she kept moving—anything to put distance between her and the camp. Toward dawn, the clouds cleared away, and the stars put in an appearance. While it was still dark, she could see better and sped up to a jog.

She'd passed the first five-mile markers by the time the sun rose. It wasn't what she'd hoped to accomplish, but it was

CHAPTER 36 - RIDLEY

better than nothing. Still, she'd lost a lot of time and needed to catch up. To do that, she had to eat first. Her stomach was empty, and her reserves were low. The same applied to Loki. "Alright, boy. Time for a quick break."

She removed several strips of dried meat and fat from her backpack, sharing it between her and Loki. Afterward, she poured him a bowl of water and emptied the rest of her canteen. Relieving her full bladder in the nearest bushes, she geared up again.

"Right, are you ready, boy? It's all or nothing now." Loki yipped and ran a few feet ahead, clearly eager to get going. With a smile, Ridley followed, glad to see he still felt his oats. *Nothing can get Loki down. Nothing.*

At first, she stuck to a moderate pace, allowing her muscles and joints to warm up. Once she hit her stride, she upped the pace and pushed her body to the limits. This was the time to build a lead. While the sun was up, the air warm, and her belly full.

The hours passed while she ran, never stopping. When she got thirsty, she took a swig or two from her canteen. When she got hungry, she chewed on nuts, seeds, or dried fruit until she felt nauseous. As hard as it was on them both, she didn't want to stop for even a second, afraid her muscles and joints would stiffen if she was inactive for too long.

Around noon, she crossed a small stream. The water was shallow, and she barely broke her stride. However, it was a lucky find for Loki, and he paused to quench his thirst before catching up to her.

The miles flew past, and her spirits rose. She was doing well. So well that she was sure she had to be in the lead. In her mind, she saw herself running across the finish line with

Loki. Her body would punch through the red ribbon, and the crowd would cheer, taking up a chant. *Ridley, Ridley, Ridley!*

It was an enchanting thought but also an illusion. Inevitably, reality set in. The brutal pace became too much for her body to maintain, her energy flagged, and her breathing grew labored. She stumbled and nearly fell but caught herself before she hit the ground. The sand was hot beneath her feet, and her throat was parched. She reached for her canteen and took a few sips, but it was almost empty. She should've refilled it at the stream, but it was too late to turn back now, and she gave the last bit to Loki. "Sorry, boy."

He looked at her with plaintive eyes, but she could only pray they'd stumble across a river. Pressing on, she focused on the horizon and ran until her legs ached and her lungs burned with exhaustion. Her lips cracked and bled, and her tongue felt like a dry stick in her mouth. There was no relief in sight—no chance for rest or recovery. Shoving a handful of trail mix into her mouth, she called to Loki. "Come on, boy. Let's go."

Late afternoon, she found the stream she so desperately needed and fell to her knees beside it. Plunging both hands into the water, she splashed the cool liquid on her face and gasped. "Oh, that feels so good."

She splashed more across her shoulders, chest, and head, relishing in the sensation. Loki followed her example, jumping and frolicking in the stream. That brought a smile to her lips, and she decided to rest for a few minutes.

The short break had revived her, and she ran with a lighter tread. She'd gotten her second wind. Or her third. Maybe it was her fourth? Whatever it was, it came at the right time, just when she needed it.

CHAPTER 36 - RIDLEY

However, her good mood was spoiled when dark clouds moved in, obscuring the sun. Thunder rumbled overhead. The wind picked up, whistling through the trees and churning the dead leaves on the forest floor into mini tornadoes. It tugged at her clothes and plucked at her hair like a fiendish foe. Shivering, Ridley kept going, intent on her goal. Pumping her arms and legs, she sped up, trying to outrun the storm. "Come on, Loki. Run!"

She was able to keep up the pace for an hour before the storm hit with its full force. The wind sped up to gale force, buffeting her from side to side. The trees shook and shuddered beneath the onslaught, and the rain poured down in sheets of silver. The rumbling thunder grew louder and louder until it vibrated through the earth and into her bones.

A deafening crack caused Ridley to jump with fright. Lightning flashed overhead and struck a nearby tree. The canopy exploded in a ball of flames, orange, red, and yellow lighting the dim clearing. Sparks rained down, turning to ash when they hit the sodden forest floor.

A tree swayed, its slim length creaking with each blast of the wind. Its wooden fibers split, and the base disintegrated from the stress. With a high-pitched moan, the tree toppled over and landed on the ground with a crash, missing Ridley by a hair's breadth. "Watch out, Loki!"

Another tree crashed down, shaking the ground beneath her feet. The rest swayed above her head in a nauseating display of nature's power, and she didn't know where to turn. When the third tree groaned before ponderously falling to the ground, she'd had enough. "Loki, on me!"

Frantic to escape, she swerved away from the destruction and ran downhill until she reached a stream. The water churned through the narrow strip, hemmed in on either side by steep muddy banks. Fed by the storm, the once tiny river had turned into a raging flood, filled with branches and other debris.

There was no way around the waterway, and Ridley judged it to be about waist deep. Desperate to find a way across, she spotted a couple of boulders sticking out above the water. Tightening the straps of her pack, she called to Loki and tied him to herself with a length of rope. With one hand entangled in his harness, she braved the river. "Come on, boy. Don't be scared. I've got you!"

The current nearly swept her off her feet, tugging at her legs and waist with icy fingers. She pushed ahead, wading through the water one step at a time. Near the middle, the levels rose to her chest, and panic rushed through her veins. Loki yelped when his head dipped underwater, his legs scrabbling for purchase.

Heaving herself forward, Ridley grabbed hold of the nearest rock. She pulled herself and Loki through the churning mess, using her free hand to hold on to the rocks.

She was almost across when a broken branch rolled toward her on a wave of water. She twisted to the side, shielding Loki with her own body. The branch hit her in the ribs, the broken end tearing through her skin and flesh. Crying out, she almost let go of the boulder, her fingers slipping on the wet surface. A fingernail tore loose, but she ignored it. It was just another hurt to add to the litany of others.

Gritting her teeth, Ridley heaved herself and Loki the last few feet across the stream and collapsed on the muddy bank. Almost crying, she hugged the wolf to her chest. "We made it, boy. We did it."

CHAPTER 36 - RIDLEY

He licked her face, just as happy as she was to escape the icy river of death. His warm tongue on her face revived her a little, and she untied the rope that bound them together with shaking hands. Next, she refilled her empty canteens and weighed up their options. "What do we do, boy? Where do we go?"

Loki barked and ran up the bank toward the shelter of a clump of bushes and deadfalls. Exhausted and shaking with the cold, Ridley dragged herself after him. The storm showed no signs of easing, and she realized they had to find shelter fast, or they'd freeze to death.

Examining the clump of vegetation, she discovered a small space between two fallen tree trunks wedged together against a rock. It wasn't much, but it was a start, and she quickly wove more branches, leaves, and twigs into the gaps above and around the area.

Afterward, she dug the hole deeper and placed her bedroll and blanket inside. She crawled into the space and used her backpack and weapons to block the entrance.

It wasn't ideal, but it was better than nothing. At least no predators could smell her with the storm, and she was safe enough for now. That drew her attention to the dull ache in her ribs, and she lifted her shirt to examine her body.

"Mother of…. Ow!" she yelled, poking the area. The flesh was bruised and torn where the branch hit her in the side, and blood seeped out in a steady trickle.

Grabbing her first-aid kit, she disinfected and bandaged the site before moving on to her other injuries: The torn fingernail, the stitches on her shoulder and scalp, and the blisters on her feet. Loki got the same treatment, and she drank her antibiotics and painkillers.

"Thanks, Doc. You were an ass, but I owe you one," Ridley muttered, burrowing deeper into her nest. Pulling the blankets up around her and Loki, she listened to the storm raging overhead.

A force of nature, it bombarded the earth and its creatures with thunder and lightning while the wind scoured the surface and sheets of rain soaked the soil. The temperature dropped beneath the bitter onslaught, permeating the atmosphere with an icy touch.

Ridley had never felt so scared or helpless and clung to Loki's familiar warmth. He whimpered in her arms, just as frightened as she was, and her heart bled for him. "I'm sorry, boy. I shouldn't have dragged you out here."

Lying there, she wondered if they'd ever make it to the finish line. Or would they die out in the storm? Fried by lightning or drowned by a flash flood? These thoughts and worries swirled around until she drifted into a fitful sleep. Ultimately, her only consolation was that nobody else could run in the storm either.

Chapter 37 - Ridley

Ridley didn't want to get up. She didn't even want to move. The rain had seeped into her rough shelter, soaking her and Loki to the bone. Huddled together, they tried to keep each other warm, but to no avail. She knew she should get up and move. It would be warmer, but she couldn't summon the will. She was too tired.

Give up. Just give up, a harsh voice whispered in her ear.

In the end, it was Loki who got her up and going. He licked her face, whining over and over. Wriggling out of their miserable shelter, he tugged at her clothes with his teeth, urging her to get up.

"Go away, Loki," Ridley said, swatting him away.

He ignored her and kept pulling on her pants.

Finally, she couldn't take it anymore and got up. Wiping her face, she pulled her sodden hair into a rough ponytail and peeled off her wet clothes. Thankfully, the spare set in her bag was still dry and felt good against her damp skin. She ate the last of her trail mix, gave Loki the last of her dried meat, drank the last of her water, and pulled on her last pair of clean, dry socks—the last of everything. *Now, there's no turning back.*

Today, she had to reach the finish line or die trying. The

others probably thought she was dead, lost somewhere in the wilderness. She hadn't shown up at the last relief camp, and they'd probably send out a search party soon.

The other racers would set out at dawn, vying for first place, not realizing she'd pulled ahead. It gave her an advantage, but a small one, just like her hold on life. If she didn't start running soon, she never would.

Forcing herself to get up, Ridley set out into the darkness. Once again, she had no torch. No light to guide her. However, some greater power must've been looking out for her because the dark clouds cleared away, revealing a full moon.

The silver orb shone down on the earth below, granting her enough sight to keep moving. At a slow jog, she hit the trail, each step an agonizing effort of will.

Loki ranged ahead, his every sense on high alert, and she watched him carefully. When he shied away from a clump of bushes, she gave them a wide berth, trusting his instincts.

The hours wore on. One, two, three.

Finally, it was sunrise, and the horizon lightened with the first rays of dawn. She embraced the heat, tilting her head back to enjoy the sun's golden glow. It helped to lighten the load, both on her body and her mind. Each step became easier than the last. The constant movement drove the chill from her body, and the sharp pain in her muscles faded to a dull ache.

She picked up the pace, envisioning the finishing line. It was only a few miles away, and she imagined crossing it first. She burst through the red ribbon, her arms flung wide with Loki at her side. Thunderous applause would greet her victory, and she'd be showered with riches—enough to help her find her father.

CHAPTER 37 - RIDLEY

The memory of her dad caused a sharp stab of pain in her chest. She missed him more than life and couldn't wait to see him again. To see his smile cheering her on, encouraging her to be her best. He'd always been her biggest fan and her biggest cheerleader.

She missed her mother too. More than she'd thought possible. She regretted their fight now, realizing that it was petty and unimportant. What did it matter when weighed against everything else? *When I see her again, I'll apologize, hug her tight, and tell her how much I love her.*

These thoughts buoyed her spirits, and she ran at a good clip, eating up the last few miles between her and her goal. She was going to win. She was sure of it.

As the sun rose overhead, she burst into the open, leaving the forest behind. In the distance, she spotted a field of white-capped tents surrounded by the ever-present chain-link fence and armed guards. A sandy track stretched out to greet her, adorned with colorful streamers, flags, and balloons. At the far end was an arch complete with a red ribbon, waiting to be broken by the winner. It was the finishing line.

With an eagle-eyed gaze, she scanned the empty field between her and the end of the race. The area was empty. There was no sign of the other contestants. That meant one of two things. Either she was dead last... or she was first. Considering the ribbon was unbroken, she knew she was first.

Joy bubbled up her chest, and she whooped with sheer happiness. "We did it, Loki! We're first!"

Loki ran ahead, every bit as excited as she was. He flew across the packed earth like a gray bullet, and she followed. Pumping her arms and legs, she ran as fast as she could, giving it everything.

The distance shrank until she could make out the crowd lining the final yards between her and the finish. They cheered and waved when they saw her, music adding to the chaotic blend of noise and colors. The air vibrated with their excitement, sending a thrill running down her spine.

A man in a tower studied her with his binoculars, the lens flashing in the sun. Picking up a loudspeaker, he announced. "The Girl and her Wolf are in the first place."

The girl and her wolf? Didn't she have a name? Ridley thought with a touch of annoyance, but she didn't care. Not when victory was so close at hand. Calling Loki, she said, "Come on, boy. Let's cross the line together."

Loki heard her command and turned back, hurtling toward her. He streaked across the ground, his tongue lolling from his jaws. She smiled and reached out to greet him. All she wanted was for the two of them to cross together. They were a team, after all.

Suddenly, a terrible howl tore from Loki's throat, a mixture of agony and fright. His front leg snapped with an audible crunch, and he went down hard. Dirt and pebbles sprayed in every direction, and a cloud of dust obscured his form.

"Loki, no!" Ridley cried, shock and horror flashing through her body. She sprinted toward him and fell to her knees beside him. "Loki, what's wrong?"

Loki whimpered, his eyes filled with liquid pain. He held up a broken front leg, the bone sticking out of the flesh at a monstrous angle. Blood leaked from the ugly wound, crimson on bone. White on red.

Ridley shook her head. "This can't be happening. I'm so sorry, boy. This is all my fault."

CHAPTER 37 - RIDLEY

Loki whined, thrusting his nose into her hand. He needed her help and trusted her to look after him in his time of need. She looked around for help, but there was none. She was all he had.

Realizing that she was on her own, Ridley got to her feet. She dumped her gear on the ground. It would only weigh her down. Bending down, she picked Loki up and cradled him to her chest. Taking care not to jostle his broken leg, she began to walk.

One step.

Two steps.

Three steps.

Over her shoulder, she spotted the first of the other racers emerge from the forest and enter the field. Two men were in the lead, followed by Maya, Jara, and Zeke. Behind them, the rest followed one by one.

There was still time. She could win if she left Loki in the field, injured and alone. She could cross the finish line, claim her prize, and return for him with medical help.

Never.

She could never treat him like that. He was her friend. Her best friend. Her only friend. "Don't worry, Loki. I'm here for you."

She kept walking, the other racers closing in behind her. One by one, they passed her by, their looks curious but unaffected. None of them would give up their chance at winning for her and Loki. Not even Maya.

Ridley ignored them, focused on getting Loki to safety. Every minute she wasted was another minute he spent in pain. Gritting her teeth, she picked up the pace, pushing through the exhaustion. Everything hurt. Every bone and muscle in her body ached. Her breath came in ragged gasps, and a blister on her heel popped, warm liquid dampening her sock. Still, she walked.

The first contestant crossed the line, breaking the ribbon to the faltering cheers of the crowd. As thrilling as it was to have a winner, all eyes were on Ridley carrying her wolf. The other racers followed, each finishing the race at their own pace. She'd officially lost the race, but it didn't matter anymore. All that mattered was Loki.

The distance closed, and Ridley entered the final stretch. Twin rows of spectators lined the field, a sea of faces staring at her. A profound hush had fallen over the scene, and no sound could be heard. Even the wind had stopped blowing, and the colored banners hung limp overhead.

The sheer weight of it all drove Ridley to her knees. Her legs buckled under the strain, and she fell to the ground. Loki yelped, nearly slipping from her arms, but she held on. She tried to get back to her feet but failed. Her strength was spent. She'd finally hit the wall, and there was no way around it. Closing her eyes, she whispered, "I'm sorry, boy. I'm so sorry."

Whispers rose from the crowd. Soon, it became a chant, the words as clear as day.

Ridley.

Ridley.

Ridley.

They're cheering for me, she realized, hot tears brimming on her eyelids. *They care. They really care.*

With a monumental effort, Ridley climbed to her feet. She stood swaying like a reed, each muscle in her body screamed. Placing one foot in front of the other, she took a step.

And another.

CHAPTER 37 - RIDLEY

And another.

The finish line drew closer. It crept toward her in inches, each requiring a battle of wills.

Finally, she stepped across the chalky white border. The crowd burst into wild cheers, and the other racers surrounded her, squeezing her shoulders, slapping her on the back, and congratulating her.

Maya was there. Jara too.

"I didn't think you had it in you, squirt, but you made it. You finished the race," Jara said. "I knew you wouldn't win, though."

"Neither did you," Ridley replied.

To her amazement, Jara burst out laughing. "See you next year. You and your dog."

"Wolf," Ridley yelled after Jara's retreating back.

"Congratulations, Ridley," Maya said, grinning from ear to ear.

"For what?" Ridley asked. "I came last."

"You finished the race, kiddo, and that's more than most people can say!"

Ridley stared at her, surprised. Then she realized it was true. *I did it. I finished. I finished the 10th Annual Vancouver to Chilliwack Endurance Race!*

Chapter 38 - Ridley

For a few moments, surrounded by well-wishers and onlookers, Ridley bathed in the glow of their adoration. It was an intoxicating sensation, but it was fleeting as well. Temporary.

What truly mattered was Loki and his need for medical assistance. Looking around, she yelled, "Doctor. I need a doctor, please!"

The crowd parted, and three people rushed forward with a stretcher. A woman with graying hair and kind eyes reached for Loki. "I'm a doctor. I'll take care of him."

With relief, Ridley released Loki into the woman's care. "Can I come with you?"

"Of course. Follow me," the Doctor said, leading the way to the medical tent.

Inside, the doctor and her assistants sprang into action. They set up an IV line, injected Loki with painkillers and sedatives, and examined his leg.

Ridley watched it all with worry gnawing at her throat. She couldn't bear for anything to happen to him, and guilt lay heavy on her heart. *It's my fault. I shouldn't have called him back to my side. I should've let him run.*

Finally, the doctor turned to her. "It's not as bad as it looks. It's a clean break, and I can set it quite easily. He'll be off his

CHAPTER 38 - RIDLEY

feet for a while, but he'll be just fine."

Ridley sobbed with relief, overwhelmed. She reached out and touched Loki's head. "You hear that, boy? You're going to be okay."

Smiling gently, the doctor led her to the tent's exit. "I need to work on him now, and it would be better if you weren't here to see it. It can be quite painful for loved ones to witness."

"Are you sure?" Ridley asked, loathe to leave Loki's side.

"I'm sure. I'll call you when he wakes. I promise," the doctor said.

"Okay," Ridley said, feeling lost. "But what do I do now?"

"Why don't you go to your friends?" the doctor suggested.

"Friends? I don't have any friends here," Ridley said, shaking her head.

"Oh, I think you do," the doctor replied, pointing to a couple waving feverishly at Ridley. The guards were holding them back, but their urgency was apparent.

"Jessica! Bear!" Ridley cried, amazed and relieved to see them. "I'm so happy to see you. You made it!" She rushed past the guards and into their waiting arms.

"Of course, we're here. We promised, didn't we?" Jessica said, pulling Ridley into a fierce hug. Bear enveloped them both in his arms, and they stood like that for a long time.

Finally, Ridley pulled away. "You know?"

"Yes, sweetheart. We saw it all. Is Loki alright?" Jessica asked.

"The doctor said it's a clean break. He'll be okay," Ridley said, wiping the tears from her face.

"Oh, my dear, sweet child. I'm so proud of you," Jessica exclaimed.

"We both are," Bear added, squeezing her arm.

Ridley stared at them in confusion. "What for? I lost the race."

"You lost?" Jessica cried. "You didn't lose, sweetheart. You won the admiration of everyone who saw you walk over that finish line."

"I did?" Ridley asked, feeling confused but also hopeful.

"Yes, you did, and I could not be prouder than I am right now," Jessica pronounced. "Heart, Ridley. You have heart."

"Really?" Ridley said, moved to tears once more.

"Really. Now, wipe away your tears, and let's get you fixed up. You look awful."

Ridley managed a laugh. "I guess I do."

"Afterward, you can meet your new fans," Jessica prompted. "There's that journalist, too. What's his name? Allen Scott."

Ridley pulled a face. "That guy? I've got a lot to say to him as well."

"Don't be too hard on him. He did make you famous," Jessica said with a laugh.

Ridley frowned. "I never wanted fame. I wanted my dad."

"We can talk about that later, sweetheart," Jessica said. "I booked a room at a nearby guest house. You can wash, eat, and rest up there."

"What about Loki?" Ridley asked.

"He's in good hands for now, and when he's ready to travel, we'll take him home," Jessica said.

"Home? I like the sound of that," Ridley said, and for the first time, she knew what it really meant. *Home.*

Epilogue I - Ridley

Several days later, Ridley packed her stuff and left it outside her door in the hallway. A driver would pick it up later and load it in the truck. It had all been carefully arranged by Imogen. Their transport from Chilliwack to Vancouver, their accommodation in Vancouver, and their final return to Prime City and the Zoo.

Imogen's generosity did not come without strings, however. Ridley was expected to appear at several functions and complete interviews with newspapers and magazines. She was the Girl with the Wolf now, even if she didn't win the race.

While she didn't look forward to it, Ridley was willing to do it for her mother and Loki's sake. Both needed medical treatment of the kind she couldn't afford, and Imogen was willing to sponsor them both.

Looking at the room that had been her home for the past few days, Ridley marveled at how much had changed. At how much she had changed. Even the mirror told a different story. She'd finally grown up, realizing how childish and rebellious she'd been.

Her mother's illness had come as a shock, and she looked forward to seeing Rogue again. She needed to apologize for the things she'd said and done. Needed to make up for all the wrongs she'd committed. *I'm sorry, Mom. I hope I see you soon. Then I can tell you how much I love you in person.*

A knock on the door drew her attention, and she turned around. "Hello?"

Jessica's smiling face popped around the corner. "Ready to go, sweetheart?"

"Yes, I am," Ridley said with a firm nod.

"Feeling better?" Jessica said.

"Much better," Ridley confirmed, looking down at her body. She'd filled out since the race, losing the gaunt look and hollow cheeks she'd sported after finishing the race. She still had stitches on her head and shoulder, and her feet still looked horrendous, chafed, and blistered, but she felt miles better. She was rested, fed, bathed, and treated.

As she left the guesthouse, Ridley waved at the small crowd waiting to see her off. She stopped to sign a few papers and race tickets, doing her best to seem pleasant and friendly. It still felt strange, however, being noticed and recognized everywhere she went.

Jessica told her it would blow over soon. She just had to be patient, and Ridley fervently hoped it was true. She did not want to live her life in the spotlight and longed for an end to her current fame.

With a sigh of relief, she climbed into the truck, shutting the crowd out with a firm click. Loki lay on the seat beside her, his splinted leg cushioned against the journey.

His tail thumped on the seat when he spotted her, and he whined softly until she lavished attention on him. "Loki! There's a good boy. Did you miss me?" she cried, ruffling his fur and rubbing his ears. He licked her on the cheek, and she mock squealed. "Eeew, gross. Doggy slobber!"

He threw her a look, and she backtracked quickly. "Sorry, I meant wolf slobber. It's still gross, though!" He laughed, eyes crinkling while his tongue lolled from his jaws.

Feeling complete for the first time in days, Ridley settled into the seat, one hand resting on Loki's ruff. With him at her side, she was ready to face anything, no matter how terrifying. "Remember what I told you as a puppy? The first time I saw you?"

Loki shot her a quizzical look, not sure what was expected of him but knowing she wanted something.

"I said, one day, you and I will have grand adventures. That's a promise." Ridley smoothed her hand over his flank. "And we did, didn't we? We had a grand adventure."

Loki's tail thumped the seat again, whacking her in the face. She laughed and pushed it aside. "Don't worry. There will be more adventures. This isn't the last. It's you and me against the world, boy."

Snuggling into her seat, Ridley laid her head on Loki's back and closed her eyes. It was time for a well-deserved nap. After all, they'd need their strength, for who knew what the morrow would bring?

Epilogue II - Rogue

Rogue drifted in and out of consciousness, her mind floating in a fog of memory. Memories were the only stuff that meant anything to her. The only things she could hold onto for any amount of time. The rest kept slipping away, and she couldn't hold onto anything but the past.

At one point, she was a young girl again, playing with her friends in the schoolyard. Her teacher called to her once the break was over. "Lilian, come inside!"

Lilian.

That used to be her name.

At least it used to be until the Shift.

It happened so quickly. A shimmering curtain that was there one moment and gone the next. Her classmates disappeared, along with the teacher and most of the room. She was left on the other side, frightened and alone in a world full of monsters.

Not for long.

The fog shifted, and she was Rogue again—a young woman scouring the streets for an easy score. A pickpocket and a thief, she stole food to survive until disaster struck. The theft of an egg cost her everything, and she was exiled from her home: Prime City.

EPILOGUE II - ROGUE

She thought it was the end, but it was only the beginning. What followed was a grand adventure filled with wonderful people, amazing friends, and more. She rediscovered her long-lost mother and met the love of her life, Seth. She could never regret stealing that egg, though she did regret the people who got hurt along the way.

The fog shifted again, and she thought of Seth. Seth, her husband, and her soulmate. He was missing. Gone. Lost. So was her daughter. *Ridley? Where are you?*

"I'm here, Mom. I'm right here," Ridley said.

"Ridley? Is that you?" Rogue asked. "It can't be you. You're gone. You ran away."

"Why is she so confused?" Ridley asked, her voice drifting somewhere in the void.

"It's the sedatives. We kept her under to give her system time to heal, but it should wear off soon," another voice replied.

"Okay, thanks," Ridley said.

"I'll give you a few more minutes, but you must not tire her too much. She needs her strength."

"Alright. I won't," Ridley replied.

"Is that really you, Ridley?" Rogue asked, desperate to be sure.

"Yes, it's me, Mom," Ridley replied. The fog parted, and Ridley's face appeared above her bed. "It's really me. I promise."

"I'm so glad to see you. I was so worried," Rogue said, tears of joy running down her face.

"I'm sorry, Mom. I'm sorry about everything," Ridley said. "That stupid fight we had, the things I said, running away... all of it."

"I'm sorry too. I tried to protect you, but I held on too tight,"

Rogue said. "I suppose I've always held on too tight, afraid to lose you."

"I understand, and it's okay," Ridley said.

"What about the race? Did you win?" Rogue asked.

"No, I lost," Ridley said. "I came in last, actually."

"It doesn't matter," Rogue said. "I'm sure you gave it your all. It's what you do."

"I did, Mom. I gave it everything I had," Ridley said.

"Are you happy?" Rogue asked.

"I am, and I'll be even happier once you're healed and back on your feet," Ridley said. "So, you'd better get well, okay?"

"Okay," Rogue said, her heart full to bursting. "Now, sit down and tell me all about the race."

"Are you sure you're up for it?"

"Of course I am. Don't leave anything out. Not one single detail," Rogue said, patting the bed next to her. "I want to hear it all."

Ridley grinned and sat down in the empty space. Her expression was animated when she talked, relaying the story bit by bit. Her hands waved around, drawing pictures in the air while her body shifted this way and that. She was quite the storyteller, weaving a tale of daring do, embellishing many of the details, no doubt.

The nurse came and went, checking on her. The attendee brought lunch: Roast chicken, rice, and carrots. Jelly with custard. The doctor did his rounds, horrified to find Ridley still there, tiring her mom.

Rogue chased them all away, determined to catch up on everything Ridley had gone through while she was gone. What she'd done. What she'd learned. What she felt about it. She wanted to know it all.

She asked a few questions. Questions about Loki, Bear, and Jessica. She wanted to make sure they were okay and that everything was as it should be.

It was. Or so Ridley assured her.

Rogue watched as much as she listened, memorizing every tiny feature of her daughter's face. It reminded her so much of Seth. They had the same coloring, mannerisms, laugh, and determination. It made her realize he wasn't gone. Not really. A piece of him would always live on in their daughter. Always.

Epilogue III - Seth

Seth lay shivering in his cell, the damp straw doing nothing to dispel the chill. He huddled close to Ronnie while Reed lay at his back. They'd learned to sleep like that, sharing their bodily warmth, however meager it might be. If they didn't, they would die from the cold.

Despite it being late spring, the damp, concrete cells held no warmth, and their threadbare clothing did nothing to help. Starved and skinny, their bodies were down to their last reserves. They had no body fat or energy to spare—nothing to fight off the daily depredations they faced.

Desperate and without hope, Seth knew they had to escape soon. If they didn't, they would die in captivity. It was as simple as that. *I can't die in here. Not like this. Trapped, beaten, and treated like a slave. If I die, it must be as a free man underneath the open skies.*

Closing his eyes, he reviewed what they'd learned over the past weeks. It wasn't much. Nuggets of information gleaned over the course of their days and pieced together like a quilt until it told a story.

Every morning at dawn, they were fed. Thin gruel and moldy bread so hard it nearly broke one's teeth.

Afterward, they were marched outside to continue clearing

the fields in readiness for the winter crops. Once the task was accomplished, they'd return to their duties inside the prison, making it harder to escape. Therefore, they had to run before that happened.

It would not be easy, though. The fields were surrounded by a stone wall, towers, and guards armed with guns. Automatic rifles.

He was almost sure the guns were for show, however. He'd gotten a closer look once, and the magazines were empty. They had no bullets. If they did possess a few, it was just for show.

The guards changed shifts at noon. Three fresh guards came to replace the old ones.

The morning shift was more alert than the afternoon shift. Especially the guard called Shanks. Sadistic and cruel, he liked to play with the prisoners. Therefore, they had to escape in the afternoon.

Seth had found a weak spot in the wall. Several stones protruded from its rough surface, providing foot and handholds. They could scale the wall and run to the forest if they were quick. From there, it was a simple matter of escaping.

Despite the other's reservations, he was sure he could get them away. All they had to do was hide their tracks from their pursuers. Even food and water didn't bother him. He was confident he could find enough to keep them alive and moving. Enough to let them escape and make it back home.

It was what he was good at, after all. Surviving, hunting, tracking, running, and foraging. The wilderness held no mystery or fear for him. He wasn't afraid of it or its inhabitants. He admired nature, and he respected its creatures, big or small. He was part of it. He belonged.

The thought of escape reminded him of better days. Days when he did what he wanted, when he wanted, with who he wanted. It was funny how much more it meant to him now. How much more he appreciated what he'd had and lost.

Escape. Freedom. Liberty. Love. Hope. Family.

They were such small words with such significant meanings. Within the span of a few letters lay an infinite universe of thought, feeling, and emotion. Things most people took for granted. That he took for granted when he still had it, but no more.

Tomorrow, he decided, his mind made up. It was tomorrow or never. If they waited any longer, they wouldn't have the strength to escape. They'd die in their cell, lost and forgotten. *Tomorrow. Tomorrow, we run.*

The End.

But wait! There's more. Primordial Earth - Book 2 is now available on Amazon. Secure your copy today and continue the adventure.

https://www.amazon.com/dp/B0C3F7V3CD

EPILOGUE III - SETH

Plus, there's more. Turn the page for a sneak peek at Primordial Earth, the series that began it all. Available here: https://www.amazon.com/dp/B0BPT8XXS2

Do you want more?

So we've reached the end of Primordial World - Book 1, and I really hope you enjoyed reading the book as much as I enjoyed writing it. If you did, please leave a review and help other readers discover the story too.

Even better, Primordial World - Book 2 is now available on Amazon. Find out what's next in store for our intrepid heroes, Ridley and Loki. Plus, I've included a sneak preview of the book for your enjoyment. Happy Reading!

Chapter 1 - Seth

Seth woke well before dawn, unable to sleep despite the exhaustion that dragged at his limbs. Huddled between Reed and Ronnie, he tried to preserve the meager body heat coursing through his veins. It was a losing battle, the morning chill leaching into his bones. Shivering, he sat upright and rubbed his arms and legs briskly.

The rest of the group awoke one by one, each more miserable than the last. Ronnie coughed, a phlegmy sound that worried Seth. If his friend didn't receive treatment soon, it would likely devolve into pneumonia—a death sentence.

"Here. Have some water," Seth said, offering him the jug.

"Thanks," Ronnie said, but he only took a sip before handing it around. They never got enough of anything, including water, and had to ration every drop.

Seth got the last sip, grateful for the bit of moisture it provided. Afterward, he relieved himself in the stinking bucket in the corner before turning his gaze to the tiny window.

The first rays of sunlight hit the rectangular opening, and the interior flooded with gold. Dust motes glittered in the light, floating around them like tiny fireflies. It was the only time of day that the cell was bearable. A brief moment in time when he could pretend he was somewhere else.

Keys rattled in the metal door, and the edge scraped across the uneven concrete floor as it swung open. "Eat up, and be quick about it," a voice said, and a wooden tray filled with crusts of hard bread and scraps of meat slid through the opening.

Seth hunkered down next to the food and carefully divided it into equal portions. The rest joined him, and they chewed on the skimpy rations one bite at a time. As hungry as they were, they'd learned to savor their food. It was all they'd get until noon.

The guard at the door handed them a fresh jug of water and stood waiting while they finished their meal. Afterward, he waved to the other guard, and the prisoners filed out of the cell in a single row. They kept their heads down and their pace measured, anything not to arouse the ire of the guards. Short-tempered and mean, they doled out punishment for the most minor infractions.

The last prisoner out of the cell carried the toilet bucket. Once outside, he'd empty it into a pit and wash it with dirty water from the mop buckets. He'd also throw a layer of sand into the bottom to help with the smell. It was a job they took turns at, as with everything else in their lives. Or the hollow shells their lives had become.

Still, today was different. Today was the day they escaped. It was decided. Come hell or high water, the day would end with their freedom or deaths.

Seth could feel the heat of rebellion rising within him as he followed the other prisoners out of the cell and into the dank hallway. This was it. The moment they had been planning for the past few weeks. As they made their way to the work yard, Seth took note of every detail around him, ready for anything.

The prison building was almost as bad as his cell. A dank, dark building made from bare rock and concrete; its walls stank of mold, and its ceiling dripped whenever it rained. The bathrooms stank of piss, shit, and blood, and Seth was thankful they no longer had to clean them. Working out in the stony fields was hard, backbreaking labor, but it was clean work.

People walked up and down the corridors, sat at steel tables in the common room, or lounged outside in one of the many courtyards, their expressions blank and their eyes empty. They seemed no better off than the prisoners, and it was no wonder the guards were so mean.

Once outside, Seth and the rest were put to work, breaking rocks with pickaxes and hauling them away in wheelbarrows, and the hours passed slowly. The sun beat down on them, and sweat dripped from their foreheads and backs. Their bellies ached with hunger, and their tongues grew dry in their mouths.

Around noon, they stopped for a short break, hunkering

down on broken rocks and sharing the meager rations they received. It was more of the same. Scraps of meat, bread, and a jug of water. Only this time, there was an apple for each of them. Wrinkled and old, but whole.

Seth stared at the fruit in amazement, and saliva flooded his mouth. He hadn't had an apple in months. He bit into the grainy flesh and relished the burst of sweetness on his tongue. It was the best thing he'd ever had, and he closed his eyes to savor the moment.

After the quick meal, the group lingered for a few seconds, slow to return to their work. One of the guards noticed and barked, "Get back to work before I break each one of your fingers!"

It was Shanks, the cruelest of the bunch. He was a sadistic man who delighted in causing pain, and the prisoners were his favorite toys. The group jumped to obey his commands, unwilling to risk his anger.

Seth followed suit but exchanged a determined glance with Reed and Ronnie. Now more than ever, they had to escape from their prison. It was either that or a slow and painful death beneath Shanks' gloating gaze. Glancing at the rest of the group, he whispered, "Are you guys ready?"

One by one, they nodded, their eyes cast low so as not to arouse suspicion. Billy, Jerry, Finn, Liam, Boyd, and Wallace. They'd all agreed the night before.

"Remember, wait for my signal," Seth whispered, his green eyes darting between the guards and the wall that loomed a short distance away. All he could think about was his family, the faces of those he loved swimming before him like ghostly apparitions. He had to get back to them. Failure wasn't an option.

The group nodded again before returning to their labor, each taking up a position as close to the wall as possible.

Seth swung his pickax through the air, splitting a rock in half. Grunting, he dug the pieces out of the hard ground and loaded them onto a waiting wheelbarrow. The sharp edge of a rock cut his palm, and he swore under his breath. Blood welled from the cut, and he sucked on it with his mouth. Though not deep, it could get infected, especially in their living conditions. It was just another reason to escape. Another reason to take a chance at freedom.

He scanned the area, keeping an eye on the guards. They were clustered in a group by the prison entrance, chatting and laughing among themselves. Seth's heart raced with anticipation. Soon, the new guards would arrive, and their attention would be everywhere except with the prisoners. Surrounded by high walls, they stood little chance at escape—captives by design.

Seth's heart pounded as the clock ticked closer to shift change. He wiped his bloody hand on his shirt, not caring about the mess. The plan was set, but he couldn't ignore the fear that threatened to consume him. What if they failed? What if they were caught?

He looked up and saw Shanks watching him with a smirk on his face. Seth wanted to glare back, defiance burning in his chest, but he dared not. The plan could not fail just because of his pride.

The bell signaled the end of the guards' shift, and the prisoners watched as the new group exited the building. They mingled with the old, talking and laughing while the prisoners went unheeded.

Seth gripped the handle of his pickax, swung it to his

shoulder, and glanced at his group. "Now!"

The word was uttered in a fierce whisper, and the prisoners exploded into action. With a burst of speed, they dashed towards the wall, muscles straining and lungs burning.

Seth's legs felt like they were filled with molten lead, but he pushed forward, driven by desperation and determination. Behind him, the alarm went off as the guards caught on. He darted a look over his shoulder and spotted Shanks yelling at them to stop, his face puce with rage.

Ignoring the guards, Seth reached the wall a few steps ahead of the others. He tossed his pickax to the other side and vaulted over the top, barely clearing the jagged rocks. The ground rushed up to meet him, and he landed with a grunt, pain shooting through his legs.

Ronnie and Reed were right behind him. They threw their tools over the wall, scaled it, and dropped down on the other side. There, they lingered, casting anxious looks at Seth.

"Go! Run for the forest," Seth shouted, waving them on.

"No, not without you," Ronnie said, shaking his head. Picking up their pickaxes, they waited with grim determination on their faces.

Grateful for their support, Seth turned back to the wall. "Give me a boost."

Ronnie helped him up, and he straddled the wall, searching for the rest of his group. Finn and Liam were the closest, followed by Billy and Jerry. With the kind of speed granted by fear and adrenalin, they scaled the wall.

That left only Wallace and Boyd, the oldest and weakest of the bunch. They lagged several steps behind, and Seth waved at them with growing desperation. "Come on. Come on"

The guards were out in full force and stormed across the

distance with roars of anger. They'd reach the wall within seconds, right behind Shanks, who was gaining on Wallace and Boyd with every step.

Boyd slammed into the barrier and dropped his pickax. He reached up, his fingers scrabbling at the stones. Seth grasped his wrist and helped him up, hoisting the older man over the top with a mighty heave. The moment Boyd hit the ground, he yelled, "Run. All of you. Go!"

Boyd hesitated for a second, his chest heaving with exhaustion. Then he got up and ran, his legs pumping with surprising speed. The rest followed, except Reed and Ronnie, who stubbornly stood their ground.

That left only Wallace inside the prison yard, and Seth turned to the man with a sense of hopelessness. Wallace still had several yards to cover, his pace excruciatingly slow. *He's not going to make it.*

"Come on, Wallace. Move!" Seth cried, leaning forward so far he almost fell off the wall.

Wallace shook his head, his cheeks flaming red. He'd long since dropped his pickax, but even that didn't seem to help. With every step, Shanks and the other guards gained on him. *I have to help him.*

Seth moved to swing his leg across, but a couple of hands grabbed his ankle and held him in place. Confused, he looked down into the fierce gaze of Ronnie. "Don't do it. You can't help him. You'll only get caught."

"But... we can't leave him behind," Seth protested.

A pained cry alerted him to trouble, and he swung back in time to see Wallace fall to the earth, his legs too weak to sustain the brutal pace.

Wallace hit the stony ground hard, his breath leaving his

lungs in an audible rush. Within moments, Shanks was on him, kicking him in the ribs with his boots. Wallace screamed.

"No!" Seth yelled, reaching out, but there was nothing he could do. Nothing but watch in horror as the scene played out before him.

Shanks delivered each kick with ferocious intent, putting his entire weight behind the blow. Each hit landed with a meaty thud followed by the snapping and crackling of bones.

"Take that, you filthy beggar," Shanks yelled through gritted teeth, an expression of glee crossing his face each time Wallace screamed in agony.

It wasn't long before the rest of the guards reached the two, and for a brief moment, Seth hoped they'd stop the torture. Instead, they joined in with whoops of delight, their boots connecting with Wallace's arms, legs, chest, and stomach until he begged for mercy.

"Stop. Please, stop!" he pleaded, blood bubbling from his lips. He cast a wild look at Seth and reached out with one hand. "Help me."

Shanks stomped on the hand, grinding the fingers into the stones. Wallace howled in anguish, blood spurting from the ragged stumps that remained.

Seth lunged forward, prepared to rush to his aid no matter the cost, but Ronnie and Reed held onto him with fierce determination.

"You can't go," Ronnie said.

"I have to help him," Seth cried.

"Think of your family," Reed said.

The word family caused Seth to pause. A vision of Rogue and Ridley drifted past his mind's eye, and he knew he couldn't let them down. He couldn't break his promise to them. Not even for Wallace.

Helpless and defeated, he watched Wallace try to evade his abusers. Like a wounded animal, the man tried to roll over, but Shanks stomped on his back until the vertebrae cracked.

He looked at Seth sitting astride the wall and grinned. "You'd better run because once I'm done with your friend, you're next."

Pulling his leg back, he delivered a tremendous kick to Wallace's face. The man's nose became a pulverized mess, and blood gushed from the injury, turning his hoarse cries into blubbering mewls.

A second and a third kick smashed his lips and crushed his cheekbone. The fourth and fifth blinded him in one eye and rendered him semi-conscious. The next few blows destroyed his face until nothing was left but mangled flesh.

Finally, the beating stopped. Wallace rolled onto his back, unrecognizable. Crimson stained the earth underneath him, and bloody foam frothed on his lips. With a shudder, he breathed his last, his body releasing its tenuous hold on life.

Shanks danced backward with a satisfied grin, wiping the sweat from his brow. Specks of blood misted his clothes, and he reached for the rifle slung across his back. He swung it toward Seth, his teeth bared like an animal. "Run, pretty boy. I'm coming for you."

"I'll kill you for that," Seth cried, his voice hoarse with grief. Rage suffused his mind, holding him in place despite the danger. "I swear it."

"You can try," Shanks taunted, aiming the rifle at Seth's chest.

The other guards streamed past Shanks, running toward Seth and the wall. None of them reached for their guns, reinforcing his belief that they had no bullets. The weapons were for show—a bluff and a good one too.

The guards screamed at Seth to get down, to surrender, but he ignored them, his full attention on Shanks. The man cocked his gun and pulled the trigger, but nothing happened. The gun was empty, just as he'd suspected.

Still, Shanks laughed as if he'd scored a hit and said, "When I catch you, I'll take you apart with my bare hands. Piece by piece. I don't need a gun for that."

"We'll see," Seth said, allowing Ronnie and Reed to drag him off the wall.

They shoved his pickax into his hands and pushed him toward the forest. "Run, damn it."

Forced into action, Seth sprinted toward the trees at full speed. His feet flashed across the uneven surface, dodging the thorny bushes and sharp stones with long strides. His lungs burned, and his muscles ached with the effort, but he dared not slow down.

Behind him, Shanks and the other guards shouted to each other, coordinating the chase, and Seth knew they had precious little time to escape. The moment he broke through the trees, he slowed and looked around. Ronnie and Reed were beside him, but he couldn't see the others. "Billy? Jerry! Where are you guys?"

"Over here," Billy said, stepping out from behind a tree. Jerry and Boyd were with him, looking pale but determined. Finn and Liam waved from the side, hidden in the shadows.

"Everyone all right?" Seth rasped, gasping for breath.

"Alive and in one piece," Finn confirmed, wincing as he tested his ankle.

"Let's keep moving," Liam urged, casting a nervous glance

back at the wall.

They plunged into the dense forest, the undergrowth clawing at their clothes, branches whipping across their faces. The sounds of pursuit were distant, but they knew it wouldn't be long before the guards were on their heels. It was a race against time, and they couldn't afford to lose.

"North," Finn instructed, taking the lead with Liam by his side. "The inland sea is our best chance. We can lose them there."

"Stay close," Seth called to the others as they followed the twins, hearts pounding, fear and hope colliding within their chests.

Each step took them deeper into the unknown, the shadows of the forest closing around them like the jaws of a predator. But Seth held onto the image of his family, their love a beacon guiding him through the darkness. They would survive, he vowed. No matter what it took, they would find a way home.

End of preview. Enjoy what you read? Then grab your copy right here and continue the adventure with Ridley and Loki at your side.

https://www.amazon.com/dp/B0C3F7V3CD

Primordial Earth - Sneak Peek

Primordial Earth - The Complete Collection
Book 1, Chapter 1

Rogue leaned against the rough stone wall of the alley with her arms folded around her aching belly. It growled, and the sound reminded her how long it'd been since she'd last eaten. Three days.

In front of her, the market was in full swing, a rough square filled with stalls heaped high with goods. It was a bustling hive of activity where the residents of Prime City traded for food and other supplies, haggling over each item's price until its worth was established. The lucky ones, those who had jobs, could pay with a coin.

She was not one of the lucky ones, nor did she possess anything valuable enough to trade. Except her body, and she was not desperate enough to go that route. Not yet, anyway. A wave of dizziness swept over her, her knees buckling as she fell to the ground. *I need to eat.*

Rogue dragged herself upright, clinging to the shreds of her pride. On unsteady feet, she left the shelter of the narrow alley she'd occupied and entered the market square.

A wall of sound washed over her. The cries of vendors hawking their wares, citizens complaining over the cost of a loaf of bread, street urchins and pickpockets screeching as they ran through the crowds, blank-eyed prostitutes calling for clients.

With the noise came the smells. Scents that had her empty stomach convulsing until she nearly collapsed once more. Salted meat, sweet oranges, freshly baked bread, and overripe tomatoes. Underlying it all was the stench of humanity—a potent mix of urine, feces, and sweat.

Above their heads, sheets of metal and cloth hid the people from view because flyers of all kinds were an ever-present threat to the city.

Rogue kept her head down, and her hood pulled up as she walked, her rough cloak blending into the crowd with seamless ease. Her eyes swept from side to side, looking for an opportunity, a moment. That was all she needed.

A loud-mouthed hag drew her attention. The woman waved a flatbread in front of the owner of a stall piled high with the crusty rounds. "Three coins for this? Are you crazy? I'll report you to the Watch."

"Madam, I…"

"Don't Madam me," the woman cried, slapping the man with the bread. "This is an outrage."

Rogue sidled closer, one hand snatching a still-warm loaf from the edge of the stall. It disappeared underneath her cloak, and she hurried away, heading toward the fountain.

Its cool steps beckoned to her, and she sank onto the cracked tiles with a sigh of relief. With shaking hands, she tore pieces from the bread and swallowed them nearly whole, too eager to fill her belly to chew. Bit by bit, the small loaf dwindled until nothing remained but crumbs.

The food revived her strength, little though it was, and Rogue leaned over the edge of the fountain to drink from the spout in the wall. It tasted stale. Each drop in the city was processed over and over again, along with the sewage. Not even the rainwater collected on the roofs in huge drums could make it any fresher.

With her thirst sated, Rogue took to the market once more. A loaf of bread would only take her so far. She needed more, or she'd starve. Thievery was against the law, however, and carried a hefty penalty. She had to be careful. The Watch was everywhere.

Haunches of meat swung in the breeze, rinds of salt crisscrossing the fatty flesh. It was dinosaur meat, of course. They were hunted by the raiding parties that scavenged around the city's outskirts whenever it was safe. She didn't dare try to steal it, though. Too bulky.

A small hand tugged at her pants, and she slapped it away with a warning glare at the little boy who'd sought to empty her pockets. He stuck his tongue out before melting back into the throng, and she turned her attention to the fruit stalls.

The oranges were small and wrinkled. The crop this year had been poor, but to her hungry eyes, they looked delicious. She was about to snatch one when she spotted it. A woven basket padded with soft white feathers. Inside, it cradled a cargo more precious than gold. Eggs.

Rogue smothered a gasp. She hadn't seen an egg in years. Memories of a previous time flooded her mind. The smell of burning toast and scrambled eggs. Bacon and coffee. The clink of cutlery and the low hum of conversation as her parents discussed the coming day of work and school.

Rogue shook her head, trying to banish the thoughts, but the feelings they'd invoked lingered. Longing rose within her breast, and without realizing it, her hand reached out and plucked one of the precious eggs from its nest. She cradled it to her chest with one palm, the smooth shell warm against her skin.

"Hey, what do you think you're doing? Give that back." A large hand clamped over the wrist of her free hand, squeezing the bones until she thought they would snap. "Nobody steals from me!"

Rogue screamed in pain as the hand raised her arm high in the air until she stood on tiptoe. Her eyes widened at the sight of the vendor, a brute of a man. His face was broad, and a coarse beard as black as sin covered his jaws, mirroring his beady eyes.

Acting on instinct, she tucked the egg into her pocket and pulled out her small knife. With a flash of silver, she opened a cut on the stall owner's cheek. Blood poured from the wound, and he stumbled back with a hoarse cry.

The moment he let go of her, she was off, darting through the stalls with every bit of speed and agility she possessed. Behind her, the vendor recovered long enough to shout for the Watch.

His angry bellows tore through the air, raising an answering cry, and Rogue knew she was in trouble. Serious trouble. Within seconds, the Watch was in pursuit. Their runners pushed through the crowd without a single care for those who got in their way.

Rogue ducked behind the nearest stall, hugging the wall as she sprinted toward an alleyway on the other side of the square. It was far, but if she made it, she could escape into the labyrinth of passages that wove through the heart of the city.

A wall of baskets blocked her way, and she turned her face aside as she plowed through, angry shouts following in her wake. She tripped over one, and a hand reached out to catch her, the fingers hooking in her hair. Long strands ripped free of her scalp, and hot tears filled her eyes as she regained her feet.

"She's over here!"

"There she is!"

The Watch had spotted her, and several runners converged on her location. Rogue pushed her body into overdrive, using every ounce of energy she possessed to outrun them. She leaped over a cart, shimmied between two poles, and rolled beneath a table, all in a frantic bid to escape.

Her body turned on her, becoming the enemy. Each breath was a struggle, every muscle screamed in protest, and her knees burned where she'd skinned them. Blood trickled down her shins.

"Halt!"

Rogue ducked beneath the arms of a Watch guard and upended a table covered in apples. The fruit tumbled to the ground, rolling beneath the feet of her pursuers and slowing them down. With a grateful cry, Rogue headed for the alley that beckoned. *Only a few more steps.*

A terrifying screech rent the air and sawed into her eardrums. Rogue stumbled, casting a horrified look over her shoulder. A gigantic shadow swooped over her head, followed by another screech. It was a sound that awoke an ancient fear within anyone who heard it. A call as old and primal as the earth itself. The triumphant cry of a predator that had found its prey. Pterosaur!

As soon as the knowledge registered, the gigantic beast plunged toward the market, its taloned claws ripping apart the sheet metal and canvas covering the square. The noise caused by her chase must have lured the beast in, rendering their flimsy camouflage useless. Screams rose as people surged to get out of the way, a tidal wave of panicking humanity trampling each other in a bid to escape.

Rogue fell to the ground and crawled between their legs and feet until she found shelter beneath a small table. Two sets of terrified eyes met hers, street urchins hiding from the chaos. Same as her.

The monstrous flyer plunged into the hole it had created. Its great beak snapped at the people running away from it in panicked terror. Rogue watched in horror as its great crested head dipped in and out of the crowd. A veritable smorgasbord of meat was at its disposal.

"Oh, my God," Rogue whispered. "It's a Quetzalcoatlus."

The very name of the flighted dinosaur inspired mind-numbing fear. It was the largest of the pterosaurs, a carrion eater, and an opportunist. Its wingspan alone numbered thirty-odd feet, and its serpentine head flashed yellow and red as it plucked the limbs from a man like he was no more than an ant.

Crimson blood sprayed into the air, and agonized cries cut through the noise. Rogue crouched in her spot, frozen by the knowledge that she'd caused this. Guilt coursed through her veins like acid.

She jerked upright when the alarms sounded. Horns blown by sentries stationed in guard towers across the city. Their deep, mournful wails shivered down her spine and vibrated through the stones beneath her feet. They signaled the call to battle, drawing out every man of the Watch. It meant one thing to all of them.

The city was under siege.

Rogue curled up into a little ball, a sob of despair leaving her lips. There would be no escape for her today. Not after the mess she'd created with her thoughtless actions. Once they'd dealt with the dinosaur, the Watch would tear the city apart looking for her. Stone by stone. They'd find her. There was nowhere to hide—no one to turn to. *Not even Moran can help me now.*

Rough commands rang out as soldiers stormed into the marketplace, their heavy armor gleaming in the sun. Bows were raised, and arrows sang in flight as the soldiers aimed the Quetzalcoatlus.

Many glanced harmlessly off its thick hide, but a few found tender spots and buried steel heads into soft flesh. The pterosaur screeched, its massive wings battering those on the ground as it sought to take flight.

With ponderous strokes, it rose into the air. Gusts of wind pummeled the ramshackle market stalls. Baskets flew, awnings came loose, and dust swirled in thick clouds, tinting the air dark yellow. Grains of sand stung exposed skin and eyes alike.

The heavier ballistae and crossbows mounted on the walls let loose. Bolts as thick as her arm slammed into the flying beast's body. It wailed in agony as a missile crushed the fine bones of its wing and tore great rents in the delicate membrane.

The flyer slewed mid-air and crashed to the ground, plowing over stalls, carts, and tables. It raised its head and let loose an ear-splitting shriek, by no means defeated. Folding its broken wings and using them as arms, it attacked anything within reach, its enormous head reaping a harvest of corpses.

Rogue pressed shaking hands to her mouth to prevent

herself from crying out at the sheer horror of it all. She watched as the monstrous bird tore apart a man of the Watch, his armor no defense against the frenzied attack. One colossal wing slammed into the ground not far from her, and the two children next to Rogue screamed. Within seconds, they were on their feet, scrambling to get away from the pterosaur's thrashing limbs.

Rogue longed to follow but remained frozen in her corner until the same wing swept across her head, turning the table into matchsticks. She screamed and covered her head before scurrying away on her hands and knees. A glancing blow tossed her into the air, and she flew several feet before crashing into a wall.

She fell to the ground with a grunt of pain, every bone in her body protesting its abuse. Through tear-filled eyes, Rogue spotted a sheltered nook created by two adjoining walls and crawled toward it on her belly, each movement an effort of will. Her lip was split, and blood filled her mouth. It drooled from the corner of her lips to the rough stones beneath.

The nook she headed for was tiny, nothing more than a gap between two overlapping brick walls. An architectural mistake, no doubt. Yet, it was big enough to fit her body. Even fully grown at twenty-five, she barely topped five feet, a side-effect of constant malnutrition. She curled up inside with the fervent hope it would keep her safe from the rampaging creature. Without realizing it, she began praying for Moran to find her, to save her. Though not her mother by blood, the fierce woman who'd raised her and become the Rebel Faction leader was the only person she truly trusted. But Moran was nowhere to be seen. Rogue was on her own.

Even as she looked, the flyer stormed across the market

square, causing mayhem and destruction until a squad of soldiers stormed in and surrounded the beast. As one, they opened fire, wasting precious ammunition in their bid to bring the creature down. Each bullet cut into the Quetzalcoatlus until it slumped to the ground in a pool of blood, its body shuddering as it took its final breath.

The remaining soldiers lowered their guns and took a step back from the corpse. The screams that had filled the square moments before faded away. They were replaced by an awful silence broken only by whimpers and sobs. People picked through the debris, looking for loved ones, while others keened next to the bodies of friends and family.

Despite the horror that pulsed through her veins and the guilt that threatened to destroy her, Rogue knew she had to move. If she was to stand any chance at escape, she had to run. Now. While the Watch was still occupied.

She knew what awaited her if she was caught. Death. There'd be no mercy for her, a street rat, and a thief. A murderer. Every mouth in the city would call for her execution.

This knowledge spurred her on, and she emerged from her hiding spot with furtive looks in every direction. With the palms of her hands, she wiped away the sand that clung to her clothes. With her hood in place once more, she turned toward the alleyway.

It was close. So close she could almost taste freedom. Its dark, smelly interior beckoned with the promise of escape and anonymity. If she could get away, burn her clothes, cut her hair, and change her appearance…maybe, she stood a chance. The rebels could hide her. Moran would see to it. "Now or never."

Rogue took three steps, each lighter than the last, before an iron fist closed on her shoulder and swept her around. Brutal fingers clamped onto her throat, crushing the tender flesh even as it cut off her air supply.

"Where do you think you're going?" a low voice asked. It came from a man dressed in the full regalia of the Watch Command. His chest gleamed with medals, and his manicured looks spoke of a life of ease—a life of privilege.

Rogue pulled at the hand that threatened to choke the life from her, but it was no use. She was no match for the man who held her prisoner, his furious eyes radiating anger. A single white streak in his otherwise dark hair identified him, and terror coursed through her veins. General Sikes. Head of the Watch, Second in Command of Prime City, a man known for his ruthlessness.

In that instant, Rogue knew she was doomed, yet she had to try. She couldn't give up. Not yet. "Ge…General, please. I didn't mean to…"

His fingers tightened, cutting off all oxygen to her brain, and he lifted his arm until she was standing on tiptoe. Her legs scrabbled for purchase on the rough ground. "Do not speak, you filthy whore, or I shall have your tongue cut out."

Rogue's eyes bulged, her face swelling with blood even as her lungs screamed for air. Spots danced in front of her eyes, and she barely registered the moment the General tossed her to the ground. Her body heaved, and she gagged through the bruised flesh of her throat.

Hands gripped her upper arms, and she was lifted to her feet and dragged away. Each breath was an effort, the crushed fibers raw and tender. Her cut lip stung, and her body ached from being thrown against the wall by the pterosaur.

But the worst of all was the knowledge that she was about to die. And for what? An egg she didn't even get to eat. The wet slimy patch inside her pants rubbed against her skin with each step she took, filled with broken shells—a mocking reminder of her failure and her doom.

End of preview - Available here: https://www.amazon.com/dp/B0BPT8XXS2

Your FREE EBook is waiting!

If you'd like to learn more about my books, upcoming projects, new releases, cover reveals, and promotions, simply join my mailing list. Plus, you'll get an exclusive ebook absolutely FREE just for subscribing!

Yes, please. Sign me up!
 https://www.subscribepage.com/i0d7r8

About the Author

WEBSITE - **www.baileighhiggins.com**

Glossary

Primordial World – Glossary

- Glossary terms are listed in alphabetical order and without reference to their locations within the book.
- Generally speaking, physical location references are not listed in the Glossary.
- Measurements are provided in both metric and US/Imperial units.

Alamosaurus – A genus of sauropod dinosaurs containing just one species that lived in the late Cretaceous period. (See Cretaceous.) Specimens suggest they could measure up to 30 meters (98 feet) in length and weigh as much as 79 metric tons (88 tons). For comparison, the largest living land animal in the present day is the African elephant, which can weigh up to 6.3 metric tons (7 tons). (Wikipedia.)

Ankylosaurus – A genus of armored dinosaurs that lived at the very end of the Cretaceous period. (See Cretaceous.) Specimens suggest they could measure up to 10.6 meters (35 feet) in length and weigh as much as 5.9 metric tons (6.5 tons). (Wikipedia.)

Buitreraptor - A genus of dromaeosaurid dinosaurs that

lived during the Late Cretaceous Period. It was a rather small dinosaur, estimated at a length of 1.5 meters and a weight of three kilograms. It has some different physical features than typical northern dromaeosaurs, such as *Velociraptors*. *Buitreraptor* has a slender, flat, extremely elongated snout with many small teeth, and the forelimbs were long and ended in very long and thin three-fingered hands. The enlarged sickle claw at the second toe of the foot formed a blade that was long although less large than in other raptors. (Wikipedia.)

Cretaceous – The Cretaceous period is defined as beginning 145 million years ago (mya) and lasting until approximately 66 mya. (Wikipedia.)

Lambeosaurus – A genus of hadrosaurid herbivore dinosaurs that lived in the late Cretaceous period. (See Cretaceous) These dinosaurs had duckbills and could feed on trees as high as 4 meters (13 feet). (Wikipedia.)

mya – an acronym for "million years ago," also "m.y.a," used in astronomy, geology, and paleontology. (Wikipedia)

Nyctosaurus – A genus of nyctosaurid pterodactyloid pterosaur that lived in the late Cretaceous period. An adult could have a wingspan of 2 meters (6.5 feet). Compared to terrestrial dinosaurs, Nyctosaurus were small-bodied and weighed less than 2 kilograms (4.4 pounds). (See Cretaceous.) (Wikipedia.)

Parksosaurus - A genus of hypsilophodont ornithopod dinosaur from the early Maastrichtian-age Upper Cretaceous.

A small, bipedal, herbivorous dinosaur. (See Cretaceous) Length: 2,5 m (Estimated) Height: 100 cm Mass: 45 kg (Estimated) (Wikipedia)

Pteranodon (genus *Pteranodon*), flying reptile (pterosaur) found as fossils in North American deposits dating from about 90 million to 100 million years ago during the Late Cretaceous Period. (See Cretaceous) *Pteranodon* had a wingspan of 7 meters (23 feet) or more, and its toothless jaws were very long and pelican-like. (The Editors of Encyclopaedia Britannica)

Pterosaur – Pronounced "tero saur." Science considers pterosaurs to be flying lizards that are distinct from dinosaurs. There are many different species. Pterosaurs existed from the late Triassic to the end of the Cretaceous period. (See Triassic.) (See Cretaceous.) (Wikipedia.)

Stegoceras - is a genus of pachycephalosaurid dinosaur that lived in what is now North America during the Late Cretaceous period, about 77.5 to 74 million years ago. (See Cretaceous) The first specimens from Alberta, Canada, were described in 1902, and the type species Stegoceras validum was based on these remains. (Wikipedia) Height: 1,2 m Length: 2 – 2,5 m Mass: 10 – 40 kg

Styracosaurus - meaning "spiked lizard," had four to six long parietal spikes extending from its neck frill, a smaller jugal horn on each of its cheeks, and a single horn protruding from its nose, which may have been up to 60 centimeters (2 feet) long and 15 centimeters (6 inches) wide. A relatively large dinosaur, reaching lengths of 5–5.5 meters (16–18 ft) and weighing about 1.8–2.7 metric tons, it stood about 1.8 meters (5.9 feet) tall. The skull had a beak and shearing cheek teeth suggesting that the animal sliced up plants for food. (Wikipedia.)

Quetzalcoatlus – Pronounced "ket suhl kow at luhs." A genus of pterosaurs. Triassic – The Triassic period is defined as beginning approx 251 mya) and lasting until approximately 202 mya. (Wikipedia.)

Triceratops - a genus of herbivorous ceratopsid dinosaur that first appeared during the late Maastrichtian stage of the Late Cretaceous period, about 68 million years ago (mya). It is one of the most recognizable of all dinosaurs and the best-known ceratopsid. It was also one of the largest, up to 9 meters (29.5 feet) long and 12 tonnes (13.2 tons) in weight. (See Cretaceous) (Wikipedia.)

Zuniceratops – Pronounced "Zooni ceratops." A genus of ceratopsian herbivore dinosaurs having two horns and a head frill. It is thought to have been a herd animal. Specimens suggest a length of 3 to 3.5 meters (10 to 11.5 feet) and a weight of 100 to 150 kilograms (220 to 330 pounds). Height at the hips was approximately 1 meter (3 feet). (See Cretaceous) (Wikipedia.)

Special note: While every effort was made to use dinosaurs of the Late Cretaceous Period existing in North America, this remains a work of fiction. Certain creative license was taken in instances where it better served the plot.

Printed in Great Britain
by Amazon